THE PENALTY

"Are you in love with me now?" he
asked wistfully

THE PENALTY

BY
GOUVERNEUR MORRIS

ILLUSTRATED BY
HOWARD CHANDLER CHRISTY

CHARLES SCRIBNER'S SONS
NEW YORK :::::::::::::::::::::::: 1920

TO MARY BALDWIN

If I should lose from my life that part of it of which you are a part, there would be but a skeleton left. Yet if you had played a larger part in my life I should have been so spoiled that there would be no living with me. And I'm spoiled enough, God knows!

In the Iliad you wrote for me, and I "drawed" for us both, 'twas Hector fixed Achilles. When I sat at your right hand and your sharp, swift knife went into the turkey, 'twas I that got the tit-bits and the oyster. And all was right with the world *then*, I can tell you!

We have ridden together over old battlefields, and I have worn the epaulettes and the swords in the attic, and listened to tales of the great brother who died of the war, and whose bull-terrier Jerry chased the cannon-balls at Gettysburg. Oh, the cutlass captured from the Confederate ram, and the wooden canteen, and the Confederate money (in a frame)! I was the hunter that used to handle the Colt (with the ships engraved on the cylinder) that shot the buffalo from the rear platform of the train, and was stolen by a genuine thief. Is Jeff Davis's bible that he gave to the brother who with Major R. caused game chickens to fight for the edification of his captivity still in your upper bureau drawer?

Are the photographs that General Gilmore had taken of Charleston siege still in the bookcase with the glass doors? Or have they vanished like the child's footprint that I made for you when we were planting the—the "plant," and I was going away?

Time has passed. *Grand*nephews are as young and hopeful as nephews used to be. *I* have written innumerable miserable grovelling tales. I dedicate this one to you; despairing at last of writing that masterpiece which should have been worthy of you.

But tell me this: Is there still a little corner of your heart that I may call mine? a corner into which no one else is allowed to put— yes—to put *foot?* Oh, but I should be glad to know that!

G. M.

BEDFORD, *February*, 1913.

ILLUSTRATIONS

THE PENALTY

THE PENALTY

I

THE number of love affairs which intervened between
Barbara Ferris's first one, when she was eleven, and
her twenty-second birthday could not have been
counted on the fingers of her two hands. Many
boys, many men, had seemed wonderfully attractive
to her. She did not know why. She knew only
that the attraction seemed strong and eternal while
it lasted, and that it never lasted long. She was
sixteen before she began to consider herself a heart-.
less, flirtatious, unstable, jilting sort of a girl. When
she made this discovery, she was terribly ashamed,
and for one long depressing year fell in love with
nobody, became very shy, and hated herself. It was
during this year that she had her first, last, and only
touch of mania. It lasted only a little while and
was not acute. She got the idea that she was being
watched, spied on, and followed. But she was too
strong in body and mind to give in for long to so
silly an hallucination. And when she had dismissed
the second man and her maid, who had particularly
excited her suspicions, the mania left her, as a dream
leaves at waking.

In her seventeenth year she was presented to society, and became an immense favorite. There were excellent reasons for this: she was lovely to look at, she
would inherit a great deal of money, she had charming natural manners, and she was sweet-tempered.

During her second season she had an unpleasant
experience. She had almost reached an understanding with a certain young man with whom she fancied
herself in love. They were spending a Saturday to
Monday at a great place on Long Island. On Sunday
night, her host, a man old enough to be her father,
invited her to see his rose garden by moonlight.
She accepted this invitation as a matter of course.
Pacing down a path between tall privet hedges, her
host, who for some minutes seemed to have lost the
use of his tongue, made her a sudden impassioned
declaration of love, seized her in his arms, and kissed
her wherever he could with a kind of dreadful fury.
For half a minute she stood still as a statue. Then,
crimson with shame and anger, she wrenched free,
and struck him heavy blows on the face and head
with her strong young fists. She beat him, not indeed to insensibility, but to his senses. They returned to the house after a time, and entered the
drawing-room talking in lazy, natural voices and
praising the beauty of the night and of the garden.
Not even Barbara's lover suspected that anything
out of the common had happened.

Barbara, having played half a dozen rubbers of
bridge with the great skill and sweet temper which

were natural to her, excused herself, went to her room, and cried half the night. It was not the shame of having been forcibly kissed that sickened her of herself, but the unforgettable, unforgivable fact that toward the last of that furious kissing she had found a certain low feline pleasure in the kisses. She wished that she might die, or, infinitely better, that she had never been born.

It seemed terrible to her that she could at once be in love with one man and enjoy the kisses of another. She had heard of girls who were thus, and had for them the contempt which they deserved. And yet it seemed that she was one of them; neither better nor worse. What Barbara did not realize was, that in the first place she was not really in love with anybody and never had been, and that it was not she herself who enjoyed being kissed by a man to whom she was indifferent, neither liking nor loathing, but nature, which for reasons, or perhaps only whims, of its own, tempts the cell to divide and the flower to go to seed.

Through the tangle of her love affairs Wilmot Allen threaded a path of hope, despair, and cynicism. There were times when she seemed to have a return of her childhood infatuation for him; there were times when he feared that in one of her moments of impressionable enthusiasm she would marry some other man in haste, and repent at leisure. And there were the cynical intervals, when it seemed to him that he could do without her, and that nothing was worth while but enjoyment, both base and innocent, and pleasure.

During Wilmot's junior year at New Haven, his father's sensational, dissipated, and stock-gambling career came to a sudden end. There was even a shadow on the name. He had done something *really* discreditable, something of course to do with money; since a man who is *merely* a gambler, a drunkard, and a Don Juan may with ease keep upon good terms with society.

Wilmot Allen failed, at least without honor, filled himself full of brandy, cocked a forty-five-calibre revolver, put the muzzle in his mouth, pulled the trigger, blew off the back of his head, and was "accidentally shot while cleaning the weapon."

The real tragedy was that so good a career as the son's should have come to so untimely an end in so good a collegiate world as Yale. He stood well in his class, he had played right tackle for two seasons and was heir apparent to the captaincy; he was well beloved and would have received an election to a senior society in the spring. But the solid ground being withdrawn from under his feet—in other words, his allowance from his father—he left amid universal regret, and found himself a very small person in a very great city; worse, a youth who had always had everything, loved pleasure, lights, games, and color, and who now had no visible means of support.

Friends found him a position in Wall Street.

She wished that she might die, or,
infinitely better, that she had never
been born

Being young, attractive, a good "mixer," not in the least shy, he was given a handsome "entertaining" allowance and told to bring in business. So he fore-gathered with out-of-town magnates, made the city a pleasant, familiar place to them, and brought much of their money into the firm's office. When Barbara was kind he despised his anomalous position and strove to free himself from it; but even the best man has to live.

And during those intervals when he thought he could do without her, Wilmot sank deeper and deeper into methods of self-advancement which, if not actu-ally base and culpable, at least smirched the finer qualities of his nature, and hardened his heart.

If the father's heritage, drink and women, were spared him, or at least that part of him which was really noble, a love of cleanness, clear-mindedness, and purity, died hard. But gambling was second nature to him. He could not enjoy a game unless he had something on it; and all book-makers and pro-prietors of gambling-houses were friends of his and called him by his first name. Sometimes through a series of lucky turns he rose to heights of picturesque affluence; more often he was stone-broke; but so much money passed through his hands in the course of a year that it was always possible for him to bor-row and live well enough on credit. Money became his passion, not for its own sake, not for the sake of what it could buy, but because it was a game upon which the best wits of the world have been engaged

for ages and ages—and because you have to have it,
or be able to owe so much that it amounts to the
same thing.

At first when he got in a hole, owed money which
he saw no way of raising, Wilmot suffered all the
anguish and remorse of the trustee who has specu-
lated with orphans' funds (for the first time) and
lost them. Gradually he became hardened. And
those who knew him best could never tell whether he
was worth fifty thousand or had just lost that much.
He drew upon a stock of courage and cheerfulness
worthy of even the noblest cause, until the term "self-
respect" dropped automatically from his inner vocabulary and his moral sense became a rotten, rusty
buckler through which the spear of temptation or
necessity passed like a pin through a sheet of tissue-
paper.

He put himself under obligation—in moments of
supreme need—to dangerous persons, and suffered
from the familiarity and perhaps the contempt of
some who were his inferiors in breeding, in heart, and
in soul.

One day, being at his wit's end, he walked rapidly,
seeking light, through a quarter of the city which
was not familiar to him. He was in that mood
when a man does not wish to be at the trouble of
nodding or exchanging a word even with his best
friend. A voice hailed him, "Mr. Allen."

He stopped and saw that the voice came from a
legless man who sat in the sun by a hand-organ on

which were displayed for sale a few pairs of shoe-laces and, to excite charity, a battered (and empty) tin cup.

"Have you forgotten me?"

The light of recognition had twinkled instantly in Wilmot's eyes, for he was wonderful at remember-ing faces. And he smiled and said:

"Of course not. How are you?"

"Pretty well," said the beggar. "And you?"

"Pretty well."

Wilmot's giving hand had slipped automatically into his trousers pocket. Then, for once in his char-itable life, he hesitated, since the pocket contained nothing but a ten-dollar bill, and that was all the money he had in the world with which to meet a pressing note of ten thousand. His hesitation lasted only a moment. He laughed and stuffed the ten-dollar bill into the cup, and said:

"For old acquaintance' sake."

The beggar studied the young man's face. Then he said: "Mr. Allen, I once had the honor to warn you against three things."

"I remember."

"Your face is innocent of wine and women. How about the gambling?"

"My friend," said Wilmot, "you read me like a book. The gambling is all to the bad. I have just given you all the money I had in the world."

"A few dollars are of no use to me," said the beggar.

"Nor to me. Don't worry."

"I am not worrying. I'm thinking that you and I have something in common. And for that reason I am tempted to ask if a few thousand would be of any use to you?"

Wilmot smiled with engaging candor. "Fifteen thousand would."

"You shall have them," said the beggar shortly. He pointed to a glazed door across which was printed in gilt letters:

BLIZZARD—MFR.
HATS

"That," said the beggar, "is my name, and that is my place of business. Come in."

Wilmot followed the beggar through the glass door, which at opening and closing caused a bell to clang. The front of the establishment was occupied by a dust-ridden salesroom, and an office with yellow-pine partitions. As he followed the beggar into this, Wilmot caught a glimpse in the distance of fifteen or twenty young girls who sat at a long table industriously plaiting straw hats. He lifted his own hat a little mechanically, and thought that he had never seen so many pretty girls at one time under one roof.

II

WILMOT buttoned his coat over fifteen one-thousand-dollar bills. Only supreme necessity could have persuaded him to take them, since, although he had not put his name to a paper of any kind, he felt a little as if he had sold himself to the devil. But Blizzard had shown him no deviltry; only kindness and a certain whimsicality of speech and a point of view that was engaging.

The transaction finished, Wilmot was for leaving, but being under obligation to the legless man was at pains not to be abrupt. He lingered then a little, and they talked.

"The first time we met," said the beggar, "you were roller-skating with a pretty child. She was so pretty that I asked you her name. And I have never forgotten it."

He did not add that he had watched that pretty child's goings and comings for many years; that he had lain in wait to see her pass; that he had bribed servants in her father's house to give him news of her; and that the day approached when, fearing neither man nor God, he proposed that she should disappear from the world that knew her, and go down into the infamous depths of that vengeance which had been the key-note of his life. Nor did he add

that there were but two contingencies which he felt
might thwart his plans: her marriage to Wilmot Allen,
or his own untimely death. And he feared the latter
but little. The former, however, had at times seemed
imminent to those who spied upon the daily life of
the heiress for him, and in lending money to Wilmot
he was taking a first step toward making it impossible. For Barbara herself Blizzard had at this time
no more feeling than for a pawn upon a chess-board.
It pleased his sense of fitness to know she was beautiful; and to be told that she was like sunshine in
her father's house.

"What has become of her?" he said.

"Of Miss Ferris?" Wilmot did not care to discuss her with a stranger. But unfortunately there
were fifteen thousand dollars of the stranger's money
in his inside pocket. "She became a great favorite
in society," he said, "and then dropped out to study
art."

"Painting?" The legless man knew perfectly well,
but it suited him to make inquiries. "Music?"

"Sculpture," said Wilmot shortly.

"Is she succeeding?"

"She works very hard, and she has talent."

"That is not enthusiastic."

"You mustn't ask me; I'm not an art critic."

"What a pity."

"A pity that I'm not an art critic?"

"No. A pity for a beautiful girl to do anything.
but exist."

Wilmot's eyebrows went up a little. The beggar's speech surprised him, and pleased him, since it expressed a favorite thought of his own.

"Is any of her work on exhibition? Having seen her once, one takes an interest, you know."

"I think there is nothing that can be seen," said Wilmot coolly, "except upon special invitation. And I think she is very shy of showing anything that she has done."

"True artists," said Blizzard, who criminally was an artist himself and knew what he was talking about, "live in the future."

Again Wilmot's eyebrows went up a little. Why should a legless beggar be able to make loans of fifteen thousand dollars, and why should he be able to talk like a gentleman?

"I am interested in art," continued Blizzard; "sometimes I have earned a few dollars by sitting for my portrait."

He did not add that he continually put himself in the way of artists in the hope that his fame as a model would reach Barbara, and touch her imagination. He did not add that he haunted Washington Square and McBurney Place, where her studio was, in the hope that his face, which he knew to be different and more terrible than other faces, might kindle a fire of inspiration in her. He believed rightly that if a woman once looked him in the eyes she would never forget him. But hitherto Barbara had not so much as glanced at him, since she carried her lovely

head very high, and looked straight before her as
she went. While, as for him, he stood upon the
stumps of his legs, a gigantic sort of dwarf, beneath
the notice of the proud-eyed and the tall.

Wilmot passed out of the place in deep thought;
not even the pretty girls plaiting straw won a glance
from him. Coupled with the relief of being out of
present difficulties was a disagreeable sense of fore-
boding. Suppose the legless man were to ask favors
of him before the money could be repaid? Suppose
they were favors which a gentleman could not grant?
And he determined to find out, from the police if
necessary, just what sort of a man it was with whom
he had had dealings.

III

It seemed to Wilmot that he had not seen Barbara
for an age. And indeed a week had passed without
their meeting. Therefore, although he had often been
forbidden to call during working hours, he had himself driven to 17 McBurney Place and climbed the
two flights of stairs to her studio.

It was a disconsolate Barbara who received him.
She had on her work-apron, but she was not working.
She sat in a deep chair, and presented the soles of
her small shoes to an open fire. Wilmot, expecting
to be scolded for disobeying orders, was relieved at
being received with visible signs of pleasure.

"You're just the person I wanted to see," she said,
"just the one and only Wilmot in the world."

"Are you dying?" he asked.

She laughed. "I'm discouraged. I've come to one
of those times when you just want to chuck everything. And there's a man at the bottom of it."

"Tell me," said Wilmot, "in words of two syl-
lables."

"Well," said Barbara, "I woke up in the middle
of the night out of a dream. I dreamed I'd made a
statue of Satan after the fall from heaven, and that
everybody said: 'Well done, Barbs, bully for you,'
'Got Rodin skinned a mile'—it was you said that—

and so forth and so on. I rose, swollen with conceit, and made a sketch of the head I'd dreamed about, so's not to forget the pose, and then I went to sleep again. Next day, early, a man stopped me in Washington Square and begged for a dime. I looked at him, and he had just the expression of the fallen Satan I'd dreamed about—a beast of a face, but all filled with a sort of hopeless longing to 'get back,' and remorse. I invited him to pose for me—not for a dime—but for real money. Well, he fell for it. And for all that morning he looked just the way I wanted him to look. But the next morning, having had the spending of certain moneys, he looked too tidy and well fed for Satan. And this morning he was hopeless. He looked smug and fatuous and disgustingly self-satisfied. So I gave him quite a lot of money, not wishing to hurt the creature's feelings, and told him to go away." She looked up, laughing at herself. "Do you know, I really believed I'd dreamed out a golden inspiration, and then to strike just the face I wanted—and then to have everything foozle out!"

Wilmot walked over to the modelling-table on which, strongly modelled in wet clay but quite meaningless, was the bust of a man.

"I think," said Barbara, "it would look better if you snubbed his nose for him."

Wilmot snubbed the long nose heavenward, and the effect was such as to make them laugh. Barbara recovered all her usual good humor.

"Get some forms out of the kitchen," she said, "and we'll turn him into mud pies."

For half an hour they diverted themselves, displaying a tremendous rivalry and enthusiasm. And then Barbara announced that there had been enough foolishness, and that if Wilmot would put fuel on the fire, he might talk with her till lunch-time and then take her out to lunch.

"Always provided," she said, "that you are not broke at the moment. In which case Barbara will pay and tip."

"I've had a funny adventure," said Wilmot. "I *was* dreadfully broke. A man I hadn't seen for years and years—and only the once at that—stopped me in the street, told me I was broke, and offered to lend me money. Wilmot accepted, and is now plenty flush enough to blow to lunch, thank you!"

Barbara reseated herself in the deep chair, and once more presented the soles of her shoes to the flames. "Look here," she said, "aren't you, just among old friends, rather flitting your life away? I don't think it's very pretty to borrow money from strangers, and to be always just getting into difficulties or just getting out of them. Do you?"

"Well, you know," said Wilmot earnestly, "I don't. When I don't hate myself, I don't like myself any too well. But there's something wrong with me. Maybe I'm just lazy. Maybe I lack an impulse. Maybe I'd do better if any single solitary person in this world really gave a damn about me."

His cheerful boyish face assumed a proper solemnity of expression, and a certain nobility. At the moment he really thought that nobody in the world cared what became of him.

"Nobody," said Barbara, "likes to back a flighty pony. You yourself, for instance, are always putting money, your own or some one else's, on horses that always run somewhere near form. Of course you have excuses for yourself."

"I? None."

"Oh, yes, you have. You were brought up to be rich, and you were left poor, and a man has to live and even secure for himself the luxuries to which he has been accustomed. Haven't you ever excused yourself to yourself something like that?"

Wilmot admitted that he had, and went further. "You can't knock livings out of a tree with a stick like ripe apples," he said. "You've either got to use your wits or begin at the bottom and work up. And it seems to me that I'd rather be a little bit tarnished than toil away the best years of my life the way some men I know are doing."

"Yes," said Barbara, "but why not go somewhere where the world is younger, and there are real chances to be a man, and real opportunities to make money in real ways? I don't blame you for living on your wits. I blame you for gambling and never getting anywhere and not caring."

"Not caring? And this from you?"

She changed color under his steady eyes.

"You just give me a certain promise, Barbs, and I give you my word of honor I'll settle to something above-board and make it hum. Look here now! How about it? Who's been so faithful to the one girl for so long? Who understands her so well? Who'd enjoy dying for her so much?"

"Good old Wilmot," she said gently and gave him her hand. He kissed it and would have liked to go on holding it forever, but she took it away from him, and after a silence said, with some bitterness: "I mustn't ever marry anybody. I've learned to know myself too well. And I've no constancy, and I don't trust myself."

"That," said Wilmot with the faith of a fanatic in his god, "is because you've never really cared."

"And besides," she said, "I have what I am pleased to call my career. And 'Down to Gehenna and up to the throne he travels fastest who travels alone.'"

"True," said Wilmot, "he arrives soonest, but all tired out, and the house is empty, and there are no children in it, and only paid servants. And it may be very showy to live for fame, but it isn't good enough. When we turned that bust you began into mud pies, we did a wise thing. We amused ourselves, and we said the last word on art as opposed to life. The best thing in this world is to *be* children and to *have* children—and the next best thing is nowhere."

"Would you," said Barbara, and her eyes twinkled a little, "really rather be a parent than a Praxiteles?"

"It looks to me," said Wilmot sadly, "sometimes —in moments of despondency—as if the honorable gentleman was never going to be either. But then again," and he spoke in a strong voice, "I believe in my heart that after you've done handling the book of life and admiring the binding, you'll open it at chapter one, and read, '*Young Wilmot* Allen——'"

"Lunch-time," said Barbara, and she rose from the comfortable chair with sharp decision. "I vote for a thick steak, being famished. Is my hair all mussy?"

"No," said Wilmot dejectedly. "I wish it was. And I wish it was my fault—and yours."

IV

"I'VE done enough for you more than once," said the legless man; "you're big enough and strong enough to work, but you're a born loafer."

"I had a job." The speaker, a shabby, unshaven man with a beastly face, whined dolefully. "And I done right; but I got the sack."

"What was the job and why were you sacked?"

"I got a job as a artist's model. I sits in a chair while the lady makes a statue out of my face, and then she gives me money, and I goes and spends it. The third day she gives me more money, and tells me I looks too well fed and happy to suit her, and sends me away."

The legless man was astonished to learn that his heart was beating with unaccustomed force and rapidity. "Who was the artist?"

"She's a lady name o' Ferris."

The legless man steeled his face to express nothing. "Ferris," he commented briefly.

"Say," said the unshaven man, "what's all that about the devil falling out of heaven and fetching up in hell?"

"Why?"

"That's how she says I looks. And she wants to make a statue of him, just when he comes to and sits up, and looks up and sees how far he's fell. She says my face has all the sorrers and horrors of the world in it."

"And then, you fool," said the legless man, "you spoiled her game by high living. You ate and you drank till you looked like a paranoiac bulldog asleep in the sun. Where was the lady's studio?"

"Seventeen McBurney Place."

"And she wants to do a Satan, does she?"

The unshaven man drew back from the expression of the legless man, in whose face it was as if all the fires of hell had suddenly burst into flame. The unshaven man covered the breast of his threadbare coat with outstretched hands as if to shield himself from some suddenly bared weapon. His eyes blinked, but did not falter.

"Say," he said presently, after drawing a deep breath, "if she could see you once."

"If I don't know," said the legless man, "how Satan felt after the fall, nobody does. The things I've been—the things I've seen—back there—down here—the things I've lost—the things I've found! Hell's Bell's, Johnson! what is it you want—food?—drink?—a woman?"

The unshaven man's eyes shone with an unholy light.

"What would you do for twenty-five dollars?"

The unshaven man said nothing. He looked everything.

"Do you know the McIver woman?"

"Fanny?"

The legless man grunted. "Yes. Fanny. She'll look at you if you've got money."

"She'd crawl through a sewer to find a dime."

"Quite so," the legless man commented dryly. "Well, it wouldn't matter to me if she went on a tear and was found dead in her bed."

"It's worth fifty." Something in the unshaven man's voice suggested that he had once been remotely connected with some sort of a business.

The legless man shook his head. "Judas Iscariot," he said, "betrayed the Lord God for thirty. Fanny McIver's scalp isn't worth a cent over twenty-five. You're just a broken-down drunk. It takes a bigger bluffer than you to make me put an insult on Christendom. Fifteen down. Ten when Fanny's had her last hang-over."

"Why don't you do some of your dirty work yourself?"

"I do all I can," said the legless man simply; "I can't find time for everything."

The unshaven man shifted uneasily on his shabby feet. In his stomach the flames which only alcohol can quench were burning with a steady gnawing fury. "How about a little drink?" he said.

"Fifteen down," said the legless man; "ten when the job's done, and a ticket to Chicago."

"With a reservation? I'll feel like the devil; I couldn't sit up all night."

"I'll throw in an upper," said the legless man.

Still the unshaven man resisted. "What's Fanny done to you?"

"None of your business."

As if that settled the matter, and removed all obstacles and moral scruples, the unshaven man sighed, and held out his hand for the money which was to bind the contract.

Twelve hours later, Fanny McIver's death was being attributed by the authorities to the insane, jealous rage of a lover. But as she had lately changed her name and address, she lay for a while in the morgue awaiting identification. It was the legless beggar who performed that last solemn rite. He was quite unmoved. Her death mattered no more in his scheme of life than the death of a fly.

But as he held up his hand and swore that the identity of the corpse was such and such, he remembered how graceful she had been at sixteen, how affectionate, how ready to forgive. He remembered with a certain admiration that during the heyday of her earning powers she had always trusted to his generosity, and had never tried to hold any of her earnings back. Prison and drink had destroyed all that was honest in her, all that was womanly. So a drop of acid will eat out the heart of the freshest and loveliest rose. She became a very evil thing—full of evil knowledge. There was even a certain danger in her —not much—nothing definite—but enough. She was better dead.

He turned and swung out of the morgue into the sunlight. And he wondered whatever had become of the child that she had borne him.

V

It would have been easier for Wilmot Allen if he could have come into Barbara's life for the first time. She was too used to him to appreciate such of his qualities as were fine and noble at their true value. And contrarily it was the same familiarity which limned his faults so clearly and perhaps exaggerated them. She often thought that if she could see him for the first time she would fall head over ears in love with him, and be married to him out of hand. Was it not better therefore, since the man's character had its disillusionments, that their life-long friendship precluded the idea of marrying in haste and repenting at leisure? "It's almost," she said to herself, "as if I had married him long ago and found out that I had made a mistake."

But she hated to hurt him in any way. And it caused her a genuine sorrow sometimes to say no to him. He had proposed to her many times a year for many, many years, and always with a passion and sincerity that made it appear as if he was proposing for the first time in his life. Twice, the strength and devotion of his physical presence had seemed to remove every doubt of him from her mind, and she had said that she would marry him, and had been ecstatically happy while he kissed her and held her in his arms. And each time better knowledge of

herself, a sleepless night, and the unsparing light of
morning had filled her with shame and remorse, and
made it quite clear that she had made one more mistake, and must tell him so, and eat humble pie. And
exact a promise that he would never make love to
her again. But she could never get him to promise
that. And she could never keep him from kissing
things that belonged to her when she was looking,
and when she wasn't. And if, as he sometimes
threatened in moments of disappointed and injured
feelings, he had gone far away, so that he could never
cross her path again, she would have missed him so
much that it would almost have killed her. And so
it is with all human beings—they care little enough
about their dearest possessions until the fire by night
consumes them, or the thief walks off with them.
Then the silver and the jewels, and this thing and
that, assume a sort of humanity—and are as if they
had been dear friends and unutterably necessary
companions in joy and sorrow.

To Wilmot a little encouragement was a great
thing, a foundation upon which to undertake pyra-
mids. Having intruded upon Barbara's working
hours without being scolded, Wilmot began to picture for himself a delightful life of intruding upon them
every day. He hoped that if she was really working,
she would not actually send him away, but let him
sit in the deep chair by the fire and wait till she was
through, and ready for talk and play. As much almost as he loved her, he hated her ambitions, if only

because they interfered with him, and because he found it impossible to take them seriously. Her work seemed surprisingly good to him—not surprisingly good for a genuine sculptor who exhibited in salons, but for a girl of his own class whom he had always known. In this estimate he did not do Barbara justice. She had a fine natural talent and she had been well trained. People who knew what they were talking about, shock-headed young fellows with neighboring studios, prophesied great things for her, partly because she was beautiful, and partly because her work, as far as she had gone in it, was really good. What she lacked, they said, was inspiration, experience, and knowledge of life. When these things came to her in due time, her technique would be quite equal to expressing them.

Wilmot's dream of being much in Barbara's studio proved negotiable only as a dream. Barbara began a fountain for her father's garden at Clovelly, and during the modelling of the central figure the studio was no place for a modest young man. He had one glimpse through the half-open door of a girl with very red hair and very white skin, and he turned and beat a decided retreat, blushing furiously. He did not repeat his visit to her studio until Barbara assured him that the nymph had put on her clothes and gone away. Then, much to his disgust, he found there a young fellow named Scupper, who smoked a vile pipe and had dirty finger-nails and was allowed to make himself at home because he

had recently exhibited a portrait bust that everybody
was praising (even Wilmot) and because he had volunteered during a delightful contemplation of Barbara's face to do her portrait and tell her all that he
had learned from his great master, Rodin.

The little beast had the assurance of the devil.
He praised, blamed, patronized, puffed his pipe, and
dwelt with superiority on topics which are best left
alone, until Wilmot wanted to kick him downstairs.
Scupper, aware of Wilmot's dislike for him, and thoroughly cognizant of its causes, did his best to goad
the "young prude" (as he chose to consider him)
into open hostility. He strutted, boasted, puffed, and
talked loosely without avail. Wilmot maintained a
beautiful calm, and the more he raged internally the
more Chesterfieldian and gorgeously at ease his manners became. Barbara enjoyed the contest between
the terrier and the Newfoundland hugely. Personally she disliked Scupper almost as much as she liked
Wilmot, but artistically she admired him tremendously and felt that his judgments and criticisms were
the most valuable things to be had in the whole city.

Wilmot not only kept his temper, but outstayed
his antagonist. The latter gone, he turned upon Barbara, and she in mock terror held up her hands for
mercy; but Wilmot was not in a merciful mood.

"When you imagine that you are uplifting the
cause of art, Barbs, are you sure that you aren't de-
basing it? You won't marry a man who has always
loved you. *Art.* You put marble and bronze higher

than little children. *Art*. You allow disreputable, unwashed men to talk in your presence as that man talked. *Art*. You hire people of bad character to sit for you, and people of no character. All art. You treat them in a spirit of friendliness and camaraderie. You affect to place art above all considerations; above character, above morals; worse, you place it above cleanliness.

"A man—yes, take him for all and all, a man—eats out his heart for you; desires only to live for you, only to die for you, only to lie at your feet afterward—that is nothing to you. You do not even care to listen. You would rather hear through a braggart, indecent mouth that ought to be sewed up what Rodin said about Phidias. It seems finer to you to be an artist than a woman, and you so beautiful and so dear!"

Barbara made no answer. She looked a little hurt, possibly a little sullen. She had a way of looking a little sullen (it did not happen often) when she could not hit upon just the words she wanted to express her thoughts. She felt that her attitude toward life was almost entirely right, almost entirely justifiable, and she wanted to explain exactly why this was thus, and couldn't. So after a silence she said:

"Oh, I'm just a little pig. Why bother about me? And besides, it's no use."

"Don't say that, Barbara. There *must* be use in it. Don't you know in your heart that some day you are going to marry me?"

"No," she said. "Sometimes I've thought so, but I don't know it." She selected an arrow from her quiver, touched the point with venom, and because she had not enjoyed being scolded shot it into him. "And at the moment I don't think so."

Wilmot spoke on patiently. "Every true lover, Barbs," he said, "comes in time to the end of his patience and the end of his endurance."

"And then he ceases from loving—and troubling."

"He does not. When he knows as I know what is best for her happiness and for his, and when he finds that humbleness, and begging, and gentleness, and persuasion are of no avail—why, then if he's a man he *makes* her love him, *makes* her marry him."

"I hope, my dear Wilmot," she said, "that you are speaking from a very limited experience."

"From the experience of ten million years. I have only one life to live. Somehow I will make you love me, make you belong to me. Just because I eat with a fork, do you think my heart is really any different from that of the cave-man from whom it descended to me, or that your heart is any different from that of the girl he wanted, who kept him guessing and guessing until he couldn't stand it, and then turned and ran and ran through the woods, and swam rivers and climbed trees and jumped down precipices until he caught her?"

There was something in Wilmot's lowered brows, a certain jerking, broken quality in his utterance, that was new to Barbara—that at once frightened

her a little, and caused her heart to beat with a sort
of wild triumph. But she did not guess that the old
cave-man was at that moment actually looking out
through her old friend's eye-places, and that ten
thousand years of civilization are but a thin varnish
over the rough and splendid masterpiece that God
made in his image.

There was a knock at the door. It was Scupper
returning. He had left his beloved pipe (on purpose). His shrewd, bloodshot little eyes took in the
situation at a glance. In two beats his little heart
was wild with jealousy.

"I beg *everybody's* pardon," he said. "I didn't
know. I—er—wouldn't have knocked—I—er—mean
I *would* have knocked just the same."

Wilmot took one slow step toward the famous
sculptor, then smiled, picked up the fellow's pipe,
and returned it to him. "I saw you put it down
just before you left," he said. "I think there is
nothing else you have forgotten, *is* there? If there
is I think it will be best not to come back for it until
I have gone. Meanwhile you will have time to shave
and bathe and make yourself presentable."

Scupper, sure that he was not actually going to be
hit, escaped with an ease and jauntiness which he
was far from feeling. And Barbara, the high tension
relieved, burst out laughing.

It was Wilmot's turn to look sullen. He had felt
that the sheer animal force of his love was holding
and even moulding Barbara to his will, as no tender-

ness and delicacy had ever done. But at the sculptor's entrance, the honest if brutal cave-man had fled, like some noble savage before a talking-machine, and left in a state of civilized helplessness a young gentleman who could not find anything to say for himself.

As for Barbara, she had never seen Wilmot look as he had looked, or heard those quivering, broken tones in his voice. The savage in her had gone out to him with open arms and, behold, the primal force which, standing like an island of refuge in a sea of doubt, she had been about to clasp was but an empty shadow. That Wilmot had not done very nobly with his talents, that there were weaknesses in his character and record, things even that needed explaining, had not at the moment of his mastery mattered to her a jot. But now such thoughts flocked to her like birds to a tree; and she was glad that she had escaped from a situation that had so nearly overwhelmed her reason and drowned her common sense in the heavenly sweetness of surrender.

Wilmot could find nothing to say. It was no mere gust of passion that had swept over him, but a storm. He was physically tired, as if he had rowed a long race. He no longer wished to play the master. He would rather a thousand times have rested his hot forehead on Barbara's cool hand, and fallen quietly asleep like a little child come in at last to his mother after too much play in the hot sun.

"Life," he said at last, "is a nuisance, Barbs.

Isn't it? Would you, honestly, be happier if I disappeared, and never bothered you again? Sometimes I feel that I ought to."

She shook her head. "If you like people," she said, "you like them, faults and all. I'm dependent on you in a hundred ways. You're the oldest and best friend I've got. If you disappeared I'd curl up and die. But now that we are talking personalities, you very nearly forgot yourself a few minutes ago. Well, I forgive. But it mustn't happen again."

He bowed his head very humbly. "I will go back to patience and gentleness," he said, "and give them another trial."

"I wish," she said, "that you would go back and begin your life over again—stop drifting and sail for some definite harbor."

"I will," he said, "on condition——"

"No—no—no," she said hurriedly, "no condition. I am in no position to make conditions, if that's what you mean. I don't understand myself. I don't trust myself. I will not undertake to bind myself to you or any one until I know that I can trust myself. It would be very jolly for you if I married you and then we found that I really loved the other fellow. I'm like that—selfish, unstable, susceptible—and very much ashamed of myself. I wouldn't talk myself down so if you didn't know these things as well as I do. Why you go on caring for me is a mystery. I'm no good. And I'm not even sorry enough to cry about it—ever. I've actually thought that I was in love—oh, ever so many times: sometimes with you. What's the use? The only things I've ever been faithful to are the dressmaker, dancing, and what in moments of supreme egoism I am pleased to call my art."

"Barbs," he said, "you're an old silly billy, and I love you with all my heart and soul. That's *that*. Don't forget it. Take pen and ink if necessary and write it down. I'll try a little more patience, and then, my blessing, if there's no good in that, I shall perpetrate marriage by capture."

They both laughed, the girl with much sweetness. And she said:

"If you and I ever do marry, it will be with great suddenness." Her eyes danced, and she added: "There are moments!"

"Thank you," he said gravely, and then with a kind of wistful gallantry: "Could I kiss the dear for luck?"

She turned her cheek to him bravely and frankly like a child. His lips touched it lightly, making no sound.

Far off in the native jungle the cave-man moaned, and shut his eyes and turned his face to the wall of his cave. The medicine-man came, examined him, and said that he was about to die of a new disease. He looked very wise and called it "predatory in-anition."

As for the cave-girl, having run and run and run, she pulled up in a flowery glade, looked behind, lis-

tened, saw nothing, heard no sound of painfully pur-
suing feet, and called herself a fool and a silly for
having run. She wanted to explain that she hadn't
meant to run away, that girls never really meant
what they said, and would the cave-man please recover at once from his predatory inanition and take
notice of her again?

"Come," said Barbara, after quite a long silence,
"let's go forth and collar a taxi. Anywhere I can
take you? I can't ask you to lunch, because I am
having seven maidens, and afterward Victor Polideon
to teach us to turkey-trot."

"I wouldn't be afraid of seven devils," Wilmot
urged in his own behalf, "if you were present."

"There are only two," she said practically, "and
they are very little devils. But I won't let you come,
because you would have much too good a time."
Then she relented. "Come later, about three, and
teach me to turkey-trot. You do it better than
Polideon. And I hate to have him touch me."

"That's something," he exclaimed triumphantly.

"What's something?"

"That you don't hate for me to touch you."

She laughed and tapped his shoulder in rag-time.
Also she whistled, and did a quiet suspicion of a
turkey-trot with her feet.

VI

One bright morning in May, divinely early, two persons of very different appearance and nature came out of two houses of very different appearance and nature at precisely the same moment, and started to move toward each other by methods of locomotion no less different than were the appearances of the respective persons or the respective houses from which they emerged.

The house from which the one issued was of speckless white marble, and looked from the advantageous corner of Sixty-something Street and Fifth Avenue upon the purple and white lilacs and the engaging spring greens of Central Park.

The other came out of a dark house at the angle of a narrow street in the shadow of Brooklyn Bridge, whose door, crossed by dingy gilt lettering, violently clanged a bell at opening and closing. The first person stepped with the long clean strides of youth and liberty. The second person cannot be said to have stepped at all. The first person, meeting a policeman, smiled and said: "Good morning, Kelly." The second, similarly meeting with an officer of the law, scowled upward, and said: "Do it again, and I'll break you." The first person came out of the uptown palace like a fairy from a grotto; the second

36

emerged from the downtown rookery like some prehistoric monster from a cave.

At a distance you might have mistaken him for an electrician or a sewer-expert coming into view.through one of those round holes in the sidewalk by which access is provided to the subterranean apparatus of cities. But, drawing nearer, you perceived that he was but half a man, who stood upon the six-inch stubs of what had once been a pair of legs. But what nature could do for what was left of him nature had done. He had the neck, the arms, and the torso of a Hercules. His coat, black, threadbare, shining, and unpleasantly spotted, seemed on the point of giving way here and there to a system of restless and enormous muscles. But that these should serve no better purpose than ceaselessly to turn the handle of an unusually diminutive and tuneless street-organ might have roused in the observer's mind doubts as to the wisdom and vigilance of that divine providence which is so much better understood and trusted by the healthy and fortunate than by the wretched, the maimed, and the diseased.

For the most part the legless man went about the business of begging among the business men of the city, since from the congested slum into which he disappeared at night it was no great feat for a man of his power to reach the more northern streets of that circle in whose midst the finances of the nation by turns simmer, boil, and boil over. It was not unusual, during the noon-time rush of self-centred individuals, for the legless man to get himself stridden into and bowled clean over upon his face or back, since nothing is more loosening to purse-strings than the average man's horror at having injured some creature already maimed; nor was it unusual for him at such times to scramble up smiling with a kind of invincible cheerfulness that more potently stirred the generosity of the man who had knocked him down than ever groans and complaints could have done. .

If the weather was fine and conducive to bodily comfort, the beggar sometimes turned north and worked his way to Washington Square or the lower blocks of Fifth Avenue. Sometimes, having agreed to pose for the head and trunk to some young art student, he left his hand-organ behind, and permitted himself the extravagance of riding in a surface car. His boarding of a street-car was a feat of pure gymnastics, swift and virile; so, too, was his ascending or descending of a flight of steps, or the high platform on which he was to pose. Incessant practice, added to natural skill and balance, enabled him to accomplish, without legs, feats which might have balked a man with a capable and energetic pair of them. He could travel upon his crutches for the length of a city block almost as fast as the average man can run, and if it came to climbing a rope or a rain-duct he was more ape than human. In his own dwelling he had for his own use, instead of the laborious stairs needed by its other inmates, a system of knotted ropes by which he could ascend from cellar to attic, and polished poles by whose aid he could accomplish the most lightning-like descending slides.

Marrow Lane, shaped like a dog's hind leg, is one of those crooked and narrow thoroughfares which the approaches and anchorings of the Brooklyn Bridge have cast into gloom and darkness. There are spots upon which the sun will not shine again until the great bridge has perished; there are corners in which drafts strong as a heaven-born wind whistle from one year's end to the other. There are thousands of children in the region, and in the more purely tenement settlements to the north, who have yet to see a green field or to handle a flower.

At the very crook of the dog's leg, on the north side of Marrow Lane, a narrow door, half glazed and sometimes burnished by the sun, has printed across it in dingy gilt letters:

BLIZZARD—MFR.
HATS

Once the door with the faded gilt letters had closed, with him inside, the legless man, who was none other than Blizzard, the manufacturer of hats, put off those airs of helplessness and humility by which so many coins were attracted into the little tin cup upon the top of his hand-organ, and assumed the attitude of one accustomed to command and to be served, to reward and to punish. He was no longer a beggar, but a magnate. He swelled with

power, and twenty girls of almost as many national-
ities, plaiting straw hats by the gas-light, cringed in
their hearts, and redoubled the speed of their hands.
About the twenty girls who slaved for Blizzard there
were two peculiarities which at once distinguished
them from any other collection of female factory-
hands on the East Side. They were all strong and
healthy looking, and they were all pretty. He had
collected them much as rich men in a higher station
of life collect paintings or pearls. If some of them
bore the marks of blows and pinchings, it was not
upon any part of them which showed. If some of
them suffered from the fear of torture or even sudden death, it did not prevent them from showing the
master rows of even white teeth between ingratiat-
ingly parted lips whenever he deigned to speak to
them. If any girl among them thought to escape
him, to find work elsewhere, to betray what she
knew of him, even, and vanish into the slums of some
far city, she was deterred by the memory of certain
anecdotes constantly related by her companions.
The most terrible of these anecdotes was that related of a certain Florence Magrue. She had fled
with her story to the nearest policeman, who had
quietly returned her to the shop, reluctantly, it was
admitted, but with the determination of a man
whose very existence depends upon the favor of another. The master had welcomed her and smiled
upon her as upon an erring child. He had sent her
upon an errand into the cellar under the shop, him-

self unlocking the door. And that was the last that any one had ever seen of Florence Magrue.

In addition to fear, the master supplied certain creature comforts, not lightly to be thrown away. If a girl could make up her mind to accept shame, bodily injury if she displeased, and a life of toil, she fared better under Blizzard's direction than her sister who worked for Ecbaum, let us say, the lace-maker, or Laskar, or any of a thousand East Side employers of labor. The man could be kind upon impulse, and generous. He paid the highest wages. He supplied nourishing food at noon, and a complete hour in which to discuss it. Furthermore, if a girl pleased him, the work of her hands was subjected to less critical inspection, and if she had any music in her, he invited her upstairs sometimes to work the pedals of his grand piano, while his own power-ful, hairy hands rippled and thundered upon the keys. He was of a Godlike kindness when his mind inclined to music, and the pedalling was skilful and sure. But let the unfortunate crouched under the key-board, her trembling hands taking the place of those feet which the master had lost, respond stupidly to the signals conveyed to her shoulder by graduated pressures from the stump of his right leg, and punishment of blows, pinchings, and sarcasms was swift and sure.

The legless man was very much at home in his own house. He had inhabited it for many years, and its arrangements were the expression of a creature immensely able and ingenious, but maimed both in body and soul.

The whole building, four stories tall, had once been a manufactory, but Blizzard had subdivided its original lofts into pens, dens, passageways, and rooms according to an elaborate plan of his own. And it was evident to the most casual glance that expediency alone, untrammelled by any consideration of purse, had been followed. Those walls, floors, and ceilings, for instance, through which no sound of human origin, unaided by mechanical device, could penetrate, must have cost a mint of money. Nor could any man who depended for a living upon occasional pennies dropped into a tin cup have got together so extensive a collection of books upon scientific subjects, many of them handsomely bound and printed in foreign countries. Works upon explosives, tunnelling, electricity, and music were especially abundant, not only in English, but in German. And there were books upon the organization of armies, and upon the chemistry of precious stones. A cursory examination of his books would have found the master of the house to be interested also in obstetrics, in poisons, and in anæsthesia; but of romance, humanity, or poetry his library had but a single example, the "Monte Cristo" of the elder Dumas.

Had all the doors and windows of the house been thrown open, and all its inhabitants expelled, so that you could have free ingress with a companion or two, and time and the mood to explore the whole of its ramifications and arrangements, you must have concluded that the designer of so much that was hideously obvious and so much that was mysteriously obscure was a most extraordinary example of viciousness, ability, purpose, and musicianship. You must have been staggered at passing from a room containing a grand piano and a bust of Beethoven to find yourself in a little operating-theatre such as any eminent surgeon might wish to be at work in, to find beyond this a small but excellently appointed gymnasium; above this, to be reached only by climbing a knotted rope, a long room, lighted from above, containing drawing-tables, many cases of drawing-instruments, and a host of workman-like designs and specifications. Thence you might pass, still wondering, into an apartment of soft divans, thick rugs, and open fireplace, a smell of incense, double windows and double doors.

Or you might descend by stairs or polished poles to the cellar under the hat factory, and find yourself, prying into the most obscure corner and lighting matches for guidance, confronted by the door of a mightily strong safety vault, the knobs of the combination lock bright and easily turned. And you might say: "Well, it's either the house of a man whose scheme of life is utterly beyond my comprehension, or of a madman."

VII

Of the two persons who left their homes this morning, the legless beggar, owing to having ridden part of the way in a street-car, was the first to reach the northeast corner of Fifth Avenue and Washington Square, whence the last rear-guard of fashion in old New York retreats before the advance-pickets of the encroaching slums, like a stag before a pack of hounds. Here he ensconced himself, placed his tin cup on the top of his organ, together with the few pairs of shoe-laces which proclaimed him a merchant within rather than a beggar without the law, and proceeded to enliven the still quiet neighborhood with the dreadfully strained measure of Verdi's "Miserère." He turned the handles of the little organ fitfully, so that now the strains of sorrow arose at such long intervals as hardly to be connected with one another, and now all huddled and jumbled like notes in a barbaric quickstep, and as he played he addressed his instrument in a quiet, cruel voice.

A house-maid opened a window in the servants' wing of No. 1 Fifth Avenue. Blizzard turned his head slowly at the sound, and looked up at her with agate eyes, coldly interrogative. There was no one else at the moment within earshot.

Nevertheless before speaking the house-maid looked

nervously into the house behind her; then up the avenue, and down into Washington Square. She was a girl of some beauty, but her face was most engaging from a kind of waggish intelligence that it had.

"Tst!" she said.

The organ squeaked and rattled. It was manœuvring for a position from which to attack the "Danse Macabre." Blizzard indicated by a lift of heavy eyebrows that he was all attention.

"You can trust Blake," she said.

Blizzard grunted. "Send him to me at six."

"Marrow Lane?"

He nodded, and turned from her with an air of finality. The house-maid hesitated, drew a long breath, pulled in her head, and closed the window.

A loose-jointed man in clerical garb came hurrying down the avenue. He made longer swings with his right arm and longer strides with his right leg than with his left. He had a white, thin face, and a look of worry and anxiety. He was perhaps distressed to think that the world contained many souls to whose salvation he would never be able to attend. Perceiving the legless beggar, he stopped hurrying, sought in his pocket, and found a few pennies. These he dropped into the tin cup.

"God bless you, reverend sir," said the beggar in a voice of deep irony.

"Don't," said the clergyman. He managed to look the beggar in the eyes. "How many hats have we?" he asked in a quick whisper.

"We're on our fourth thousand."

The clergyman was visibly upset. "Six thousand to go," he muttered. "I shall be caught."

The beggar smiled. "Come to me at six-thirty," he said.

The man of God's eyes brightened. "You'll help me again?"

"Tst," said the beggar. "Move on. Here's a plain-clothes man."

The shepherd moved on as if he had been pricked by an awl, since it was not among the police that he felt called upon to separate the black sheep from the white.

The plain-clothes man approached loitering. He might have been a citizen in good standing and with nothing better to do than hobnob with whatever persons interested him upon his idle saunterings.

"How many pairs of laces have you sold this morning?" he asked.

"Nary a pair, charitable sir," returned the beggar.

"Speaking of shoe-laces," said the plain-clothes man, "what is your opinion of head-gear?"

"Bullish," said the beggar. "Straw hats will be worn next winter."

The eyes of both men sparkled with a curious exhilaration. The plain-clothes man drew a deep and sudden breath, and appeared to shiver. So a soldier may breathe at the command to charge; so a thoroughbred shivers when the barrier is about to fall.

"There will be nice pickings," said the beggar; "there will be enough geese to feed ten thousand."

The plain-clothes man dropped a penny into the tin cup. "By the way," he asked professionally, "where can I lay hands on Red Monday?"

The beggar shook his strong head curtly. "Hands off," he said.

"When did *he* join the church?"

"Last night, with tears and confession. A strong man Red, now that he has seen the light."

The plain-clothes man laughed and passed on, still loitering.

The "Danse Macabre" had come to a timely end, if that which is without tempo may be said to have any relation with time, and the trio of Chopin's "Funeral March" was already in uneven progress. The legless man sat on the bare pavement, his back against the handsome area railing of No. 1 Fifth Avenue, and steadily revolved the mechanism of the organ with his hairy, powerful hand.

Passers were now more frequent. Some looked at him and continued to look after they had passed, others turned their eyes steadfastly away. Some pitied him because he was a cripple; others, upon suddenly discovering that he had no legs, were shocked with a sudden indecent hatred of him. A lassie of the Salvation Army invited him to rise up and follow Christ; he retorted by urging her to lie down and take a rest. Then, as if premonition had laid strong hands upon him and twisted him about, he turned, and looked upward into the fresh, rosy face of Barbara Ferris.

Their eyes met. Always the child of impulse, and careless of appearance and opinion, she felt her thoughts, none too cheerful or optimistic that morning during her long walk down the avenue, drawn by the expression upon the legless man's face to a sudden focus of triumph and solution. She struck the palm of one small workman-like hand with the back of the other, and exclaimed: "By George!"

The face that was upturned to hers was no longer the insolent, heavy face of success which we have attempted to describe, but one in which the sudden leaping into evidence of a soul dismissed facts of color, contour, and line as matters of no importance. If there was wickedness in his glance, there were also awe and wonder. He had a tortured look, the look of a man who has fallen from unknowable heights—from an Elysium which he regrets and desires with all a strong man's strength, but to which the way back is irrevocably barred by the degradation and the sin of the descent—and who, all but overwhelmed by the knowledge that he can never return whence he came, yet bears his eternal loss with an iron courage that has about it a kind of splendor.

Barbara Ferris felt that she was looking upon Satan in that moment when he first realized that his fall from heaven was for eternity and that, against every torturing passion of conviction, he must turn his talents and his fearful courage to the needs of hell.

In that first moment of their meeting, she realized nothing about the man but the terribly moving ex-

pression of his face. Nothing else mattered. If her
plastic training was equal to catching and fixing that
expression in clay or marble, she would be made according to the mould of her ambition. The flame of
art burned white and clear in the inmost shrine of
her being. She saw before her, and beneath her, not
a human being, but an inspiration. And since inspiration is a thing swift, electric, and trebly enticing
from the fact that it presents itself shorn of all those
difficulties which afterward, during execution, so terribly appear and multiply, her heart beat already
with the exquisite bliss of an immortal achievement.
In her vocabulary at that instant it would have been
impossible to discover under B the aggressive But,
or under I the faltering If. She was inspired. It
was enough.

Then she, in whose mind strong wings had suddenly sprouted, perceived that the person directly
responsible had not even a pair of legs, and felt
throughout her whole being a cold gushing of horror
and revolt.

This was not lost upon Blizzard. It was an ordinary enough human sensation, whose reflections had
often enough given the iron that was in his soul
another twist and refreshed in him vengefulness and
hatred. Yet on the present occasion the knowledge
that he was physically loathed roused in the man a
feeling rather of that despair which may be experienced by the drowning at that precise moment when
the straw so eagerly clutched has proved itself a

straw, and he winced as beneath a shocking blow between the eyes.

On discovering that the creature was maimed it had been Barbara's first impulse to pass swiftly on. But another glance at the face which had arrested her held her. She took some coins from her purse and dropped them into the tin cup which the beggar held out to her. And he looked upward into her face.

"Did you ever pose for any one?" she asked.

"Yes, miss."

"I should like to make a bust of you. I'll see that it pays you better than—better than earning a living this way."

For the first time Blizzard smiled. "Do you want me to come now?" he asked.

"Yes," she said. "My studio is in No. 17 McBurney Place." Here she stopped upon a somewhat embarrassing thought. But the legless man read what was in her mind.

"Two flights up?" he queried. "Three? I can climb. Don't trouble about that."

"You will come as soon as you can?"

"I have to meet a man here in half an hour. Then I'll come."

"Please," she said, "ask for Miss Ferris."

At the name a tremor went through the legless man from head to stump. He blanched, and for the thousandth part of a second all that was devil in him rushed with smouldering lights to his eyes. But

She took some coins from her purse
and dropped them into the tin cup

of this Barbara perceived nothing; her repugnance mastered, she had already brightly smiled, nodded, and was walking swiftly away, her head high, spring air in her lungs and inspiration in her heart.

The beggar's eyes playing upon her, she passed through the peaceful warm sunshine of the quiet old square, and vanished at last into the still brighter sunshine and still older quiet of McBurney Place.

To work with her own hands, at least until she had made something beautiful, seemed to her a better aim than any other which the world offers. She had at first been the victim of private lessons, amusedly approved by her father, and only intermittently attended by herself, since it is not in a day that a fashionable idler is turned into a steadily toiling aspirant for eternal honors. Just so long as she remained an amateur and occasional potterer in her father's house she was applauded by him and assumed by the world in general to be a very talented young lady; but when, her artistic impulses—if not her technique—having strengthened amazingly, she insisted upon the steadier routine of an art school, she met with an opposition as narrow, it seemed to her, as it was firm. Her own will in the matter, however, proved the stronger. And having passed with excellent rapidity through those grades of the school in which the student is taught to make cubes and spheres, she modelled from the antique, and at last, upon a day almost sacred in her memory, was promoted to the life class.

And here, one morning, Dr. Ferris, interested in spite of himself in her swift progress, found her, with a number of other young ladies and gentlemen, earnestly at work making, from different angles of vision, greenish clay statuettes of a handsome young Italian laborer who had upon his person no clothes whatever. That fastidious surgeon, to whom naked bodies, and indeed naked hearts, could have been nothing new, was shocked almost out of his wits. He had left only the good sense and the good manners not to make a scene. He beat instead a quiet, if substantial, retreat, and put off the hour of reckoning. His daughter was soiled in his eyes, and when she explained to him that a naked man was not a naked man to her, but a "stunning" assemblage of planes, angles, curves, lights, and shadows, he could not understand. And they quarrelled as furiously as it is possible for well-bred persons to quarrel. He commanded. She denied his right to command. He threatened. She denied his right first to create a life, and then to spoil it. He advanced the duty of children to parents, and she the duty of parents to children. Finally Barbara, thoroughly incensed at having her mind and her ambition held so cheap, flung out with: "Have you *never* made a mistake of judgment?" And was astounded to see her father wither, you may say, and all in an instant show the first tremors she had ever seen in him of age and a life of immense strain and responsibility. From that moment the activity of his opposition waned. She knew that her will had conquered, and the knowledge distressed her so that she burst into tears.

"My dear," said her father, "I once made a very terrible mistake of judgment. There isn't a day of my life altogether free from remorse and regret. I have given you money and position. It isn't enough, it seems. My dear, take the benefit of the doubt into the bargain. If I am making another terrible mistake, you must bear at least a portion of the responsibility."

It is curious, or perhaps only natural, that Barbara was at the moment more interested to know what her father's great mistake of judgment had been than in the fact that her ambition had won his tolerance and consent, if not his approval and support. If she had asked him then and there, for he was still greatly moved, he might have told her, but reticence caught the question by the wings, and the moment passed.

And they resumed together their life of punctilious thoughtfulness and good manners. Dr. Ferris continued to cut up famous bodies for famous fees, while Barbara continued to do what she could to reproduce the bodies of more humble persons, for no reward greater than the voice of her teacher with his variously intonated: "Go to eet, Mees Barbara! go to eet."

VIII

It was a discouraged but resolute Barbara who stepped forth from her father's house that bright morning in May and passed rather than walked down the quiet upper stretches of Fifth Avenue. That she might fail in art, and make a mess of her life generally, sometimes occurred to her. And it was a thought which immeasurably distressed her. It would be too dreadful a humiliation to crawl back into the place which she had so confidently quitted for a better; to be pointed out as a distinguished amateur who had not succeeded as a professional; and to take up once more the rounds of dinners, dances, and sports which serve so well to keep the purposeless young and ignorant.

To society the tragedy of Barbara's back-sliding into art was very real. Dozens of men said very frankly that they missed her like the very devil. "There is nobody else," they said, "quite so straightforward, or quite so good-looking."

Hers was a face not less vivid than a light. It seemed that in her, the greatest artist of all, abandoning the accepted conventions of beauty, had created an original masterpiece. If she had been too thin, her eyes, tranquil, sea-blue, and shining, must have been too large. Her nose was Phidian Greek; her chin, but for an added youthful tenderness, was almost a replica of Madame Duse's; a long round throat carried nobly a gallant round head, upon which the hair was of three distinct colors. The brown in the Master's workshop had not, it seemed, held out; she had been finished with tones of amber and deep red. The brown was straight, the red waved, the amber rioted in curls and tendrils. Below this exquisite massing of line and color, against a low broad forehead, were set, crookedly, short narrow eyebrows of an intense black; her eyelashes were of the same divine inkiness, very warm and long; a mouth level to the world, resolute, at the corners a little smiling, was scarlet against a smooth field of golden-brown.

If she had a certain admiration of her own beauty it was the admiration of an artist for the beauty of a stranger. Since she had had neither hand nor say in her own making, the results were neither to her credit nor against it. For success in her chosen line she would have exchanged her beauty very willingly for a plain mask, her glorious youth for a sedate middle age. She would have given perhaps an eye, an ear, or so at least she thought in this ardent and generous period of early beginnings and insatiable ambition. In her thoughts nothing seemed to matter to her but art.

There was no sustaining pleasure in the fact that her father had given in to her. Opposition—unspoken, it is true, but not to be mistaken—remained in his attitude toward her. He found indirect means for conveying his idea and that of her friends that she was wasting herself upon a folly, and was destined, if she persisted in it, to only the most mediocre success. An exhibition of her works, undertaken with the avowed wish to know "just where she stood," had been discouraging in its results. The art critics either refused to take her seriously or expressed the opinion that there were already in the world too many sculptors of distinguished technique and no imagination whatsoever. Her friends told her that she was a "wonder." And there were little incidents of the farce which caused her to bite her lips in humiliation.

That the critics should be at the pains of telling her that she was without imagination angered her, since it was a fact already better known to herself. And in one moment she would determine at all costs to prove herself an imaginative artist, and in the next "to chuck the whole business." But she could not make up her mind whether it is worse for a captain to wait for actual defeat or, having perceived its inevitability, to surrender. To go down with colors flying appeals perhaps to noble sides of man; but it is a waste of ships, lives, and treasure.

Passing swiftly down the avenue, she did not know whether, upon arriving at her studio in McBurney Place, she should get into her working-apron or make an end, once and for all, of artistic pursuits. But with the lifting of the legless beggar's face to hers, all doubts vanished from her mind like smoke from a room when the windows and doors are opened. Whatever his face might have revealed to another, to her it was Satan's, newly fallen, and she read into it a whole wonder of sin, tragedy, desolation, and courage; and knew well that if she could reproduce what she seemed to see, the world would be grateful to her. She would give it a face which it would never make an end of discussing, which should be in sculpture what the face of Mona Lisa is in painting. It would be the face of a man whom one jury would hang upon the merest suspicion; for whom another would return a verdict of "not guilty" no matter what the nature of his proved crimes; and whether the face was beautiful or hideous would be a matter of dispute for the ages.

Upon arriving at No. 17 McBurney Place, and having climbed two flights of stairs, the door of her studio was opened before she could lay hand to the knob, and a very small boy with very big eyes, and no more flesh upon his bones than served to distinguish him from a living skeleton, appeared on the threshold, smiling, you may say, from head to foot. He was dressed in a blue suit with bobbed tails and a double row of bright brass buttons down the front, and when she had gathered him from the gutter in which he had reached to his present stunted stature, a child half gone in pneumonia, he had told her that his name, his whole name, was "Bubbles" and nothing but "Bubbles."

"Good morning, Miss Barbara," he said; "the

plumber's bin and gone, and the feller from the hardware store has swore he'll be around before noon to fix the new knobs in the doors."

"Good!" said Barbara. "Well done, Bubbles."

And she passed into the studio, wondering why a little face all knotting with smiles, affection, and the pleasure of commands lovingly received and well obeyed, should remind her of that other face, massive, sardonic, lost, satanic, which had looked up into hers across the battered tin cup on the top of a battered street-organ. She turned to a little clay head that she had made recently and for which Bubbles had sat; touched it here and there, stepped back from it, turned her own head to the left, to the right, and even, such was the concentration of her mood, showed between her red lips the tip of a still redder tongue. But no matter what she did to test and undo her first impression there persisted between the two faces a certain likeness, though in just what this resemblance consisted she was unable to say.

"Bubbles," she said, "you were telling me about beggars the other day and how much they make, and how rich some of them are. Did you ever run across one that sells shoe-laces, plays a hand-organ, and hasn't got any legs?"

"Sure," said he; "there's half a dozen in the city." And he named them. "Burbage: he's the real thing, got his legs took off by a cannon-ball in the wars. Prior: he ain't no 'count. Drunk and fell under a elevated train. He ain't saved nothing neither. He drinks *his*. Echmeyer: he's some Jew; worth every cent of fifty thousand dollars. They calls him congen*eye*tul, 'cause he was born with his legs lef' off him. Fun Barnheim: he's German, went asleep in the shade of a steam-roller, and never woke up till his legs was rolled out flat as a pair of pants that's just bin ironed. Then o' course there's Blizzard."

Barbara was smiling. "What became of his *legs*, Bubbles?"

"God knows," returned the boy. "Blizzard don't boast about it like the others. But he ain't no common beggar. He's a man."

"A good man?"

"Good? He ain't got a kinder thought in his block than settin' fire to houses and killin' people. But when he says 'step,' *it* steps."

"It?"

"The East Side, Miss Barbara. He's the whole show."

"What does he look like?"

The boy at first thought in vain for a simile, and then, having found one to his liking, emitted with great earnestness that the beggar, Blizzard, looked exactly like "the wrath of God." Whatever the boy's simile may convey to the reader, to Barbara, fresh from seeing the man himself, it had a wonderful aptness.

"That's my man," she exclaimed. "Blizzard! He's got a wonderful face, Bubbles, and you said just what it looks like. I'm going to make a bust of him."

"He's coming here?"

"Yes. Why not?"

The boy was troubled. "Miss Barbara," he said earnestly, "I wouldn't go for to touch that man with a ten-foot pole."

"I sha'n't touch him, except with compasses to take measurements. He's civil-spoken enough."

"He's bad," said Bubbles, "bad. And when I say bad, I mean millions of things that you never heard tell of, and never will. If he comes in here—and, and raises hell, don't blame *me*."

Barbara laughed. "He will come here, and sit perfectly still," she said, "until he wishes he was dead. And then he will receive money, and an invitation to come to-morrow. And then he will go away."

Bubbles looked unnaturally solemn and dejected.

"Besides," said Barbara, "I have you to protect me."

Though Bubbles made no boast, a world of resolution swept into his great eyes, and you knew by the simultaneous rising toward his chin of all the buttons upon the front of his jacket that he had drawn the long breath of courage, and stiffened the articulations of his spine.

Barbara's studio was a large, high-ceilinged room, whose north wall was almost entirely composed of glass. It was singularly bare of those hangings, lanterns, antique cabinets, carved chairs, scraps of brocade, brass candle-sticks six or seven feet high, samovars, pewter porringers, spinning-wheels, etc., etc., upon which so many artists appear to depend for comfort and inspiration. Nor were there any notable collections of dust, or fragments of meals, or dirty plates. There was neither a Winged Victory, a Venus de Milo, nor a Hermes after Praxiteles. And except for the bust of Bubbles there was no example of Barbara's own work by which to fish for stray compliments from the casual visitor. Of the amenities the studio had but a thick carpet, an open fireplace, and a pair of plain but easy chairs. Upon a strong tremorless table placed near the one great window, a huge lump of clay, swathed in damp cloths, alone served to denote the occupant's avocation.

Off the studio, however, Barbara had a pleasantly furnished room in which she might loaf, make tea, or serve a meal, and this in turn was separated from the tiny room in which Bubbles slept, by a small but practical kitchen.

Barbara having withdrawn to roll up her sleeves and put on her work-apron, the legless beggar arrived in silence at the outer door of the studio, and having drawn a long breath, knocked, and Bubbles, not without an uncomfortable fluttering of the heart, pulled it open. The boy and the beggar, being about the same height, looked each other in the face with level eyes.

"*So*," said Blizzard, "this is what has become of you. You were reported dead."

"No, sir," said Bubbles, "I wasn't dead, only sick. She brought me here, and had her own father and a nurse to take care of me. And now I'm Buttons." And he went on glibly: "Come right in; Miss Ferris is expecting you. I guess she wants you to sit on the platform over in the window."

Blizzard, having unslung his hand-organ and slid it with a show of petulance into a corner, crossed the room, swinging strongly and easily between his crutches, like a fine piece of machinery, climbed upon the model's platform, and seated himself in the plain deal chair which already occupied it. From this point of vantage he turned and looked down at the boy.

"So," he said, "her father *is* Dr. Ferris."

"He's *the* Dr. Ferris," Bubbles returned loyally.

"So—so—so," said the legless one slowly, and he closed his eyes for a moment as if he was tired. Then, opening them, and in abrupt tones: "Pay you well?"

"Yes, sir."

"Many people come here?"

Bubbles, who had gone to school—not in the schools, but in the city of New York itself—could lie without the least tremor or change of feature, and with remarkable suddenness. "Lots and lots of 'em," he said. "*She's* well known."

Blizzard merely grunted. "Tell her I've come."

But it was not necessary for Bubbles to give the message at the door of the inner room, since at that moment Barbara entered, her round arms bare to the elbow and her street dress completely hidden by a sort of blue gingham overall. Bubbles, whose presence was not required during working hours, at once withdrew to his bedroom.

Here he changed his tunic of brass buttons for a plain gray jacket, snatched his cap from its hook, gained the street by a back stair, and set off at the tireless street-boy trot that eats up the blocks. Half an hour later he returned, his face no longer wearing a look of anxiety, changed back into his many-buttoned jacket of dependence, and sitting upon his bed, his back against the pillows, proceeded with astonishing deftness and precision to figure with the stump of a pencil, upon the leaves of a small dog-eared note-book. Then, appearing to have achieved a satisfactory solution of whatever problem he had had occasion to attack, he began to go through a series of restless fidgetings, which ended with a sigh of relief and a guilty look, and producing from a hiding-place a cigarette, he smoked it out of the window, so that his room might not carry forward the faintest trace of its telltale odor.

IX

WHEN Barbara at length told the legless man that he might rest, he appeared to think that she had invited him to converse. He leaned back as far as he could in the deal chair. His expression was no longer that which had struck Barbara so hard in the imagination, but one of easy and alert affability. He looked at her when he spoke, or when she spoke, but casually and without offence. Whatever feelings surged in him were for the moment carefully controlled and put aside. In his manner was neither obtrusiveness nor servility, only a kind of well-schooled ease and directness. In short, he behaved and spoke like a gentleman.

"You're the first person I ever sat for," he said, "who hasn't asked me how I lost my legs."

Barbara, regarding the rough blocking of his head which she had made, smiled amiably. That first impression of him, still vivid and lucid in her mind, appeared already, almost of its own accord, to have registered itself in the lump of clay. And she could not but feel that she had laid the groundwork of a masterpiece. If the beggar wished to converse, she would converse—anything to keep him in the mood for returning to pose as often as she should have need of him. And so, though entirely absorbed by the face which she had found, and at the moment almost uncharitably indifferent to the legs which he had lost, she raised her eyes to him, still smiling, and said:

"It wasn't from want of interest, I assure you. I'm sorry you lost them, and I should like to know how it happened."

"Bravely spoken," said the beggar.

"I have been told," said Barbara, "that you are a great power in the East Side, a sort of overlord."

"Even a beggar has flatterers. They overrate me." The accompanying shrug of his great shoulders had an affectation of humility. "Now, if I had a pair of legs—but I haven't. And if I had I shouldn't be an East-Sider. For the maimed, the crippled, the diseased, it is pleasantest to be in residence on the East Side. You have company. You may forget your own misfortunes in contemplating the greater misfortunes of others."

"Do you mind telling me," she asked, "where you learned your English?"

"My father," Blizzard explained, "was rather a distinguished man—Massachusetts Institute of Technology man, University of Berlin, degree from Harvard and Oxford. He had a prim way of putting things. I suppose I caught it."

The usual whine about better days was missing from the beggar's voice. If he seemed a little proud of his high beginnings, he did not seem in the least perturbed by the contemplation of his fallen estate. Barbara was by now frankly interested, and proceeded with characteristic directness to ask questions.

"Is your father living?"

"No. But it would hardly matter. We became thoroughly incompatible after my accident. He had very high ambitions for me, and a chronic disgust for anything abnormal—such as little boys who had had their legs snipped off. I didn't like it either. I suspect it made an unusually vicious child of me, a wicked, vengeful child."

Blizzard's candid expression implied that he had, however, soon seen the evil of his youthful ways, and turned over a whole volume of new leaves.

"What happened?" Barbara asked.

Blizzard laughed. "I cannot be said to have run away," he answered, "but I got away as best I could, and stayed away. My father settled money upon me. And that was the end of our relations."

"And then," said Barbara, "you, being young and foolish, lost your money."

"Oh, no!" he exclaimed. "I was a very bad little boy, but much too ambitious to be foolish. And you know you can't get very far in this world without money."

"Still," said Barbara, "a hand-organ and a tin cup?"

"A loiterer in the streets of New York," the beggar explained, "picks up knowledge not to be had in any other way. Knowledge is power."

"Then you don't have to beg, don't have to pose, don't have to do anything you don't want to do?"

"Oh, yes, I do. I have to crawl while others walk.

I have to wait and procrastinate, where another might rush in and dare."

Again that first expression of Satan fallen overpowered the casual ease and even levity of his face. But he shifted his eyes lest Barbara see into them and be frightened by that which smouldered in their stony depths.

Without a word, Barbara stepped eagerly forward to the rough model that she had made of his head, and once more attacked her inspiration with eager hands. The beggar held himself motionless like a thing of stone, only his eyes roved a little, drinking in, you may say, that white loveliness which was Barbara at such moments as her own eyes were upon her work, and turning swiftly away when she lifted them in scrutiny of him. Now and then she made measurements of him with a pair of compasses. At such times it seemed to him that her nearness was more than his unschooled passions could bear with any appearance of apathy. Though a child of the nineteenth century, he had been enabled for many years to give way, almost whenever he pleased, to the instincts of primitive man, which, except for the greater frequency of their occurrence, differ in no essential way from the instincts of wild beasts.

Had she been a girl of the East Side he would not have hesitated upon the present occasion or in the present surroundings. But she was a girl of wealth and high position. It was not enough that his hands could stifle an outcry, or that the policeman upon the nearest beat was more in his own employ than in that of the city. Cold reason showed him that in the present case impunity was for once doubtful.

Her hands dropped from their work to her sides.

"How goes it?" asked the beggar.

"If it goes as it's gone," she said—"if it only does!"

"It *will*," said the beggar, and there was a strong vibration of faith and encouragement in his voice. "May I look?"

"Of course."

He came down from the platform, and she could not but admire the almost superhuman facility with which he moved upon his crutches. Halting at ease, before the beginning which she had made, he remained for a long time silent. Then, turning to her, he freed his right hand from the cross-piece of his crutch, and lifted it to his forehead in a sort of salute.

"Master!" he said.

The blood in Barbara's veins tingled with pleasure. He had thrown into his strong, rich voice an added wealth of sincerity, and she knew, or thought she knew, that at last the work of her hands had moved another, who, whatever else he might have been, was by his own showing no fool, but a man having in him much that was extraordinary. And she felt a sudden friendliness for the legless beggar.

His eyes still upon the clay—knowing, considering, measuring, appraising eyes—he said shortly and with decision: "We must go on with this."

"To-morrow—could you come to-morrow at the same time?"

"I *will*," he said.

"Good. Are you hungry?"

But the legless man did not appear to have heard her. A sound in the adjoining room had arrested his attention. He listened to it critically and then smiled.

"A good workman," he said, "is turning a screw into wood."

"How clever of you," said Barbara. "There was a man coming from Schlemmer's to put on some glass knobs for me. Bubbles has brought him in by the back stairs."

The faint crunching sound of the screw going into the wood ceased. There was a knock on the door.

"Come in," said Barbara.

Bubbles appeared in the opening. "We're all through in here."

It did not at once strike Barbara that to have finished his work in the next room the man from Schlemmer's must have arrived upon the scene very much earlier than he had promised. And she could not by any possibility have guessed that Bubbles, in a state of nervous alarm, had slipped down the back stairs and run all the way to the hardware store to fetch him.

"He may as well begin in here, then," she said; "I'm through for this morning." And she turned to the beggar. "To-morrow—at the same time?"

He nodded briefly, but did not at once turn to go. He wished, it seemed, to have a good look at the young workman who now followed Bubbles into the studio. And so did Barbara, the moment she saw him.

To her critical eye he was quite the best-looking young man she had ever seen "in the world or out of it." He was tall, broad, round-necked, narrow in the hips, and of a fine brown coloring. He carried with easy grace a strong, well-massed head, to which the close adherence of the ears, and the shortness of the dark-brown shiny hair, gave an effect of high civilization and finish. Brown, level eyes, neither hard nor soft, but of a twinkling habit, a nose straight, thick, finely chiselled, an emphatic chin, and a large mouth of extraordinary sweetness, were not lost upon Barbara, but that which served most to arrest her attention was that resemblance which she at once perceived to exist between the young workman and the legless beggar. Yet between Bubbles, who also resembled Blizzard in her eyes or in her imagination, and the youth from the hardware store, she was unable, swiftly comparing them, to find anything in common. To the one nature had denied even full growth and development; upon the other she had lavished muscle, blood, and bone. The small boy had a ragged, peaked, pathetic face, hair that sprouted every which way, the eyes of an invalid, ears of unequal size and different shapes, that stuck straight out from his head—all the stampings, in short, of street-birth and gutter-raising. The workman had an efficient, commanding look, the easy, strong motions of an athlete trained and proved. Neither in the least resembled the other, yet both resembled the legless beggar, who in turn resembled Satan after the fall—and Barbara was inclined to laugh.

"I am so obsessed with one man's face," she thought, "that I see something of it in all other faces."

"Good-morning, Harry." It was the beggar's voice, cool, and perhaps a little insolent.

"Good-morning, Blizzard." The young man nodded curtly and turned to Barbara. "Do you wish all the knobs changed?"

"Please."

Without another word, the young man knelt at the door by which he had entered and began with the aid of a long screw-driver to remove its ancient lock of japanned iron and coarse white china.

"What's the best news with you, Harry?"

The young man did not look up from his work. "That the water'll soon be warm enough for swimming," he said.

To Barbara that answer seemed pleasantly indicative of a healthy nature and a healthy mind.

"It's a curious thing," observed the beggar, "how many more people drown themselves when the water is nice and warm than when it is cold and inhospitable. And yet it's in the cold months that the most people receive visits from despair."

Bubbles looked up, wondering. In his experience the legless beggar had no manner of language different from that of the streets to which he belonged. But

now he spoke as Miss Barbara spoke, only, perhaps
we may be permitted so to express it, very much
more so.

Barbara turned to the beggar. "I haven't paid
you."

But he retreated in smiling protest, picked up his
hand-organ, and slung it across his shoulders. "The
door, Bubbles."

Bubbles sprang to let the beggar out.

"To-morrow," said Barbara, "at the same time.
Good-by, and thank you."

"Good-by, and thank *you*," said Blizzard.

Bubbles followed him to the head of the stairs and
watched, not without admiration, the astounding ease
of the legless one's rapid descent.

Harry, the workman, having disengaged the old
japanned lock from the door, rose to his feet, and
turned to Barbara with a certain quiet eagerness.
"Look here," he said, "it's none of my business, but
I know, and you don't. That man," he waved the
screw-driver toward the door by which Blizzard had
departed, "is poison. There's nothing he'd stop at.
Nothing."

"Quite so," said Barbara coldly; "and, as you say,
it's hardly anybody's affair but mine."

The workman was good-nature personified. "If
you *must* go on with him," he said, "haven't you a
big brother or somebody with nothing better to do
than drop in, and," his eyes sought the clay head of
Blizzard, "watch the good work go on?" He stepped

closer to the head, and examined it with real interest. "It *is* good work," he said; "it's splendid."

Barbara was mollified. "What," she said, "is so very wrong about poor Mr. Blizzard?"

"Oh," said the young man, "we know a great deal about him, and we are trying very hard to gather the proofs."

"*We?*"

"I'm a very little wheel in the machinery of the secret service."

"I *knew*," said Barbara, "the moment I saw you that you weren't *only* a locksmith or a carpenter. Does Mr. Blizzard know what you are?"

"He can't prove it, unless you tell him."

"I sha'n't do that."

"How often will he have to pose for you?"

"Heaven only knows. But I think"—and she looked the young man in the face, and smiled, for his face had charmed her—"I think that if ever I finish with Mr. Blizzard, I shall ask you to be my next model."

The admiration with which the young man regarded Barbara was no less frankly and openly expressed than was hers for him. "Until this moment," he said, "I have never understood the eager desire which some people have to sit for their portraits. Whenever *you* say."

She laughed. "And the new door-knobs?"

"Just because a man belongs to the secret service," returned the youth, "is no reason why he shouldn't

attempt once in a while to do something really useful."

And he knelt once more and took up his work
where he had left off. Barbara stood by and watched
him at it. "I would like to do his hands, too," she
thought, "when I can get round to it." They were
very strong, square, able hands. She found herself
wishing to touch them. And since this was a wish
that she had never experienced for any other pair of
hands, she wondered at herself with a frank and childish wonder.

"Your taxi, Miss Barbara."

"Thank you, Bubbles."

She slipped out of her overall, and with swift touches
adjusted her hat at a small mirror. The secret-service
agent once more rose from his knees.

"Good-by," said Barbara, "and thank you, and
don't forget."

"Never," said he.

She shook hands with him, and his firm strong clasp,
literally swallowing her own little hand, was immensely
pleasant to her and of a fine friendliness.

"Good-by, Bubbles. See you in the morning."

"Good-by, Miss Barbara."

She was gone. The man resumed his work. The
boy watched.

"Harry."

"What?"

"Was I right?"

"Right."

Harry, the workman, . . . rose to
his feet, and turned to Barbara with
a certain quiet eagerness

"A wonder—or not?"

"A wonder."

"Harry."

"What?"

"You won't leave Blizzard up to me all alone, will you? Not *now*, you won't?"

"No, Bubbles, not now. Whenever he's posing in this room, you and I won't be far off."

"Because," said Bubbles, smiling with relief, "I'd do my best, but if it came to a show-down with *him* there ain't a thing I *could* do."

"One time or another," said Harry, "we'll *get* him. You and I will."

"I betcher," said Bubbles.

And in his little peaked face there was much that was threatening to the ultimate welfare of the legless beggar.

X

BARBARA, ordinarily clear-minded and single-minded, drove uptown with her thoughts in a state of chaos. She wished to think only about her newly begun head of Satan fallen, since nothing else seemed to her at the moment of any importance, but the face, hands, and voice of the young secret-service agent refused to be banished, and kept suing for kindly notice.

In almost the exact degree in which the legless beggar was repulsive to her sense of perfection the secret-service agent was attractive. She had never seen a man so agreeable to her eyes. And yet, as a marine artist might see fame in painting a wreck upon a sea-shore, rather than a fine new ship under full sail, so she felt that, artistically considered, there was no comparison whatever between the two men. The face of the elder compelled attention and study, and loosed in the observer's mind a whole stream of conjecture and unanswerable questions. The face of the younger began and ended perhaps in the attractions of youth and high spirits. It was a face of which, should the mind back of it prove wanting, you might tire, and learn to look upon as commonplace.

In the midst of unguided thinking Barbara laughed aloud; that small boy whom she had lifted from the cold gutter to comparative affluence and incomparable affection for his rescuer came unbidden into the flurry-scurry of her thoughts, and remained for some time. And she knew that if all her friends should fail her, if the beggar returned no more to be modelled, if the secret-service agent proved but a handsome empty shell, Bubbles would always show up at the appointed time and place while life remained in him.

Then, again, as she tried to concentrate upon her bust of Blizzard, the secret-service agent stepped forward, you may say, and smiled into her eyes. And she smiled back. Again she seemed to feel the strong clasp of his hand, and to hear the agreeable and even musical intonation of his strong voice. Odd, she thought, that he should come to put on door-knobs, turn out to be a secret-service agent, and have at the same time, if not the characteristics of a fine gentleman, those at least of a man of education and sensibility infinitely superior to the highest type of day-laborer or detective. One of her new acquaintances talked like a gentleman and claimed to be the son of a distinguished man; the other, claiming nothing, was infinitely more presentable; and there was only the small boy who remained frankly representative of his class. In spite of his coat of bright buttons, he was of the streets streety; a valiant little ragamuffin, in all but the actual rags. He had the morals of his class and the point of view, and differed only in the excellence of his heart. This was a heart made for loving, devotion, and sacrifice. Yet it was crammed to the brim with knowledge of evil, and even tolerance therefor. That certain men in certain circumstances would act in such and such a way was not a horrible idea to Bubbles, but merely a fact. In the boy's code stealing from a friend was stealing, but stealing from an enemy was merely one way of making a living.

Upon arriving at her father's house, Barbara met Wilmot Allen just turning away from the door. His handsome face brightened at the sight of her, and he sprang forward hatless to furnish her with quite unnecessary aid in stepping out of the taxi.

"Oh, *there* you are!" he said. "Sparker said you might be home for lunch and again you might not. Please may I graft a meal?"

"Of course," said Barbara, "but unless somebody else drops out of the skies we'll be all alone."

"Your father off on a case?"

"Yes," said Barbara, as they went in, "he is operating, but in Wall Street. And what's the best news with you?"

"That spring's come and summer's coming. When do your holidays begin?"

"*That*," said Barbara, with a certain air of triumph, "is a secret of the workshop. Let's sit in the dining-room. It's the only way to hurry lunch."

To persons used to humbler ways of life Dr. Ferris's dining-room would have proved too large and stately a place for purposes of intimate conversation. Warriors and ladies looked down from the tapestried walls upon a small round table set with heavy silver and

light glass for two, and having the effect, in the midst
of an immense deep-blue rug, of a little island in a
lake. But Barbara and Wilmot Allen, well used to
even larger and more stately rooms, faced each other
across the white linen with its pattern of lotus-plants
and swans, and chatted as comfortably and uncon-
cernedly as two children in their nursery.

"As for holidays," said Barbara, "I have a new
model, Wilmot; a wonderful person, and that means
work. I may stay in town right through the summer."

Allen sighed loudly, and on purpose. "You make
me tired," he said. "Bring a lump of clay down to
Newport, and *I'll* sit for you."

Barbara affected to study his face critically. Then
she shook her head. "My new model," she explained,
"has got the face of a fallen angel. I think I can do
it. And if I can do it, why, I see all the good things
of sculping coming my way."

"An ordinary every-day angel face wouldn't do?"
her guest insinuated. "I could go out and fall."

"I don't doubt it!" she returned somewhat crisply.
"I feel very sure that you could disgrace yourself
without trouble and even with relish. But it wouldn't
show in your face. You see, you couldn't really be
wicked."

"Couldn't I though!" exclaimed the young man.
"A lot you know about it. I could eat you up for
one thing without turning a hair, and that would be
wicked."

"It wouldn't," Barbara laughed. "It would be

greedy. My new model has the face of a man who has never stopped at anything that has stood in his way. I fancy that he has murders up his sleeve and every other crime in the calendar. And sometimes memory of them brings the most wonderful look of sorrow and remorse into his face, and at the same time he looks resolved to go on murdering and burning and sinning because he can't get back to where he was when he began to fall, and must go on falling or perish. Don't you think that if I can cram that into a lump of clay I'll make a reputation for myself?"

"I think," said Wilmot, "that if you've got that kind of a man sitting for you, you'll need all the reputation you can get. You talk of him with the same sort of enthusiasm that a bird would show in describing being fascinated by a snake."

Barbara considered this judicially. "Do you know," she agreed, "it is rather like that. He fascinates me, and at the same time I never saw a brute I hated so. He must be wicked to deserve such pain."

"Oh, he suffers, does he?"

"Of course. Wouldn't you suffer every minute of your life if you had no legs?"

Barbara, intent upon what was on her plate, did not perceive the sudden astonished darkening of Wilmot Allen's face, nor that the interest which he had hitherto only feigned in her new model had become genuine.

"What is he?"

"I was going to say 'just a beggar,'" said Barbara.

"But he isn't just a beggar. I've gathered that he's rather well off, and that he's one of the powers on the East Side. And he looks money and power, even if he doesn't talk them."

"Is his name by any chance Blizzard?"

She looked up in astonishment. "How did you know?"

"Oh," he said cheerfully, "I've knocked about the city and known all sorts of curious people, and heard about others. So Blizzard's your new model. Now look here, Barbara, are we old friends, or aren't we?"

"Very old friends," she said.

"Then let me tell you that you're a little fool to have anything to do with a man like that. You can't touch pitch, you know, and——"

"I only touch him with a pair of compasses," she interrupted sweetly.

"Don't quibble," said Allen with energy; "it's not like you. That man is so bad, so unsavory, so vile, that you simply *mustn't* have him about. He's dangerous."

"So is a volcano," said Barbara, "but there's no reason why the most innocent bread-and-butter miss shouldn't paint a picture of a volcano if she felt inspired."

"I see that there's only one thing to do. I shall tell your father."

Wilmot Allen was genuinely troubled. And Barbara laughed at him.

"I'm not a child," she said.

"That's just it," said he; "that's why you ought to be ashamed of yourself. And anyway you are a child. All girls say they aren't until they get into a mess of some sort, and then they excuse themselves to themselves and everybody else by protesting that they were. 'I was so young. I didn't know,' and all that rot."

"Blizzard," said Barbara, "is quiet, polite, and a good talker. He comes, he sits for me, and he goes away."

The butler having left the room, Wilmot fixed his rather tired eyes on Barbara's face, and spoke with a certain earnest tenderness. "Barbs," he said, "take it from me, happiness doesn't lie where you think it does. I think the very highest achievements of the very greatest artists haven't brought happiness. Look here, old dear; put a limit to your ambition. Say that by a certain date you'll either succeed and quit, or fail and quit, and then see if you can't take a little more interest in your own people, in your own heart—even in me."

"Wilmot," she said seriously, "if I fail with my head of Blizzard, I think I *shall* give up."

"Wouldn't it be better," he pleaded, "to give up now? And then, you know, you could always say if *only* you'd kept on you would have made a master-piece."

"And who would believe that?"

"*I!*" said Wilmot. "It's easy for me to believe anything wonderful of you. It always has been."

"And a moment ago," she smiled, "you called me a little fool and said you'd tell my father on me."

She rose, still smiling, and he followed her into the library.

"Are all the studios in your building occupied?" he asked.

"They are," said Barbara, "and they aren't. Kelting, who has the ground floor, has gone abroad. And Updyke, who has the third floor, has been in Bermuda all winter." She sank into a deep leather chair that half swallowed her.

"There's a janitor?"

"No. There's a janitress, a friendly old lady, quite deaf. She has seen infinitely better days."

"To all intents and purposes, then," said Wilmot, and the trouble that he felt showed in his face, "it's an empty house, and you shut yourself up in it with some model or other that you happen to pick up in the streets, and you don't know enough to be afraid. You'll get yourself murdered one of these bright mornings."

"Oh, I think not!" said Barbara. "There's Bubbles, you know."

"Oh, Bubbles!" exclaimed Wilmot. "He doesn't weigh eighty pounds. This Blizzard—look here, get rid of him. I can't tell you what the man is." He laughed. "I don't know you well enough. But take my word for it, if a crime appeals to him, he commits it. And the police can't touch him, Barbs."

"Why can't they?"

"He knows too much about them individually and collectively. They're afraid of him. Get rid of him, Barbs."

Wilmot Allen's voice was strongly appealing. The fact that he sat forward in his chair, instead of yielding to its deep and enjoyable embrace, proved that he was very much in earnest. But Barbara shook her lovely head.

"You ask too much, Wilmot. My heart's in the beginning I've made. I've got to go on. It's a test case. If I've got *anything* in me, now is the chance for it to show. You see, when I made up my mind seriously to try to do worth-while things with my own hands, everybody was against me. And the sympathy that I am going to receive if I fail to make good is of a kind that's almost impossible to face."

"Then do me a favor. It won't interfere with your work, and it may be very useful at a pinch." He drew from his hip pocket a small automatic pistol. "Accept this," he went on, "and keep it somewhere handy as a sort of guardian. It's much stronger than the strongest man."

"How absurd!" she said. "And what are you doing carrying concealed weapons? I'm beginning to think that you're a desperado yourself."

He rose, smiling imperturbably, and laid the pistol in her lap

"At least," she said, "show me how it works."

He explained the mechanism clearly and with patience, not once, but several times. "Point it," he said, "as you would point your finger, and keep pulling the trigger until the enemy drops."

"One every two hours," Barbara commented, "until relieved."

"May you never need it," said Wilmot, earnestly.

"I never shall," said Barbara. "Must I really keep it?"

"Yes."

"But you," she exclaimed, "you will be quite unprotected all the way from here to the nearest shop where such things are sold."

"I shall be armed again," he smiled, "before I am threatened. Indeed, to know that you are armed has heartened me immensely. What are you doing this afternoon?"

"I don't know," she answered with provoking submissiveness; "you haven't told me."

"It's just possible," he said, "that the turf courts at the Westchester Country Club have been opened. I might telephone and find out. Then we could collect some clothes, jump into a taxi, and go out and open the season."

"You can't afford taxis, Wilmot. And you never let anybody else pay for anything."

"Oh," he pleaded, "I can afford a taxi this once, believe me."

"In that case," said Barbara, "I surrender."

"If you only would, Barbs."

"'Phone if you are going to, and don't be always

slipping sentiment into a business proposition." She affected to look very stern and business-like.

"I shall engage the magic taxi," he affirmed.

"The what?"

"Don't you know? There's a magic taxi in the city—just one. You get in, you give your order, and lo and behold, rivers and seas are crossed, countries and continents, until finally you fetch up in the place where you would be, and when you look at the meter you find that it hasn't registered as much as a penny."

"Time," said Barbara, "flies even faster than a magic taxicab. So if you are going to 'phone——"

"Is there no drop of sentiment in that exquisite shell which the world knows as Barbara Ferris? Didn't any man ever mean anything to you, Barbs?"

She flushed slightly, for there had come into her thoughts quite unbidden the image of a certain young man in workman's clothes, kneeling at a door, and removing an old japanned iron lock. She shook her head firmly, and smiled up at him insultingly.

"Men, Wilmot," she said, "are nothing to me but planes, angles, curves, masses, lights, and shadows. They are either suited to sculpture or they aren't."

Wilmot laughed, and while he was busy with the telephone, Barbara tried to think of the secret-service agent in cold terms of planes, curves, masses, etc., and found that she couldn't. Which discovery annoyed and perplexed her.

XI

THE girls who plaited hats for Blizzard had just finished luncheon and were taking their places at the long work-table. The entrance door having clanged its bell, twenty heads bent earnestly over twenty hats in various stages of construction, and twenty pairs of hands leaped into skilful activity.

The master passed up and down on his crutches, observing progress and despatch with slow-moving, introspective eyes. Presently he came to a halt and clapped his hands sharply together. Twenty pairs of eyes, some cringing, some with vestiges of boldness, some favor-currying, sought his, and twenty pairs of hands ceased work as when power is shut off from as many machines. Blizzard's eyes passed slowly over the girls in a sort of appraising review, once, and a second time.

"Miss Rose."

"Yes, sir."

The speaker was one of those flowers of girlhood which bloom here and there in the slums. She might have been a princess in exile and disguise. Even her hands and feet were fine and delicate. And if in her expression there was a certain nervousness, there was none of fear.

"Stand up."

She rose in her place; the corners of her mouth trembled a little, but curled steadily upward.

"Stand out where I can see you."

She did so, with a certain defiant grace.

"Turn around, slowly."

She might have been one of those young ladies at a fashionable dressmaker's upon whom the effect of the latest Parisian models is continually tried. While she slowly gyrated, the legless man, looking up at her, spoke aloud.

"Muck! Muck!" he said. "And yet she's the pick of the bunch."

The girl kept on turning.

"Stand still."

She did as ordered, but it so happened that her back was squarely turned upon the master.

"No monkey business," he shouted. "Face me! Face me!"

She faced him, still scornful, but white now, and biting her lips.

"The rest of you," he said, "will have the rest of the day off. Get out."

Seventy-six chair-legs squeaked, and Miss Rose's nineteen companions, with murmurs and occasional nervous giggles, hurried off to the coat-room. A few minutes later the bell of the outer door clanged once —they were going; clanged a second time—they were gone.

Meanwhile the legless man had not taken his hard, calculating eyes off the girl who remained. Presently

She faced him, still scornful, but white
now, and biting her lips

he spoke. "We're alone," he said. "I'm between you and the door." He spread his great arms, as if to emphasize the impassability of the barrier which confronted her. "Are you afraid?"

"Yes."

The legless man laughed. "Well said," he remarked, "and truthfully said. And why are you afraid?"

"Everybody's afraid of you."

He regarded her for some moments in silence. "You needn't be. Have I ever hurt you?"

"No."

"How long have you worked for me?"

"Five months."

"And you are the cleverest worker I have. You admit that?"

"I don't know."

Again he laughed. "Once," he said, "I thought you were the prettiest girl I'd ever seen. But I've seen a prettier."

"I believe you."

"But you've got a certain spirit. You don't cringe."

"Don't I?"

"No!" he bellowed, "you don't." And when he saw that she didn't cringe, he laughed once more.

"You live with Minnie Bauer?"

"Yes, sir."

"You have no father—no mother?"

"No, sir."

"Burnt alive in a tenement fire, weren't they?"

She answered with a great effort, and seemed upon the verge of tears. "Yes, sir."

"You will leave Minnie, and come here to live."

"Why?"

"Because I make it my business to reward the skilful, the laborious, and the deserving."

She shook her head. "That's not good enough," she said.

"You will keep my house in order," he said; "you will learn to help me with the piano. You will have fine clothes to wear, and the spending of plenty of money."

"Not good enough," she repeated.

"I have read you these five months as if you were a book. You are loyal to your friends. You can keep secrets. I admire you. There are many things that I wish to talk about. But I cannot talk about them except to some one that I can trust. Will you stay?"

She shook her head, but the legless man smiled, as he might have smiled if she had nodded it.

"I am suffering," he said, "the tortures of the damned. I ask you for help and for comfort, and you refuse them."

A look curiously like tenderness swam into the girl's eyes. The beggar moved sideways upon his crutches.

"If you want to go," he said, "the way's open."

"Can I really go if I want to, and not come back?"

"You really can," he said. "Most things that I

want I take, but a man can't take help and comfort unless they are freely given."

She moved slowly forward as if to discover the truth of his statement that the way was open. He made not the least gesture of interference. When she was between him and the outer door and rather nearer the latter, she turned about sharply.

"What's troubling you?" she asked.

"The fact," he said, and there was a something really charming in the expression of his mouth and eyes, "that though I can give orders to very many people, and be obeyed as a general is obeyed by his soldiers in war times, I have no friend. Fear attracts this person to me, self-interest attracts that person, but there's no one that's held to me by friendship."

"You're only asking me to be your friend?"

"You will be as safe in my house as in the rooms of the Gerry Society."

"If you want me for a friend why did you call me *muck* just now?"

"I don't want the others to know that we are friends. I want them to think—what they always think."

"How do I know you trust me?"

"Lock the street door," he said; "you're younger than I. It's easier for you to move about."

She locked the door and returned.

"Are you staying," he asked, "through curiosity or friendship?"

"Look here," she said, "it's neither. Can't you
guess what ails me?"

"Tell me."

She took his strong, wicked face between her young
hands, and bending over kissed him on the forehead.
Then she drew back, flaming.

The legless man was touched. "Why?" he asked.

"I don't know. It just came to me," she said.
"God knows I didn't want it to. I guess that's all."

Rose found it hard to control her jumping nerves.
A curious thing had happened to her. Having at last
wormed her way into the master's confidence, and
brought a long piece of play-acting to a successful
conclusion, a certain candor and frankness which were
natural to her made the thought of divulging what
she had already found out, and whatever he might
confide to her in the future, exceedingly repugnant.
And she acknowledged with a shiver of revolt that
the creature's fascination for her was not altogether
a matter of make-believe. She was going to find it
very hard to keep a proper perspective and point of
view; to continue to regard him as just another
"case" and all in the day's work.

"In my house," he said, "you shall do as you
please. You're a dear girl, Rose."

"I feel at home in your house," she said, "and
happy."

A cloud gathered in Blizzard's face. "Happiness!"
he exclaimed. "There is no such thing—neither for
you, nor for me. The world is a torture-chamber,

and remember, Rose, we are to be allies; we are to have no secrets from each other.''

She shrugged her shoulders. "That was what you said," she complained. "But have you really shown me any confidence?"

He smiled as upon a wayward child. "You shall know everything that there is to know—when the time comes."

She pouted.

"And what, by the way," he went on, "have *you* told *me?*"

"I have told you," she answered with dignity, "my one secret."

"The way you feel about me?"

She nodded and blushed. It was going to be a hard lie to keep telling.

"And you've no other secret? Nothing else that you ought to tell me?"

There was more meaning in his voice than in his words, so that for a moment Rose was startled. Was it possible that the man suspected her, and was playing with her as a cat plays with a mouse?

"What else could I possibly have to tell you of any importance?"

"I was joking," said the beggar.

Rose sat at the window of her room looking upward into a night of stars. She could not sleep. Twice she had heard the legless man pass her door upon his crutches. Each time he had hesitated, and once, or so she thought, he had laid his hand upon the door-knob. She wondered how much of her wakefulness was due to fright, and how much to the excitement of being well launched upon a case of tremendous importance, for the secret service knew that Blizzard was engaged upon a colossal plot of some sort, and just what that was Rose had volunteered, at the risk of her life, and of her honor, to find out.

XII

THE next morning, at the appointed hour, Blizzard climbed the stairs to Barbara's studio, knocked, and was admitted. That he was welcome, if only for his head's sake, was at once evident.

"Something told me that *you* wouldn't fail me," said Barbara.

"You can be quite easy about that," said Blizzard. "I am in the habit of keeping my word."

He climbed to the model's platform and seated himself as upon the previous morning, with a kind of business-like directness.

"Ready when you are," he said.

Barbara withdrew the damp cloths from the clay, looked critically from the bust to the original and back again. "My work," she said, "still looks right to me. But you don't."

Blizzard smiled.

"Yesterday," she said, "you looked as if you were suffering like," she laughed, "like the very devil. To-day you look well fed and contented. Now that won't do. Try to remember what you were thinking about when I first saw you."

At once, as a fresh slide is placed in a magic-lantern, the legless man's expression of well-being vanished, and that dark tortured look of Satan fallen which had

so fired Barbara's imagination, once more possessed
his features. Barbara's eyes flashed with satisfaction.

"It wasn't hard for you to remember what you
were thinking about, was it?" she said.

"It was not," said Blizzard, and his voice was cold
as a well-curb. "When I first saw you, I was thinking thoughts that can never be forgotten."

"Lift your chin, please," she said, "just a fraction.
So. Turn your head a fraction more toward me.
Good. And please don't think of anything pleasant
until I tell you. Anybody can make an exact copy
of a head. Expressions are the things that only
lucky people can catch."

"I believe you are one of them," said Blizzard.
"I believe you will catch mine—if you keep on wanting to."

"I must," she said simply.

And then for half an hour there was no sound in
the studio but the long-drawn breathing of the legless man. Barbara worked in a kind of grim, exalted
silence.

Meanwhile Bubbles was climbing the back stair to
his bedroom, where he had left Harry, the secret-
service agent, on guard over Barbara. The boy, all
out of breath with haste, opened his right fist and
disclosed a narrow slip of paper with writing on it.

"The minute *he* came out of his burrow and started
uptown," said Bubbles, "and was out o' sight, I
begun to spin my top up and down Marrow Lane.
Rose she's moved upstairs, like she said she would."

Harry's eyes sparkled with interest and approbation. "Good girl!" he said.

"I seen her," Bubbles went on, "at an upper window, and when she seed me, she winked both eyes, like as if the sun was too bright for 'em. I winked the same way, and then she lets the paper drop."

Harry took the paper out of the boy's hand, and read: "Nothing done, much doing."

"She's a grand one," said Bubbles. "If he ever gets wise to her, he'll tear her to pieces."

"I'm not worrying about Rose—yet," said Harry. "She knows what she's up against, and she can pull a gun quicker than I can. We used to play getting the drop on each other by the hour."

"What for?" asked Bubbles, always interested in the smallest details of sporting propositions.

"Poker-chips," said Harry, and Bubbles looked his disgust. There was a minute's silence, then:

"Harry," said Bubbles, "what do *you* think he's up to?"

"By George," said Harry, "I can't make out. What do *you* think?"

Bubbles's sensitive mouth quivered eagerly. "You tell me," he said, "what he's making hats for—he don't sell 'em—and I'll tell you what he's up to."

"Some of the labor leaders in the West are mixed up in it," said Harry; "we *know* that."

"Labor leaders, Harry!" The small boy's face was comic with scorn and facetiousness.

"You know the ones I mean, Bub. Not the men

who lead labor—that's only what they call themselves; but the men who betray labor for their own pockets, the men who find dynamite for half-witted fanatics to set off. The men—" He broke short off, and listened. "Better butt in to the studio, Bub, and see what's doing."

"Did you think you heard something?"

"I know that I haven't heard anything for half an hour."

In a few minutes Bubbles returned. "He's just sitting there with a hell of a face on him," he said, "and she's working like a dynamo."

And although Barbara actually was working with great speed and gratitude, the entrance of the small boy had seemed to disturb the train of her inspiration. Somewhere in the back of her head appeared to be some brain-cells quite detached from the important matter in hand, and to these was conveyed the fact that a door-knob had been turned, and at once they began to busy themselves upon the suggestion. Something like this: door-knobs—old door-knobs—new glass door-knobs—man to put on new glass door-knobs—wonderfully prepossessing man—name Harry—charming name. Harry—charming smile—wonder if anybody'll ever see him again.

Gradually other cells in Barbara's brain took up the business, until presently she was entirely occupied with unasked, and unwelcome, and altogether pleasant thoughts of the young secret-service agent. It was almost as if he laid his hand on her shoulder, and said: "You've worked long enough on this dreadful beggar—come with me for a holiday."

Twice, sternly, she endeavored to go on with her work, and could not. Something of the May-weather message, that all is futile except life, had filtered into her blood. Her hands dropped to her sides, and her face, very rosy, became so wonderfully beautiful that Blizzard almost groaned aloud. Something told him that his morning was over, his morning filled with the happiness of propinquity and stolen looks, with the happiness that is half spiritual and half gloating.

"Thank you," said Barbara, "ever so much. I sha'n't do any more to-day. I'm not fit. But we have gotten on. Want to look?"

She turned the revolving-table so that Blizzard could look upon his likeness. And you may be sure that he did not lose the opportunity thus presented. He regarded the clay steadily, for a long time, without speaking. Then he drew one very long breath, and the expression upon his face softened.

"That man," he said, "has had a hard life, Miss Ferris. It is all written in his face. When he was a little boy, he was the victim of a mistake so atrocious, so wicked, that the blood in his body turned to gall, and all his powers of loving turned to hatred. Instead of facing disaster like a man, he turned from it, and fled—down—down—down, and fell down—down—grappling with all that he could reach that was good or beautiful, and dragging it down with him —to destruction—to the pit—to hell on earth. And then he lived a long time, pampering all that was base in him, prospering materially, recognizing no moral law. He was contented with his choice—happy as a well-fed dog is happy in a warm corner. And then the inevitable happened. An idea came to him, a dream of peace and beauty, of well-doing and happiness. But that chance was torture, since, if he was to live it, he must undo the evil that he had done, unthink the thoughts that had been meat and drink to him, and he must get back to where he was before he fell."

He paused, and extending his right forefinger pointed at the bust of himself and exclaimed:

"That man—there—that you've made in my image—line for line—torture for torture, must go on living in the hell which he has prepared with his own perverted mind. He can never get back. It is too late—too late—too late!"

His voice rose to a kind of restrained fury. The room shook with its strong vibrations.

Then he turned to Barbara, smiled, all of a sudden, gayly, almost genuinely, and said in a voice of humble gallantry:

"But I've done you a good turn. If you never proved it before, you're proving these days that you are a heaven-born genius."

A harder-headed girl than Barbara must have been pleased and beguiled. She blushed, and laughed. "I've only one thing to wish for," she said.

"What is that?"

"I wish," she said, "that you were the greatest art critic in the world."

He leaned forward, and in a confidential whisper: "A secret," said he, "between us two. I am."

Then they both laughed, and the beggar, not without reluctance, climbed down from the platform. Swift and easy as were his motions, he appeared to terrible disadvantage, and he knew it. So did Barbara, who a moment before had been on the point of really liking him. She steeled herself against the sudden disgust which she could not help feeling, and smiled at him in a steady, friendly way.

"To-morrow?" she said.

"To-morrow."

"At the same time, please. Good-by, and good luck to you."

"Good luck to *you*, Miss Ferris." And he was gone.

Barbara, opening the door into the next room, surprised a sound of voices. They ceased instantly. "Bubbles," she called.

He came, looking a trifle guilty.

"Who's that with you?"

"Harry," he said simply.

"The man who was here before?"

"Yes, Miss Barbara."

"What's he doing in my rooms?"

"He was just sitting, and chinning," said Bubbles.

Miss Ferris was displeased. "Tell him," she said, "that I can't have my apartment turned into a Young Men's Club."

"Yes, miss."

Bubbles retired, reluctantly, with the message, only to return in a moment.

"He says will you let him speak to you a moment, please."

She hesitated. And then, "Yes," she said. "I suppose he wishes to apologize."

He was even more charming-looking than the memory of him. She made an effort to look a little displeased, and a little unfriendly. She failed, because the May-weather message had gotten into her blood, and because certain forces of which as yet she knew little had established connecting links between herself and the young secret-service agent.

"I am going to scold you," said Barbara. "Bubbles has his work to do."

"But I was helping him with it."

"He said you were just sitting and—and chinning."

"When we had finished working."

"Have you been here long?"

The young man looked her steadily in the face, and said gravely: "Ever since Blizzard came."

Barbara lifted her chin a little. "I am quite able to take care of myself," she said.

He shook his head sadly.

"Do you make it your business"—she had succeeded in making herself angry—"to keep an eye on all young women whom you fancy unable to take care of themselves?"

"I only wish to God I could," he said earnestly.

"But of course it's impossible. So I just do the best I can."

"And why have you chosen me? Surely others are even *more* helpless than I am." She managed to convey a good deal of scorn. "Why," she continued, "must I be the particular creature singled out for your chivalrous notice?"

"I don't know," he said simply.

All the anger went out of Barbara, and a delicious little thrill passed through her from head to foot, leaving in its wake a clear rosy coloring.

"Bubbles," said the young man, "would die for you; but he is only a little boy. I am very strong."

Barbara refused to rise at the implication that the strong young man was also ready and even eager to die for her. "Tell me more about Blizzard," she said.

"He's one of the half-dozen men in the city that we would like to have an eye on night and day. We want him."

"Oh," she said, "then you are not here entirely on my account? It is also your business to be here?"

He nodded, not altogether pleased with the turn the matter had taken.

"In that case," she said, "I have no wish to stand in your way. But—I don't propose to be a cat's-paw. You may sit in Bubbles's room if you like, but I won't have you on your hands and knees at the studio door listening at the key-hole. That must be understood."

The young man flushed with righteous anger.

"You don't *look*," he said, "as if you could say a thing like that to a fellow."

Instantly, and almost humbly, she begged his pardon.

"Then I may come to-morrow?" he asked.

"And the next day," said Barbara. "And, by the way, what is your name?"

"Harry," he said.

"Harry what?"

A look very much like pathos came into his handsome eyes. "I want to be honest with you," he said. "I don't own any other name. I call myself West. But I've no right to it. I don't know who my father was or what he was."

"You don't have to explain," said Barbara. "I think you would have been quite within your rights in saying that your name was West and letting it go at that."

It was not her intention to receive Mr. West's confidences either at this time or any other. And so, of course, ten minutes later, as she drove uptown, she was "dying" to know all that there was to be known about him. He had gone downstairs with her, and put her into her cab. He might have been a prince with a passion for good manners. He seemed to her wonderfully graceful and at ease, in all that he did.

XIII

DR. FERRIS smiled tolerantly, and said to the footman who had brought the card: "I shall be very glad to see Mr. Allen." And he kept on smiling after the footman had gone. The interview which he foresaw was of that kind which not only did him honor but amused him. Wilmot Allen would not be the first young man to whom the rich surgeon had had the pleasure of putting embarrassing questions: "What can you tell me of your past life and habits?" "Can you support my daughter in the way to which she has always been accustomed?" etc., etc.

But Wilmot Allen did not at once ask permission to address Barbara. He entered with that good-natured air of easy laziness which was rather attractive in him, and without looking in the least troubled announced that what he had come to say embarrassed him greatly.

"And furthermore," he said, "if Barbara hears of it, she'll be furious. She would take the natural and even correct point of view that it's none of my business, and she would select one of the thousand ruthless and brutal methods which young women have at their disposition for the disciplining of young men. So, please, will you consider my visit professional and, if you like," he grinned mischievously, "charge me the regular fee for consultation?"

Dr. Ferris laughed. "I shall be delighted to play father confessor," he said, "if you'll sit down, and smoke a cigar."

Mr. Allen would. He lighted one of Dr. Ferris's cigars with the care due to a thing of value, settled himself in a deep chair, and appeared by slightly pausing to be gathering scattered thoughts into a focus.

"Yes," he said at last, "there's no doubt about it. I am about to be very impertinent. If you like you shall turn me out of your house, with or without kicks, as seems best to you. Barbara needs a nurse, and it seems to me you ought to know it; because in a way it's a reflection on you."

"Quite so," said Dr. Ferris. "I am not at all pleased with Barbara. What has she done?"

"Do you suppose it would be possible to get her interested in anything besides this sculpture business —before it's too late?"

"Too late?"

"Before she gets a taste of success."

"But will she—ever?"

Wilmot Allen nodded eagerly. "She will," he said. "She is doing a head. It's far from finished; but even now, in the rough state, it's quite the most exceptional inspired thing you ever saw. She will exhibit it and become famous overnight. I can't bet much—as you may perhaps suspect—but I'll bet all I've got. And of course, once she gets recognition and everybody begins to kow-tow to her—why, goodby, Barbara."

"Still," said Dr. Ferris, "if she's developing a real talent, I don't know that I ought to stand in her way. And, besides, we've fought that all out, and," he laughed grimly, "I took my licking like a man."

"Of course," said Allen. "When a girl that ought to go in for marriage and that sort of thing takes to being talented—I call it a tragedy. But, passing that, the model for the head she's doing isn't a proper person. That's what I'm driving at. He's one of the wickedest and most unscrupulous persons in the world. Barbara ought not to speak to him, let alone give him the run of her studio and hobnob with him same as with one of her friends. He's a man too busy with villainy to sit as a model for the fun of sitting. The pay doesn't interest him. And if he shows up every morning at nine and stays all morning, it's only because he's got an axe to grind. He talks. He lays down the law. He appeals to Barbara's mind and imagination; and it's all rather horrible—one of those poison snakes that look like an old rubber boot, and a bird all prettiness, bright colors, innocence, and admiration of how the world is made. Look at it in this way. She makes a great hit with the bust. Who's responsible? Well, the creature that supplied the inspiration, largely. She'll feel gratitude. He'll take advantage of anything that comes his way. And frankly, Dr. Ferris, I may be making a mountain out of a mole-hill, but I'm worried to death. Suppose I told you that, say, Duane Carter spent hours every day in Barbara's studio?"

Dr. Ferris jumped to his feet, white with anger. "Do you mean to tell me that my daughter is friendly with that person?"

"Oh, no," said Allen calmly. "I think Barbara's new friend is a very much more dangerous person for her to know. Whatever Duane Carter is he wouldn't dare. This other man——"

"Look here, Wilmot"—Dr. Ferris began to pace the room in considerable agitation—"you're an old friend of Barbara's. Is friendliness at the root of your worry, or is it some other feeling, not so disinterested as friendship?"

Wilmot Allen rose to his full height, and Dr. Ferris paused in his pacings. They faced each other.

"If I was any good," said the young man slowly, "if I had any money, if Barbara would have me, I'd marry her to-morrow. But I'm not any good—never was. I haven't any money, hardly ever have had, and Barbara would no more have me of her own free will than she'd take a hammer and smash the bust she's making. So much for motives. Have I disposed of jealousy?"

Dr. Ferris nodded.

"The man," said Allen, "isn't a man. He's a gutter-dog, a gargoyle, half a man. And his position in the city—in the whole country, I think—is so fortified that with the best will in the world the law cannot touch him. Duane Carter—well, he's been a gay boy with the ladies—a bad man if you like—but at least he is not accused by gossip of murder, arson, abduction, and crimes infinitely worse than these. He may have beguiled women, but at least his worst enemy would never suppose that he had trafficked in them. Barbara's model is all the things that you can imagine. And all of them are written in his horrible face. To see them together, friendly, reparteeing, chummy, would turn your stomach—Barbara so exquisite and high-born, and the man, his eyes full of evil fires, sitting like a great toad on the model's chair. And at that—good God, you might stand it, if he was a whole man! But he isn't. It's horrible! He has no legs—and you want to stamp on him till he's dead."

Dr. Ferris had turned white as a sheet. "To me," he said quietly, "that is the most horrible form of mutilation. I can't tell you why. It is so. And you will believe that in my practice I have encountered all sorts. But who is he?"

"He's a man named Blizzard—he passes for a beggar, grinds an organ, sells shoe-laces and that sort of thing. As a matter of fact, he's very well off, if not rich. Why don't you visit Barbara's studio to-morrow, look things over, and put a stop to it? You can say things to Barbara that I can't, that no young man can say to a girl. Go as far as you like. Whatever you tell her about him will be true even if you can't prove it. You can make her see what thin ice she's skating on. Or if you can't nobody can."

"I'll go to the studio to-morrow," said the surgeon. "I am very much disturbed by what you have told

me: the more so because as a physician I have learned
how many impossible things are true. Have you told
me all you wish to? Or is there more? Do you
think," he spoke very steadily, "that Barbara *cares*
for this beast? Such things happen in the world, I
know."

"God forbid," said Allen, "but I think he has a sort
of fascination for her, and that she doesn't realize it.
You'll let your visit appear casual and accidental,
won't you? You won't let Barbara suspect that I
had anything to do with it?"

Dr. Ferris promised, and the two parted with
mutual good-will; but neither the next morning, nor
the morning after that, was Dr. Ferris at liberty to
pay a visit to Barbara in her studio. Nominally retired from active practice, and devoting whatever of
life should remain to surgical experimentation and
theory, the sudden and acute jeopardy of an old friend
caused him to put all other considerations aside for
the time being, and once more to don the white harness
of his profession. For two days Dr. Ferris hardly left
his friend's side; on the morning of the third day,
quite worn out, his jumping nerves soothed by a small
dose of morphine, he called a taxicab, gave Barbara's
number in McBurney Place, leaned back against the
leather cushions, relaxed his muscles, and fell asleep.

The taxicab and the legless man reached the curb
in front of Barbara's studio at the same moment.
The driver of the cab lifted one finger to his hat.
The legless man nodded, and peering into the cab

recognized the handsome features of the sleeping doctor. He smiled, and said to the driver:

"Take him back to his house."

The driver said: "If I do he'll enter a complaint."

"No," said the legless man; "you will tell him when he wakes that he gave you the order himself. He won't know whether he did or not. So-long."

The driver once more lifted one finger to his hat and obediently drove off.

It was very silent in McBurney Place; the double row of ancient stables made over into studio-buildings appeared deserted. The legless man could not but flatter himself that his actions had been unobserved. He chuckled, and with even more than his usual deft alacrity climbed the stairs to Barbara's studio.

Meanwhile, however, a young man and a small boy, looking through the curtains of the latter's bedroom window, had been witnesses of all that passed.

"That was Miss Barbara's father in the taxi," said Harry West.

"Looks like he'd been out all night," said Bubbles.

"He may have been drugged."

"Doubt it. The taxi turned north at the corner. If the ole 'un had had the doctor drugged o' purpose he'd 'a' sent him south where he could use him. I guess he's sent him home."

"He doesn't want his morning with Miss Barbara interrupted."

Harry West sighed and said: "I don't smoke, Bub. Give me a cigarette."

Bubbles accommodated his friend with eagerness.

"And now," said West, "the road's clear to Marrow Lane; better slip down and see if Rose has any word for us. I'll keep a good ear on Blizzard."

Bubbles changed from his buttons to his street-jacket, and departed by the back stairs. Harry West took a small automatic pistol from his breast pocket and played with it, but in the expression of the young man's face was nothing bellicose or threatening; only a kind of gentle, patient misery.

He passed fifteen minutes in taking quick aims with the little automatic pistol at the roses on the wall-paper. Short of actual target-practice, he knew by experience that this was the best way to keep the hand and eye in touch with each other. He let his thoughts run as they would. And presently he heard the sound of Bubbles's feet upon the back stairs.

"All serene here," said West.

"All serene there," said Bubbles, and he produced a slip of paper upon which Rose had written:

"Don't come so often. You've been noticed. He'll tell me things before long—or wring my neck."

"She worked her hands some," said Bubbles, and he made letters of the deaf and dumb alphabet upon his fingers. "She said O'Hagan's in the city. They had him to eat with them last night. He's growed a beard, and trained off twenty pounds, so's not to be knowed."

The air of revery had left Harry West. "O'Hagan in the East!" he exclaimed, rather with exhilaration than excitement. "Things are coming to a head."

"Yep," said Bubbles, "and we don't know what things is——"

"Bubbles! Oh, Bubbles!"

The boy disappeared in the direction of the studio.

"Mr. Blizzard has gone," said Barbara. "Ask Mr. West if he will speak to me a moment."

Mr. West would; and he, the athlete, the man of trained poise, actually overturned a chair in his willingness.

"Mr. West," she said, "you know all sorts of things about people, don't you? And if you don't know them, you can find them out, can't you?"

"Sometimes, Miss Barbara."

"I want to know about the man who comes here to pose—not vague things, but facts; who his people were, what turned him against the world."

"You're troubled, Miss Barbara?"

"I am terribly troubled. He has told me a terrible story. But how do I know if it's true or not? If it's true, he ought not to be hounded and hunted, Mr. West; he ought to be pitied."

"Then I'm sure it's not true," West smiled quietly. "What did he tell you?"

"No matter. But will you find out what you can about him?"

"Why, yes, of course. But believe me, it's not his beginnings that are of importance. It's his subsequent achievements and his schemes for the future."

"Another thing," she said, "I'm sure he means no harm where I'm concerned. He has never known that I have a protector within call, and yet his whole attitude toward me has been gentle, humorous, and even chivalrous. I think," and the color came into her cheeks, "that he feels a fatherly sort of affection for me. So thank you for all the trouble you've taken."

"I, too, have reason to think that he means no harm," said West, "and if that is true, I am wasting my time."

There was a look of bitterness in his eyes that was not lost upon Barbara. And she was troubled.

"Of course," she said, "if you *like* to waste your time——"

He looked her straight in the eyes. "I do," he said, "I love to. No man's life would ever be complete if he didn't waste the best part of it—throw it away on something or other—on an ambition—on an ideal—on a woman."

Barbara returned his glance. "Just what, Mr. West," she said, "is the idea?"

And here, Mr. Harry West might have found the sudden courage to speak out what was in his heart, had he not remembered that to all intents and purposes he had no father, and consequently in the eyes of the great world to which Barbara belonged could not be considered to have any existence.

"Oh," he said, "I was just talking through my hat."

Barbara, who, you may say, had been unconsciously putting out tentacles of affection toward Harry West, at once withdrew them, and said coolly: "So I supposed."

"May I look at the bust?"

"Certainly."

She removed the damp cloths from her work, and Harry found himself looking into the legless man's face. The features at once attracted and repelled him, and these sensations mingled with them feelings of wonder. Some subconscious knowledge told the young man authoritatively that he was looking on a master work. Barbara noticed this, and her heart warmed, and her pride was gratified.

"I'm going to hurt your feelings," she said.

"Mine? Don't. Please don't."

"If you," she said, "devoted the next twenty years of your life to wickedness and vengeful thoughts you would get to look like my friend, Mr. Blizzard."

Now that same thought had occurred, and not for the first time, to Harry West, but he did not care to admit it. So he laughed gently, and said:

"In that case I shall devote the next twenty years of my life to philanthropy and—loving thoughts."

He turned toward her, all smiling. And she avoided his eyes without appearing to do so.

XIV

THE next morning Blizzard was fifteen minutes late to his appointment with Barbara. He had sat up all night with O'Hagan, talking energetically, and for once in his life he felt tired. To this feeling was added the fear—almost ridiculous under the circumstances —that Barbara would scold him for being late. Unscrupulous brute that he was, his infatuation for her was humanizing him. And in the whole world he dreaded nothing so much, at this time, as a look of displeasure in a girl's face.

He had left off the threadbare clothes in which he usually went begging, and had attired himself in clean linen and immaculate gray broadcloth. His face was exquisitely shaved; his nails trimmed and clean. And there hung about him a faint odor of violets. In short, the male of the species had begun to change his plumage, as is customary in the spring of the year.

His mouth full of apology, he hurried up the stairs to the studio, only to find that Barbara herself had not yet arrived. Upon the seat of the chair in which he always posed, the legless man perceived an envelope addressed to himself. This contained a short note:

DEAR MR. BLIZZARD:

I can't be at the studio till eleven. Please find somewhere about you the kindness to wait, or at least to come again at that time. You will greatly oblige,

Yours sincerely,

BARBARA FERRIS.

Blizzard read his note three times; it was very friendly. The "Yours sincerely" touched his imagination. Especially the "Yours."

"Yours," he said, "mine," and with a sudden idiocy of passion he crushed the note to his lips. And then, as if with remorse at having been rough with a helpless thing, he smoothed out the crumpled sheet, and placed it, together with its envelope, in that pocket which was nearest to his heart. Then he seated himself on the edge of the model's platform, laid his crutches aside, closed his eyes, and for perhaps five minutes slept, motionless as a statue, except that now and then his ears twitched. At the end of five minutes, he waked, greatly refreshed, and ready, if the need should arise, to sit up the whole of the following night.

There was a sound of a man's steps mounting the stairs. And then a brisk knocking on the studio door.

"Come in," said Blizzard.

Dr. Ferris entered, hesitated, and then closed the door behind him.

"You'll pardon me," said Blizzard coolly, "if I don't get up?"

"Yes—yes," said Dr. Ferris, and in his handsome eyes was a look of pain and pity.

"It isn't easy for me to get up," Blizzard continued in the same cool, emotionless voice, "you can see for yourself. I can't spring to my feet—like other men. Do you know who I am?"

"Yes," said Dr. Ferris, "I'm afraid I do. But they told me the name of the man who has been posing for Miss Ferris was Blizzard. Your name——"

"My name," said Blizzard, "is forgotten."

Dr. Ferris bowed gravely. "Quite so, Mr. Blizzard," he said.

"Miss Barbara," said Blizzard, watching closely the effect upon the older man of the familiarity, "will not be here till eleven. And as you and I cannot possibly have anything pleasant to say to each other, and as you, although the older man, are far better off than I am for means of locomotion, and as even *thinking* of you has something the effect upon my stomach that mustard and warm water would have——"

"If you have any mercy in your heart," said Dr. Ferris, his mouth distorted with emotion, "don't talk to me that way. What made a hell of your life has made a hell of mine."

The look of cold hatred in Blizzard's face changed at once to curiosity. "Really?" he said; "you mean that?"

"It is the truth."

Blizzard considered, and then shook his head. "No," he said, "it couldn't be the same. It may have stretched you on the hot grid now and then, but between times of remorse you've had long, long stretches of success and happiness. I haven't. I have burned in hell fires from that day to this."

"I told you on that day," said the surgeon, "that if there was ever anything under heaven that I could do for you, I would do it. You've never called upon me for anything—money—or service."

"I've not forgotten," said Blizzard, "and some day I may hold you to your word. Right here and now I will ask something of you—an absolutely truthful answer to a question. Do you hate me?"

Dr. Ferris turned the question over in his conscience, and presently said: "I am sorry. Yes."

"Thank you," said Blizzard, who was not in the least disturbed. "I've often wondered, and even, putting a hypothetical case, thrashed the matter out with my friends. You *would* hate me. It's thoroughly human. With me, for instance—I feel non-committal about a man. I decide to injure him. I do so. *And then* I hate him. Now, if you have any message for Miss Barbara—or perhaps you came to see the bust. I will call Bubbles. He and Miss Barbara are the only persons allowed to touch the cloths. I think she'd let me uncover the thing, but, as you and I know so well, I am not tall enough."

"My business with my daughter," said Dr. Ferris, "concerned you."

Blizzard chuckled. "Her friends," said he, "have been at you to interfere. They have persuaded you that her model should be *persona non grata* in the best studios. They have, in short, begged you to take me by the scruff of the neck and kick me out into the gutter where I belong. Well, kick me. You know as well as I do, that I can't kick back."

"You hurt me very much," said Dr. Ferris simply, "if that is any pleasure to you."

"It is," said Blizzard.

"What your intuition has told you," continued Barbara's father, "is the truth. I had made up my mind to interfere."

"Well, why should you?"

"I have heard terrible things about you, Mr. Blizzard."

"That I have done things which the world regards as terrible is true," returned the legless man imperturbably. "What of it? Haven't you?"

Dr. Ferris turned away and slowly paced the length of the studio and back. "I owe you," he then said, "anything you choose to ask. But that is not the whole of my obligation to this world as I see it."

"You will oblige me," said Blizzard, "by spitting out the moral homily into which you are trying to get your teeth. It is very simple. I do not wish to be sent away. I ask you not to send me. If your statement that you owe me anything I choose to ask amounts to two pins' worth, I think that I shall continue to pose for your daughter as long as she needs me."

"Oh, I'm quite helpless," said Dr. Ferris; "I realize that."

"Spoken like a man," said Blizzard. "And to

show that my nature isn't entirely cruel, I'll tell you for your comfort that in Miss Barbara's presence the bad man is a very decent sort. We are almost friends, Doctor, she and I. She talks to me as if I were her equal. As for me, in this studio I have learned the habit of innocent thought. Only yesterday I took pleasure in the idea that in the world there are birds, and flowers, and green fields."

The beggar's eyes glittered with a sardonic look. He watched the surgeon as a tiger might watch a stag. There was quite a long silence. Dr. Ferris broke it.

"For God's sake," he said with great energy, "tell me one truth. Is it part of your scheme of life to revenge yourself on me through my daughter?"

Blizzard raised a soothing hand. "Dr. Ferris," he said, "what would cause you suffering would cause her suffering. So, you see, I am tied hand and— Pardon me! I shouldn't now think of hurting you through her unless it might be for her own happiness."

"I don't understand."

"Then you don't understand the hearts of women. Then you know nothing of the heights to which even fallen men can raise their eyes."

"What are you telling me?"

"Very little—very much. Perhaps I love your daughter."

Horror and loathing swept into the surgeon's eyes, but he controlled himself. "Mr. Blizzard," said he presently, "I find it hard to take you seriously. *Are*

you joking?   Whether you are or not, the thing is a
joke.   If you really care for my daughter, I am very,
very sorry for you.   I can't say more.   If nothing
worse threatens her than the possibility of her heart
being touched by you, there is no need for me to be
anxious about her.   As for telling her the truth about
you and me, why not?"

"*You* tell her."

"I will.   To-night."

"Won't you be playing into my hands?"

"No," said the surgeon curtly, "she has too much
common-sense."

"But you won't tell her what I've said?"   The
beggar was suddenly anxious.

"No," and Dr. Ferris smiled, "I may safely leave
that to you."

"Damnation," cried Blizzard, "you are laughing
at me."

Dr. Ferris's face became serious at once.   "God
forbid that!" he said.   "If you have spoken sincerely I feel only sorrow for you and pity—more
sorrow and pity for you even than I ever felt before."

"S-s-s-s-t," exclaimed the beggar, and his ears
twitched.   "She's coming."

"I shall wait," said Dr. Ferris, "and take her uptown, when she has finished working."

"Well," said Blizzard, with a kind of humorous
resignation, "I'd kick you out if I could; but I can't."
And he added: "You haven't got an extra pair of
legs about you, have you?"

"Why!" said Barbara when she saw her father. "Art *is* looking up. *You* in a studio!"

Secretly his presence pleased her immensely. She had always hoped that some day he would take enough interest in her work to come to see it uninvited. And she now felt that this had happened. And she thanked Blizzard with sincerity for having waited.

"Mr. Blizzard and I," she told her father, "are doing a bust. And whatever anybody else thinks, we think it's an affair of great importance. Mr. Blizzard even gives me his time and his judgment for nothing."

"Well," Dr. Ferris smiled, "I am willing to give you the latter, on the same terms. May I see what you've done?"

Barbara removed the cloths from the bust, and so life-like and tragic was the face which suddenly confronted him that Dr. Ferris, instead of stepping forward to examine it closely, stepped backward as if he had been struck. And then:

"My dear," he said gravely, "the thing's alive."

He looked from the bust to his daughter, and felt as if he was meeting some very gifted and important person for the first time. Barbara laughed for sheer pleasure.

"What do you think of it?"

"I will buy it as it stands," said her father, "on your own terms."

"If you think it's good now," said Blizzard quietly, "wait till it's finished."

"If I had done it," said Dr. Ferris, "I wouldn't dare touch it."

"Yes, you would," said Barbara, "if you knew that you could make it better. It's still a beginning."

"When do you expect to finish?"

"I'm going to keep on working until I know that I've done the best I can. We may be months on it."

Blizzard smiled secretly, and Dr. Ferris managed to conceal his annoyance.

"I wish, my dear," he said, "that I had taken you more seriously in the beginning. But it is not too late to get some advantage by studying in Paris and Rome."

"I don't believe it's ever too late for that," said Barbara, "and of course I've always been crazy for the chance, but knowing how you felt——"

"Say the word," said her father, "and you shall go to-morrow."

Blizzard's face was like stone; he felt that his high hopes were on a more precarious footing than ever. If she had the whim, Barbara would go abroad, far beyond the reach of even his long arms.

"You could finish your bust any time," said Dr. Ferris persuasively.

But Barbara shook her head with complete decision. "A bird in the hand," she said, "is worth two in the bush. And—I hope I'm wrong—but I have the conviction that this head is going to be the best thing I shall ever do. I can look at it quite impersonally, because half the time it seems to model itself. *I* think it's going to be good. If it is good, it will be one of those lucky series of accidents that sometimes happen to undeserving but lucky people."

Dr. Ferris sighed inwardly, but the expression of his face did not change. "Do you mind if I stay?" he asked. "I think it's time I knew what you look like when you are at work, don't you?"

"*High* time!" exclaimed Barbara. "I'll just get into my apron." She went into the next room and closed the door.

"Your innocents abroad," said the legless man, "wasn't a success." His face was a jeer.

XV

"BARBARA," said her father when they had finished dinner, "I made a threat this morning, and I'm going to keep it. If you have no especial objection, will you come into the library?"

Her face was radiant; he had been praising her work for the tenth time. "It sounds," she said, "as if I was going to be whipped. That wasn't what you threatened to do, was it?"

"No," said he. "*I'm* to be punished. I'm going to tell you about a mistake of judgment I once made. But not as a warning, or a moral lesson—merely, my dear, that you and I may learn to know each other better. First, though, I want to talk to you about your model."

"He's rather fascinating, don't you think?"

"He is very clever," said her father, "and when he chooses he can talk very well. He proved that this morning. To me, personally, he is most repugnant, but I admit that when he once launched out, I listened as a school-boy listens to stories of treasure and pirates. He's lived and observed and suffered. There is no doubt about that. But I shall be greatly relieved to hear that your bust is finished. I don't like the idea of such a man being in the same block with you. I hope that you will not feel inspired to do another head of him."

"He's a splendid model," said Barbara. "Of course this morning he didn't keep still—and he did talk. But then I wasn't really working. When I wish he keeps almost as still as the clay I work with."

"Doesn't looking at him ever give you—oh, a disagreeable creepy feeling?"

"Not any more. I'm so used to him now. No, I feel a genuine friendliness for him."

"I thought," said her father, "that to you artists, models were absolutely impersonal—just planes and angles and—what was it you used to say?"

Barbara flushed slightly, remembering a former and very disagreeable conversation. "Your memory is much too good," she said.

Dr. Ferris frowned. "I'm not trying to interfere," he said; "you're old enough to know what's best for you, but if I could instil in you a proper distaste for your friend, Mr. Blizzard, I should be delighted. Beauty and the beast do *not* go well together."

"*Please*," said Barbara, "don't bother your head about me. When the bust is finished, you and I go abroad for to look, for to see, for to learn. That's agreed. We shall not invite Mr. Blizzard to go with us, and all will be well. There's my hand on it!"

She laughed rosily, and they shook hands.

"Until recently," said Dr. Ferris, "I have taken, as you know, very little interest in your career as a sculptor. Haven't you thought that rather an unnatural attitude?"

"Why, yes," said Barbara, "I have."

She took a box of safety matches from a cigar-table, and kneeling, lighted the fire in the big chimney-piece.

"I hope you don't mind," she said; "I'm shivery."

She knelt on, watching the little flames grow into big flames, and spreading her hands to the warmth. Her face, arms, throat, and the front of her white dress became golden. She looked more like some lovely vestal of fire-worship than an ambitious American girl, determined to achieve fame in the battle-ground of the world.

"Why, yes," she repeated, "it has seemed strange to me. When I've thought that I wanted to do things, you always took a lot of interest and trouble, but when I *knew* that I wanted to do one thing, you gave me a dreadfully cold shoulder." She smiled whimsically. "I shall do an allegory in bluish-white marble —The Cold Shoulder."

She retreated a little from the fire, and sat at her father's feet. He laid his hand on her many-colored hair.

From childhood Barbara had resented parental caresses. On the present occasion, she felt a sudden tenderness for her father, and leaned a little against him, in answer to the touch of his hand.

"Did it ever," said he, "strike you as strange that you never took any interest in *my* career?"

"I've always been tremendously proud of you," she said. "You know that."

"You liked my results," he said, "the show pieces —newspaper notoriety—speech-making—the races in special trains against death. But you don't even know what has chiefly interested me during the last thirty years; nor the goal which I have felt I must reach before I could be resigned to parting with this life."

"No," she said gently, "I don't. Tell me. I *want* to be interested."

"You know, of course, that I experiment with animals."

"Yes. I have seen crates of guinea-pigs and monkeys at the laboratory door. I'm afraid it always made me a little unhappy. But I suppose it's the only way to get certain results. And you always give them something, don't you?"

"Always. They don't suffer more than a man would while healing a deep clean cut. In other words, they don't suffer at all. And they're not unhappy, and they don't bear malice. And still I wouldn't do it, if I could help myself. I think, my dear, that I have been chosen for my sins to introduce a great benefit to mankind. It seems now only a question of perfecting the technique. I've already had extraordinary results."

"What's the idea?"

"You know, of course, that a piece of skin from one man can be successfully grafted on another man. Well, so can a liver, a finger, a hand, a foot, an arm, a leg. I have two monkeys now: a black and a gray. The black monkey has the gray hands and forearms, the gray monkey has the black. I made the exchange eighteen months ago. And they have developed the same strength and skill with the grafted members that they had with their own. I have a monkey who had only one eye when he came. Now he has two—they aren't a good color match, but he sees as well with one as the other. When these ideas are perfected it will be possible, perhaps, to make old people young. The secret is absolute cleanliness and the accuracy in joining of a Chippendale or an Adams. So you see," he smiled, "that in a way you and I are chasing the same ambition—how to express the thing imagined through perfection of technique."

"Are you the only man working along these lines?"

"Heavens, no! Aristotle probably believed in animal grafting. But I think that, owing to a natural talent for doing close and accurate work with my hands, I have gone farther than anybody else. What gave you the impulse to be a sculptor, Barbs?"

She laughed gayly. "The statues in the Metropolitan that have lost their arms and heads and legs. I felt very sorry for them. I was very young and foolish, and I invented a game to play. I'd select a statue that needed an arm, say, and then I'd hunt among the other statues for an arm that would fit, or for a head or whatever else was missing. Through playing that game I got the idea of making whole statues from the beginning and not bothering with fragments."

"And to think," said Dr. Ferris, "that we have

failed to understand each other. Why, Barbs, your ambition is a direct lineal descendant of mine. It was a maimed marble that showed you your life's work. It was a maimed child that showed me mine. It seems that at heart we are both menders."

"I began on dolls," said Barbara.

"And I began on guinea-pigs."

A footman entered with whiskey and soda on a tray. Barbara rose.

"Shall I pour you a drink?"

"A very little one, please."

She poured him his drink, and once more seated herself at his feet.

"After I graduated from the P. & S.," said Dr. Ferris, "I did ambulance work for two years, accidents, births, fires. I was ambitious to learn, and worked myself sick. One morning, after I'd been all night bringing a most reluctant young Polack into the world, I was called to the house of a world-famous man in East Thirty-fourth Street. The house was full of servants mad with grief and fright. The man and his wife had gone out of town, and their son, a beautiful boy about ten years old, had got himself run over by a truck. His governess, I gathered, a German fool, had been in some way directly responsible. But that is the small end of the matter. The boy's legs were horribly crushed and mangled. It seemed to me that if his life was to be saved, they must come off at once. The family's physician was the famous old Doctor Watson Bell. I sent for him.

He didn't come at once, and when I had waited as long as I dared, I took upon my own shoulders the very heavy responsibility of operating. I put the child under ether, and with the help of one assistant took his legs off just below the hip-joints. Then Dr. Bell came. He was a very old friend of my father's, and he had always been very good to me. First he looked to see that what had been done had been well done. Then he examined the legs that I had taken off. Then he sent the nurse out of the room. Then he turned and looked at me, and his face was gray and cold as a stone. He said: 'You fool! You imbecile!' And he showed me, clear as a flash of lightning, that the legs never should have been amputated. Then he said, more gently: 'For your father's sake I will save your face, young man. I shall set my approval to this catastrophe. For your father's sake, and for your mother's. I have always looked on you as an adopted son. Are you drunk?' I told him that I had been up all night, and had had no sleep since five o'clock the morning before. He shrugged his shoulders, and said: 'In your right mind, you couldn't have done it,' and I knew that I couldn't. 'Horrible!' he said, 'horrible! This poor baby to be a wreck of a thing all his life, because a healthy and hearty young man cannot get along on a little sleep. But, thank God, the child will never know that the operation wasn't necessary.'

"By common accord, we turned to look at the little boy. His eyes were open. He had come out

of the ether with miraculous suddenness. And we
saw by the expression of his face that he had heard—
and that he had understood."

Barbara took her father's hand in both hers and
pressed it hard. "Poor old dad," she said.

"Of course," Dr. Ferris went on, "the child told
his parents. But Dr. Bell lied up and down to save
my face. He said that what the child thought he had
heard was part of an ether dream. And I lied. And
nobody believed the little boy. I had told him, before Dr. Bell could stop me—I was hysterical and
crazy—that if there was ever anything under heaven
that I could do for him, I would do it—no matter
what it was. And the boy told his parents that I
had said that, but it was only taken by them as evidence that I felt terribly sorry for what I had had to
do, and that I had a tender heart."

"Poor old dad!" said Barbara. "And what became of the little boy?"

"He grew vicious," said Dr. Ferris. "I don't
blame him. Quarrelled fearfully with his father,
dropped into all sorts of evil ways and companionship—all my fault, every bit of it—and finally disappeared completely out of the station to which he
had been born. I had reason until the other day to
believe that he was dead. Then I saw him."

There was quite a long silence. The fire burned
brightly. Dr. Ferris, greatly agitated by tragic memories, closed his eyes very tightly, as if to shut them
out.

"And of course," said Barbara at last, "the small boy is my Mr. Blizzard. Well, what can we do for him?"

"*You* owe him nothing," said her father sharply.

"Oh, yes," said Barbara gently, "oh, yes. Your obligations are mine. I shall tell him. It's like owing a frightful sum of money. We can't be happy till we've paid up, can we? You and I?"

"It seems," said Dr. Ferris, "that I have made two terrible mistakes. And the second is having told you about the first. My God, but this life is hard to bear!"

"But—why—what have I said? If there is *anything* we can do for him, we ought to do it."

"Are you going to say that to him?"

"Of course," she said.

"Suppose," said her father, "that in all this world he wanted only one thing—you?"

This suggestion was most unexpected to Barbara and odious. And she said coldly: "I hope he is not quite such a fool."

"But if he is?"

"My dear father," said Barbara, "I have been told that somewhere along the Milky Way there is a bridge between stars. Let's cross that when we come to it."

A footman entered carrying a large pasteboard box on which, in gilt letters, was the name of a Third Avenue florist. But the jonquils in the box were very fresh and lovely. They were, however, unaccompanied by a card.

"Some unknown person," said Barbara, "has formed the habit of sending me flowers." She smiled. "I shall ask my friend, Mr. Harry West," she said, "to find out who it is."

And then, suddenly, she turned away, so that her father should not see that she was blushing. The thought, not in the least disagreeable, had occurred to her for the first time, that perhaps Mr. Harry West himself was anonymously going down into his pocket for her sweet sake.

XVI

THE legless man was not in the habit of waiting for things that he wanted, when the chance to take them had come. And he did not propose to endure the torture of sitting perfectly still hour after hour, morning after morning, while any young woman made a bust of him. Yet he allowed a number of mornings to pass without taking any definite steps toward the vengeance which he felt to be so dear to him.

That Barbara was a high-born lady was the chief obstacle in his plans. If she were to disappear suddenly out of the world which knew and loved her, there would be raised a hue and outcry greater, perhaps, than his utmost powers and resources could check. He would be run to earth without much doubt and put where even the sweet memory of vengeance would taste bitter in his mouth. It is perhaps pleasant to pluck the fruits of vengeance, but a man requires time in which to eat and digest them. If they are snatched from his hand the moment they are picked, his vengeance fails of all sweetness and justification.

On the other hand, Blizzard, in order to revenge himself on the man who had maimed him, was willing to give, if not his liberty, his life.

If he could not abduct Barbara and go free, he would kill himself when they came to take him. But he did not wish to kill himself. He wished to live a long time after, gloating on his memories. He had also on foot a scheme which, starting almost as a pleasantry, had developed in his mind, and was still developing, until its latent possibilities staggered his own imagination.

A certain Jew, proprietor of a pawnshop, was in reality a receiver of stolen goods. It was common knowledge among certain crooks in the city, that the recently stolen Bland diamonds had come into this man's hands. Blizzard thought that it would be funny to take these diamonds away from the Jew, hold them for a while, and then, since the fellow was after all a friend, return them. To break into Reichman's store at night would be dangerous. Reichman himself was no coward, and he employed a savage night-watchman, just out of Sing Sing. So Blizzard planned a robbery in a spirit of farce, and in the broad and crowded light of day.

Six stalwart young fellows entered Reichman's pawnshop at eleven-thirty in the morning. Each one had a watch or an overcoat to pawn. They crowded about Reichman, all talking at once. They were strangers to him. At exactly the same time the attention of the six policemen on the six nearest beats was attracted by the drunken and disorderly behavior of six more stalwart young fellows—one to each policeman. In the end six arrests were made, the six young drunkards were marched off to the station house, and the beats of the six policemen were for the time being deserted.

Sharp at eleven-thirty-seven, five of the six young men in Reichman's shop flung an overcoat over his head and rushed him into a dark corner, choking him so that he could not scream. A person in the street, however, saw the struggle, and rushed off to find the nearest policeman, who of course could not be found. Meanwhile the sixth young man ran lightly upstairs, looked under the mattress of the palatial Reichman bed, where he had been told to look, and secured the stolen diamonds. The farce came to a proper conclusion. Reichman could not complain to the police that he had been robbed of stolen goods. And he went about for many days with a sour face.

Blizzard came every day to condole with him, and finally to return the diamonds. Then he told Reichman, a man he could trust, how the robbery had been worked, and the two put their heads together.

If six policemen could be so easily put out of commission at a given moment, why not many? If a pawnshop could be so easily looted, why not Tiffany's, or one of the great wholesale jewellers in Maiden Lane? Why not the Sub-Treasury?

In Blizzard's mind the idea became an obsession; and he worked out schemes, in all their details; only to think of something bigger and more engaging. One or two details were present in all his plans: a hiding-place for the treasure when he should get it, and a large number of lieutenants whom he could trust. He could, he believed, at the least throw the whole city into a state of chaos for a few hours—for half a day—for a whole day. And during that period of lawless confusion anything might happen to anybody—to Barbara for instance. But his plans were not ripe, nor his trusted lieutenants as yet sufficient in number. He must therefore either put off his vengeance indefinitely, or run the risk of having his own career as a criminal come to a very sudden end. For once in his life he vacillated. But it was something more than the desire for vengeance which decided him to risk everything on immediate action.

His plan was very simple. Sometimes a messenger-boy brought a note to her studio. And Blizzard had observed that Barbara's invariable habit with notes was first to read them, and then to burn them. She never tore them into pieces and threw them into the fireplace. She struck a match, lighted them at one corner, and saw to it that they were entirely consumed. When Barbara had finished with a note, or a circular, or a letter, Sherlock Holmes himself could not have recovered the contents or the name of the sender. Banking on this habit, Blizzard wrote Barbara a note and sent it to her father's house by a man he could trust. She received the note at six o'clock, while she was resting prior to dressing and dining out. It read as follows:

81 Marrow Lane.

DEAR MISS FERRIS:

My affairs don't seem to be prospering here, so I am
going away. I am sorry the Bust isn't finished. You will
be disappointed. I am leaving at 8 o'clock for the West.
I have enjoyed sitting for you. I wish you all the success
and happiness you deserve.

Very truly yours,

BLIZZARD.

Her mind working very rapidly, Barbara rose at
once, and quite unconsciously, so strong was habit
in her, struck a match, set the beggar's note on fire,
threw it into the fireplace, and watched it burn to
ashes. On the way to the fireplace she pressed a
button to summon her maid. When this one came,
Barbara, already out of her dressing-gown, spoke
imperatively:

"I am going out. I want a taxi called at once.
Then come back and help me dress."

But when the maid returned there was little for
her to do. Barbara was in a hurry.

She found a taxi waiting at the door. She glanced
at the driver—he was not one of those who usually
drove her.

"Do you know where Marrow Lane is?"

"Is it near the Brooklyn Bridge, miss?"

"I think so. Marrow Lane, No. 81. You can
make inquiries. Hurry."

The strange driver drove skilfully and swiftly down
the avenue. Two thoughts occupied him: the beauty

of his fare, and the docility with which she came to the master's hand when he called.

In Barbara's mind there was but one thought: not that she was going to visit a disreputable man in a disreputable part of the city, but that she was going to keep that man in the city and finish her bust of him, or know the reason why. Fame was in her grasp. She felt astonishingly sure of that. She was not going to let it escape for a mere matter of convention. It had been her first idea to send Blizzard a note by messenger. But she had more confidence in her personal powers of persuasion. If her model needed money or was in some scrape that could be righted by money and influence, she believed that she could keep him in New York.

It was not yet dark, but all the city lamps were lighted, and the East Side had that atmosphere of care-free gayety habitual to it after business hours when the weather is rainless and warm. The taxi-cab moved slowly, because the children had over-flowed the sidewalks and played games which kept them in blissful danger of their lives. Twice the taxi stopped. Instantly a crowd gathered about it, and Barbara became an embarrassed but amused centre of criticism and admiration.

It became dark. The streets were less crowded. There were fewer lights. There was an unpleasant smell of old fish and garbage. The people Barbara now observed seemed each and all intent upon something or other. They were not merely loafing in the pure evening air, but hurrying. There were no more children. The taxi passed slowly (because of the uneven pavement) through a short, narrow street. The few lights in this street were nearly all red.

Save for the light in Blizzard's manufactory, Marrow Lane was dark and deserted. For some reason or other the city lights had gone out, or had been passed over by the lamplighter.

Through the glazed door Barbara saw the vast black shadow of Blizzard's profile on the white wall of his office. There was no bell. She turned the knob and pushed open the door. A bell clanged almost in her ear with fierce suddenness. It was like an alarm. Her heart beat the quicker for it; the number of her respirations increased. She was sorry that she had come. She was frightened; still she stepped through the door-way, and called in her clear, resolute voice:

"Mr. Blizzard! It's Miss Ferris."

His vast shadow remained motionless like a stain on the wall. And for a moment he did not answer. Could she have seen his face itself, instead of only its shadow, she must have turned with a cry of fear and found that the door which had closed behind her, clanging its bell, was locked, and that there was no escape that way.

If she had turned her head she must have seen that her taxi had gone quietly away.

In the dim light she looked wonderfully young and beautiful. The parted opera-cloak disclosed her round straight throat and the broad smooth modelling of the neck from which it rose. She seemed taller and more stately than in street-dress, and at once younger, more defenceless, more virginal. There was not enough light in the place to bring out the contrasting colors of her hair. She looked like a black-haired beauty with ivory-white skin, instead of an amber, red, and brown beauty, with rosy, brown skin. Her head, small, round, and carried very high, lent her an air of extraordinary breeding and distinction. She had no thought for the short rose-brocade train of her dinner-dress, and let it trail over the dirty floor.

"Mr. Blizzard!"

This time he answered. It sounded less like a voice than the hoarse bass croak of a very enormous bull-frog.

"Please step this way."

Her head, if anything, a little higher than ever, she walked swiftly forward right into the legless man's office.

His face was very white, swollen, it looked, and blotched with purple. The veins in his forehead looked like mountain ranges on a topographical map.

"I've only a minute," said Barbara.

He lowered his head now over his ledger, but said nothing. Then he looked up and into her face steadily, and one by one the purple blotches in his own face paled, and vanished, like the extinguishing of as many hellish lights. And then to Barbara's horror a low groan, more like a dog's than a man's, passed his tightly pressed lips, came out, and was cut short off, as if with a keen knife.

"Are you sick?" she asked, not kindly, but imperatively and with a tone, perhaps, of disgust.

"Yes," said the legless man briefly, but without going into any explanation of his ailment. "You came to tell me that I mustn't go away till the bust is finished. Is that it?"

Barbara felt more at her ease. "Yes," she said, "I am selfish about it. It means so much to me."

"Well, you needn't have come," said Blizzard, and it was almost as if he was angry with her for having done so. "I've changed my plans. I've had to change them. I stay."

Barbara was immensely pleased. "I wish I could tell you how glad I am," she said.

"The thing now," said Blizzard, "is to get you back to your house. You shouldn't have come to this part of the city at all; and especially not dressed like that. But you didn't stop to think. You had an idea in your head. And you came. Did anybody know where you were going when you left home?"

She shook her head.

"Something dreadful might have happened to you," he said, and a curious smile played about his mouth for a moment, "and no one the wiser. Suppose you hadn't found me here to look after you? Suppose you'd found some drunken crook just out of Sing Sing, or something worse?"

"But I *did* find you," said Barbara, "and all is well."

"Yes—yes," he said, "all *is* well. And you may thank your stars for that. Why didn't you tell your taxi to wait?"

"But I did."

Again the curious smile flickered about the legless man's mouth. "Well, he's gone."

Barbara followed the lead of Blizzard's eyes, and saw that the street in front of his manufactory was empty. He reached for his crutches, and swung himself down from his chair.

"Perhaps he's dropped down to Jake's saloon. Wait here. I'll see."

The bell of the outer door clanged with horrid suddenness. And then she heard a piercing loud whistle twice repeated. And a few moments later the sound of a motor.

"All right, Miss Ferris, I've got him."

She drew her cloak together, and joined the legless man on the sidewalk.

"Thank you very much," she said, "and good-by till to-morrow."

The taxicab driver's face had no expression whatever. He who understood driving so well could not make out what the master was driving at.

Blizzard held open the door of the taxi, and Barbara got in. But he did not at once close the door. Instead he turned his head and looked up the street. Then he called out sharply:

"Hurry up! Can't you see the lady's waiting."

One came, running; a tall well-built youth, with an expression on his face of cool, cynical courage and good humor.

"Miss Ferris," said Blizzard, "this young fellow will ride in with you if you don't mind. You can drop him when you get out of the East Side, and reach your own part of the city. He will see that no harm comes to you. If you ask him questions he will answer them. Otherwise he will not speak unless you wish."

The youth grinned a little sheepishly, and Barbara made room for him on the seat beside her.

"He will answer for your safety," continued the legless man, "with his ears. Where to?"

She gave the number of the house at which she was to dine, and the legless man repeated it to the driver.

"Good-night, Mr. Blizzard, and thank you."

"Good-night, Miss Ferris, and welcome."

The legless man watched the taxicab until it had rounded the corner of Marrow Lane. Then he looked upward at the stars for a while. Then he swung slowly and wearily back into his rookery, and having extinguished the light, sat for a long time in the dark.

What was it that had come over the man to let his victim escape when she was so mercilessly in his power? Ask the stars to which he turned. Ask the darkness in which he sits, alone, thinking. Better, perhaps, ask the man's warped and tormented soul.

It seems that while he sat in his office waiting for her, a champion rose up to defend her, a champion in

He turned with one foot on the sidewalk, and one in the cab. . . .
"Here I wishes you salutations . . ."

his own heart. A champion who made such headway against the brute's lawless and beastly intention as to overthrow it.

Blizzard was in the power of that which all his mature life he had feared more than hanging or the electric chair, more even than prisons. He had fallen quietly, even gently, in love.

"I'm not going to ask you any questions," said Barbara, "because I don't think of any. But if you like to talk, please do."

Without comment or preamble the youth who was to answer for her safety with his ears, began to talk.

"Might have knocked me over with a feather," he said, "to find a lady like you sitting in a cab in front o' Blizzard's place. At first look I says to myself: 'One o' these high-fliers I've heard talk about that likes to fly low.' Then I flings your eyes one penetrating peep, and says to myself: ''Spect she ain't one o' that kind.' And I make out just this about you that you're O. K. from A to Xylophone, and I takes this opportunity to remark aloud to myself that I don't know what your game is, and it's none o' my haterogeneous business, but if I was you I'd cut Marrow Lane out o' my itenerary, and stay home nights playin' a quiet rubber o' tiddle winks-the-barber."

Barbara laughed gayly. "Everybody," she said, "thinks that my friend, Mr. Blizzard, is a very bad man. But he does nothing to prove it. He has been very considerate of me in every way."

"Did I say anything against Blizzard? You'll tell him I did? Not you. And I did not. If it *wasn't* for him, I says, Marrow Lane *would* be hell's kitchen, and on the chanct that he ain't always going to be on the spot, nor me, cut it out, I says. But," continued the talkative youth, "in case you don't cut it out, in case you're ever in trouble down our way you take this," bluntly he handed her a small, dark metal whistle, "and blow her good. I knows the note, and if my ears is on the job, you gets help. You gets it sudden. You gets it good. And here, without fear or comment, I leaves you."

He signalled to the driver to stop. They had reached the southern boundary of Washington Square. Barbara held out her hand. She was greatly taken with her escort.

"And whom," she said, "am I thanking for the whistle?"

"Kid Shannon."

"Don't tell me," said Barbara, "that *you're* the man who put Hook Hammersley out in the third!"

"A right to the solar plexus," said Kid Shannon simply, "to bring him in range and a left to the jaw. Even his friends admits that he begun to take his gloves off while he was still in the air. But I'm in the saloon business now, if it's all the same to you, having been light-weight champion, and spoke a monologue over three circuits—nice-behaved ladies and gentlemen o' both sexes always welcome, pay as you consume; but for you or any friends o' yours the drinks will be on the house."

He turned with one foot on the sidewalk, and one in the cab.

"Lady," he said, "what I've poured in jest, drink in earnest. All that's yellow isn't butter. But if anybody was to ask you—say, a man who shall be as nameless as he is legless—what I says to you during our discursive promenaid, you answer back and say, 'Kid Shannon, whenever I speaks to him, merely says, "Ha! Hum!"—*or words to that effect.*' Here I wishes you salutations, and may your life contain nothing but times when you looks and feels your best."

Barbara shook hands with him again. "Come to 17 McBurney Place," she said, "some morning. Ask for Miss Ferris, and see what you think of the bust she's making of Mr. Blizzard." She smiled mischievously. "He's supposed to represent the devil just after falling into hell."

Shannon nodded with complete understanding. "Then," said he, "I bet he looks a ringer for Hook Hammersley that time he hit the resin."

"Thank you for protecting me," said Barbara, "and for the whistle. Will you tell the man to hurry, please? Thank you! Good-by."

She was very late to her dinner, but much too amused with recent events to care. And nobody could have made her believe that her going to Blizzard's place had been fraught with terrible peril.

She prized the whistle that Kid Shannon had given her, and resolved that some time she would adventure again into his part of the city, and see if she could bring him running to her side.

"I am sorry I am late," said Barbara, "but I couldn't help it." She vouchsafed no further explanation, and because she was so young and beautiful all those who had been kept waiting forgave her.

Wilmot Allen took her in to dinner, and looked much love at her, and talked much nonsense. He was, indeed, so gay and foolish that she imagined that he must have got himself into trouble again.

XVII

BLIZZARD was an acute student of human nature.
And a certain softening in Barbara's manner toward
him was proof that she had learned his story from
her father, and no longer regarded him as a stranger
off the streets, but as a human being definitely connected with her outlook upon life. Still, the suggestion that their relations had changed did not come
from him, for he knew that pity or sympathy given
by request lacks the potency of that which is spon-
taneously offered. So he held his peace in order that
Barbara might be the first to speak, and during those
days his heart became filled with mad hopes for the
future.

Upon one thing he was determined, that when in
the course of events Barbara should touch upon her
father's criminal mistake, he would conceal, as something precious from a thief, the hatred and vengefulness that were in him, and unroll for her benefit a
character noble and forgiving. He was content, or
appeared content, day after day, for a number of
hours, to be with her, and to play the hypocrite so
ably as to defy detection.

And Barbara, knowing how the man had been
abused, guessing how he must have suffered, and still

suffered, came to look upon him, not indeed as upon a person wholly noble, but as upon one who, with an impulse in the right direction, had in him possibilities of great nobility.

Just as a fine motor-car, perfect in mechanism, punctures a tire and is stalled by the side of the road, so works of genius like Barbara's head of Blizzard do not progress in one swift rush from start to finish. There were whole mornings during which it seemed that things went backward instead of forward, and when she was so discouraged that, had it not been for the legless man's almost fiery confidence in her ability to overcome all obstacles, she must have taken a hammer and pounded her fine sketch back into the lump of clay from which it had been evolved.

Blizzard's eyes had undergone a most thorough schooling. They had learned, to the flicker of an eyelid, when Barbara was going to look their way, and at such times were careful not to meet her eyes. When, however, they knew her to be intent for a period upon the work and not the model, they studied her always with zest, and always with more and more understanding.

Suddenly, one day, after he had been sitting motionless for half an hour, the beggar broke his pose.

"Please don't," she said. "I'm not through."

In his eyes, soft and full of understanding, there was a gentle, if masterful, smiling. "Yes, you are," he said, "for now. I haven't watched you at work all these mornings without learning something about the way you go at it. Do you know what a blind alley is?"

"Yes," she said petulantly, "and I'm in one."

"Quite so," said Blizzard. "And you're not taking the right way out. First you tried to climb up the house on the right, then the house on the left, and when I interrupted you, you were making a sixth effort to shin up the lightning-rod of the house that blocks the alley."

Barbara laughed. "But," she objected, "I've got to get out somehow—or fake—or call the thing a fiasco, and give it up."

"Of course you've got to get out," said Blizzard, "and it's very simple."

"Simple!" she exclaimed; "a lot you know about it."

"Quite simple," he repeated; "you merely face about and walk out. In other words, remove that lump of mud which one day is going to be more like my ear than my ear itself, and begin over."

And it came home to Barbara that the man was right. "Thank you," she said simply. "You're a great help. That is precisely what I shall do."

"But don't do it now."

"Why not?"

"Because you've wasted the freshness of your early-morning zeal with vain efforts. Destroy what you've done—there's always satisfaction in that; but either leave the re-doing alone for to-day, or try something else."

"When," said Barbara, beginning to feel soothed and confident again, "did I put myself in your hands for guidance?"

"The moment you lost your presence of mind," said the beggar; "that's when a woman always puts herself in a man's hands.   Put a cloth over his satanic majesty's portrait, and sit down and relax your muscles, and talk to the devil himself."

Barbara did as he commanded with the expression of a biddable child.   She flung herself into a deep chair, and drew a long, care-free breath.

"There," she said, "I knew I wasn't fit."

"You can't spend the night at a Country Club, dance till 4 A. M., catch the 7 A. M. for town, and do good work—not always."

"How did you know all that?"

Blizzard laughed.   "From a man," said he, "who had planned to rob the Meadowbrook Club last night. There is a fine haul of scarf-pins, and sleeve-links, and watches and money in the bachelors' quarters.   He came to me in great dejection and explained what very hard luck he had had.   He said the whole place was lit up and full of people and music, and no chance for an honest man to earn a cent.   I happened to ask if you were there, and he said you were.   The train was a guess, and so of course was the 4 A. M.   Will you take a piece of well-meant advice?   Either be a society girl or a sculptor.   But don't burn the candle at both ends.   You even look tired, and that's nonsense at your age."

He laughed like a boy.

"They tell me," he said, "that I could do the new dances. They tell me they are just like clinches in a prize-fight, and that only the novices move their feet."

Barbara's brows contracted. "I'm going to ask you a favor," she said. "If you want to talk about your misfortune, God knows I'm ready to listen. I feel some of the responsibility. But please don't joke about it. We're friends, I think. And I like to forget that you're not exactly like other people. And sometimes I do."

"Truly?" His eyes were full of suppressed eagerness and elation.

"Yes," she said, "when you talk high-mindedly and generously, as you can, when you want to, I enjoy being with you, in touch with a mind so much more knowing and able than my own. But, now we've made a beginning, I'd really like to talk about —all this dreadful mess that's been made of your life, and how things can be made easier for you, and for my father."

Figuratively, Blizzard's tongue went into his cheek at the mention of Dr. Ferris, but the expression of his face underwent no change. "Of course," he said simply, as if it was the most natural thing in the world, "I have forgiven your father. He was very young—very excitable—inexperienced."

"*Actually*," she said, "in your heart, you've forgiven him? And you're not saying things just to make me comfortable?"

"I am afraid," he confessed, "that I am too selfish to say or do things just to make other people comfortable. Did you ever hate anybody?"

"I think so."

"Did you like it?"

"For a while it was rather fun to think up things to do to the person, and then it got to be disagreeable, and feverish, like a cut that's festered, and then I made a strong effort, and found that hating was very poor company and led nowhere."

"Exactly," said the beggar. "Do you mind if I talk frankly? My hatred for your father persisted a great many years, until I found that going to bed with it every night and getting up with it every morning was a slow poison that was affecting all the rest of me—my power to think out a line of action, my power to stick to it, even my power to like people that were good to me and faithful to my interests. I found that I was beginning to hate everybody and everything in the world and the world itself. Meanwhile, Miss Barbara, I did things that can never be undone."

He was silent, and appeared to be turning over the leaves in the books of his memory. Suddenly he spoke again.

"And it was all so silly," he said, "so futile. The cure was in my head all the time—just longing to be used. And fool that I was, I didn't know it."

"What was the cure?"

"It was the sovereign cure for all our troubles,

Miss Barbara—reason, and crowds. Stand morning or evening at the entrance to the Brooklyn Bridge—stand there with your trouble, and consider that among the passers, better carried than yours, are troubles, far, far greater than yours, more poignant, lives lived in dungeons deeper and more dark. Your father has lived a life of most admirable utility: should he be hated for one mistake? Suppose that it had been some other small boy's legs that he wasted, instead of mine? Would I hate him for it? Why, no. I'd say it's too bad. But since it was I that lost the legs I lost all sense of proportion and justice and was a long time—a long time coming back to it."

"May I know what brought you round?"

The beggar felt that he might dare a little. He smiled. "Of course. What brought me around was the discovery that he had created something far, far more important than what he had destroyed. At first I thought you were like so many other girls of your class—well dressed, and good to look at. Then that you had a very genuine talent, and were going to count in the world. Then, and this is best, it came over me that you were one girl in a million—that you would do whatever seemed right to you, not without fear of criticism, and pain and sacrifice, but regardless of them. And so, you see, the reparation is made. The father hurt, and the daughter cured."

Barbara's face had become very grave. "However wrong you are about my character," she said, "the reparation is not yet made. And you may be sure of

this—that, whatever the criticism, I owe you friendship and you shall have it."

The beggar trembled inwardly, but he shook his
head. "You could hardly pull me up to a level," he
said, "upon which friendship between us would be
possible. Imagine that I have sunk to the chin in
mud, and that at the last time of calling I have been
pulled out. Still the mud clings to me."

"Nonsense," said Barbara, "you can be washed."

They both laughed, and at once became grave
again.

"You don't know," he said, "what I've been or
what I've done. You can't even imagine."

"That is not the point," said Barbara, "and this
is: Are you sorry? If you really have been rotten,
do you want to be sound and fine? If you do I'm
your friend, and whatever help I can give you, you
shall have."

"If you knew," he said humbly, "how I dread the
bust being finished! I'll be like a child stealing a ride
by the strength of his arms, I'll have to drop off
then—won't I?—back into the mud."

"I'm not offering you friendship," she said, "merely
while you are useful to me. Do well, Mr. Blizzard,
and do good, and I will always be your friend."

"Do you believe that I want to do well, that I
want to do good? That I want to wipe the past from
the slate?"

"You have only to tell me," she said loyally, "and
I shall believe."

"Then I tell you," he said, and Barbara jumped impulsively to her feet and shook hands with him.

"And I may come to you," he pleaded, "for advice, and help? Old habits are hard to shake. My friends are thieves, crooks, and grafters. My sources of income are not clean. Even now I have dishonest irons in the fire. Shall I pull them out?"

"Of course."

"But people who have trusted me will be hurt."

"You must work those problems out in your own conscience."

To Blizzard, believing that he was actually making progress into the fastnesses of her heart, and that he might in time gain his ends by propinquity and his own undeniable force and personality, a sudden, cheeky knocking upon the door proved intensely irritating. It was a very small messenger-boy with a box of jonquils. Blizzard watched very closely the expression of Barbara's face while she opened the box. She held up the flowers for him to see.

"Aren't they pretty?" she said.

"They are very pretty," said Blizzard, and he found it difficult to control his voice. "And it was very sweet of him to send them. Isn't that the rest of the speech?"

"Of course," said Barbara gayly.

She lifted the flowers until the lower half of her face was hidden.

"Mr. Allen, I suppose," said the beggar.

"Why should you suppose that?" said Barbara, a little coldly. "There is no card."

Blizzard felt his mistake. And Barbara felt that he felt it. She went into the next room for a vase of water, and returned presently with heightened color. She had heard Harry West's slow grave voice explaining something to Bubbles. Her heart told her that West had sent the flowers, and she meant to get rid of Blizzard and find out. So, the vase of flowers in one hand, she held out the other to him, and said:

"To-morrow."

Blizzard was loath to go, but he felt that there was a certain finality in her voice, and he swung out of the studio, his heart gnawed with jealousy.

XVIII

Through Bubbles, Harry West received the happy news that Miss Ferris wished to speak with him. But when he saw her with the vase of jonquils in her hand, and the empty box in which they had come at her feet, his stout heart failed him a little.

"Mr. West," said Barbara, "some person is annoying me."

"Annoying you?"

"I am continually receiving flowers without card or comment."

"Is it the flowers which annoy you or the lack of comment?"

"I love the flowers, but anything in the shape of anonymity is unfair, and I resent it."

"I can think of cases," said West, "in which a man might properly send flowers without disclosing his identity—just as I may pass a fine statue and praise it, without telling the statue who I am." He smiled.

"Flowers don't resemble statues in the least, and your comparison is unnaturally far-fetched. Another thing, and this annoys me even more: my secretive friend sends flowers from the cheapest florist he can find. I argue from this that he is poor, and cannot afford to send me flowers at all."

"Perhaps his home and business in the city are too far from the Fifth Avenue shops."

"You are not saying gallant things, Mr. West. I —an unprotected young woman—tell you that I am being annoyed by a strange man. Instead of flying into a chivalrous rage and threatening to wring his neck when you catch him, you stand up for him. Very well. I shall set Bubbles to find out who the man is, and take my own steps in the matter."

Her expression was grave and unruffled, though a certain look of amusement might have been detected in her eyes, by a youth less embarrassed than Mr. West was.

"Don't do that," he said; "Bubbles could never find out. You wish to know who is sending you flowers?"

"Very much. Can *you* find out?"

"I think so. I mean, I'm sure I can."

"And when you have found him will you point out to him that in the future he must be open and above-board, or something disagreeable will be done to him?"

Mr. West bowed humbly.

"How long," she asked, "will it take you to run the creature down?"

"Well," said Mr. West, "I could go to the florist whose name is on the box, show my badge, and exact a description of the man who bought the flowers. Then I could give you the description, and if you knew any such man——"

"The florist," said Barbara, her expression Sphinx-like, "is just 'round the corner."

"I hear," said Mr. West, "and I obey."

"I will read a book till you come back," said Barbara.

But she didn't read a book; she leaned instead from a window and watched for Mr. West to come out of the studio-building. He came presently, but did not turn east in search of the florist. Neither did he descend the steps. Instead, he took out his watch and sat down, and waited. Barbara in great glee watched him for ten minutes. She was possessed of a devilish longing to fashion out of paper a small water-bomb and drop it on his head. Memories of water-bombs brought up memories of Wilmot Allen and old days. She drew back from the window and was no longer gleeful. Why should men trouble her heart, since she wished and had elected to live, not a woman's life but a man's? She paced the studio, her soul at odds with the rest of her.

Had she ever encouraged Wilmot? Yes. West? Yes. And about a dozen others. And here she struck her left palm with her right fist. She had even encouraged a man who had committed all the crimes in the calendar and was only half a man at that! Half a man? She was not sure. There was a certain compelling force about him which at times made him seem more of a man to her than all the rest of them put together. "I can't imagine him in love," she thought. "It's really too revolting. But if he

was, I can imagine nothing that he would let stand
in his way.   I wonder if he is married.   And if he is
I pity her.   And yet she could say to other women,
'My husband is a man,' and most of the women I
know can't say that."

And she remembered her father's perfectly ridiculous suggestion that perhaps the man so wronged by
him had lifted his eyes to herself.   The idea no longer
seemed ridiculous; but quite possible and equally
dreadful.   She made up her mind that she would
sacrifice her immediate chances of recognition and
fame and tell the beggar to discontinue his visits.
Then she withdrew the cloth from her work, and it
seemed to her that what she had made was alive and
had about it a certain sublimity, and that to surrender
now was beyond her strength.   She had a moment of
exultation, and she thought: "In a hundred years my
body will be dust.   It doesn't matter what becomes
of it now or hereafter; but people will gather in front
of this head, and artists will come from all over the
world to see it.   And there will be plaster casts of it
in city museums and village libraries.   And I suppose
I'm the most conceited idiot in the world, but—but
it's good.   I *know* it's good!"

She had forgotten West, and Allen, and Blizzard,
so that when the first-named knocked, she had some
ado to come out of the clouds and recall what they
had been talking about.   Then, not wishing to drive
West into a lie, she said only:

"Have you the man's description?"

"He is not," said West gravely, "a man in your station in life. He is, I imagine, some young fellow to whom, in passing, you have been carelessly gracious."

"Is he handsome?" Mischief had returned to her mind.

"He is only bigger and stronger than usual."

"Dark or light?"

"Medium."

"And how long did it take you to find out all these interesting items?"

"Twelve minutes," said West gravely.

"By the clock?"

"By a dollar watch. . . . Miss Ferris, I haven't done right. I'm not doing right."

This came very suddenly. He had lowered his fine head and was frowning.

"I'm the man who's been sending you flowers. I didn't know it was wrong. I'm not a gentleman. But once I'd seen you, I could never see flowers without thinking of you, so I kept sending them, hoping that they would give you pleasure for their own sake. I had no business even to look at you. To win the kind of race I'm up against, a man ought to keep his eyes in the boat, and not look right or left till his race is won or lost. And even then it ought to be right or left that he looks, and not up, and certainly not down. I didn't keep my eyes in the boat. I looked up, 'way up, and saw you, and caught a crab that threw the whole boat out of trim. I've no excuse, only this—that I haven't ever before even looked right or left or down. But it's all right now. Nobody's hurt. I won't come any more to watch over you. The lines are closing round Blizzard, and he knows it. His claws are pulled. He's got to toe a chalk-line, and you're as safe with him as with the Bishop of London."

Barbara said nothing. She felt very unhappy.

"One thing more. As long as I did forget the work in hand, as long as I did look up, why, I'd like to thank God, in your presence, that it was you I saw. Because in all the whole world there is nobody so beautiful or so blind."

He thrust out his hand almost roughly, caught hers, said good-by, and turned to go.

"Please wait," said Barbara. And she said it quite contrary to reason, which told her that it would be kinder to let the young man go without comments.

"You've done nothing wrong," she went on, "and I can't help being pleased by the flowers and knowing that you think I am all sorts of things that I'm not. If you really like me a good deal, don't go away looking as if the world had come to an end. I think you are a fine person, and I shall always be glad to be your friend."

There was agony in West's eyes. "My friendship," he said, "can never be any special pleasure to you. And seeing you—even once a year—would keep alive things that hurt me, and that never ought to have been born, and that were better dead."

"'Faint heart—'" Barbara began, and could have bitten out her tongue, since she had so often promised herself that she would never again encourage anybody.

The agony died in Harry West's eyes, and there came instead a look of great gentleness, compassion, and understanding.

"May I say things to you that are none of my business?" he asked. She nodded briefly, and he went on: "You mustn't say things like that. You have a race to row, too, but your beautiful eyes are all over the place!"

"I knew I was a rotter," said Barbara, "but I didn't know it was obvious to everybody."

"To eyes," said West gently, "in a certain condition lots of things are obvious that other people wouldn't see. May I still say things?"

"Don't spare me."

"You love to attract men. And if you happen to hurt them, you think you are a rotter. That isn't true. You're being pulled two ways. Art pulls you one—the way you *think* you want to go—and nature pulls you the way you really want to go. Men attract you to a certain extent. I can almost feel that —and you tire of them, and think it's because you haven't got the capacity for really caring. That isn't true either. You have infinite capacities for caring, but as yet you haven't been attracted to the man you are really going to care for."

Barbara looked him straight in the eyes. "How do you know I haven't?"

He returned the look, as if doubting what he should say or do. Then he drew a deep breath to steady himself.

"Perhaps you have. But I know very well that it is not the man you think, at this moment. You are in the hunting stage, and you didn't know it. Now that you do know—unless I am greatly mistaken —I think you will try very hard not to hurt people, not to let them have wild dreams of something doing in the future."

"But if I really think——"

"Then be secret until you *know*."

"And if everything that is me seems to be going out to a certain man——"

"Then be secret until it has really gone out to him."

"I don't know why I let you talk to me like this."

"There you go again," he said, and she bit her lips. "It is very awful for me," he said, "to think that I have raised my voice in any criticism or disparagement of you."

"Oh, it's all true, and it's all deserved."

"But you are like that. And all at the same time it's your greatest strength and your greatest weakness, and for the right man, when he comes along, it will be his greatest treasure. . . . I don't like to say good-by. It comes hard."

"If I said, 'Don't say good-by,' would I be breaking the rules?"

"Yes," he said, "for I could never be the right man."

"Not even if——"

"Not even if—and you will have forgotten any kindness that you felt for me, while I am still wondering why the city is so empty, that once seemed so full."

The tears sprang into Barbara's eyes. "Is there anything about me that you don't know?" she asked bitterly.

"Oh, yes," he said.

"Do you know that if you asked me to marry you, I should say yes?"

"And I know that I am not going to ask you. There are two reasons. You don't love me. And I do love you."

Her arms dropped limply to her sides.

"And it shall never be said of me," he said proudly, "that I dragged any one down. . . . Will you promise me something?"

"If you care to trust me to keep promises or to do anything that's right and honest."

"Only promise to keep your eyes in the boat. Don't help a poor dog of a man into love with you. And don't help yourself into love with him. When the right man comes along, he will *make* you love him, and then you will be sure."

"I will promise," said Barbara simply, "and I never knew how rotten I was. And I'm glad you've told me. If it's any comfort to you—you've helped. And nobody ever helped before. I shall always be proud to remember that you loved me. And I'll keep my eyes in the boat."

"And that," said Mr. West, "is where I'll keep mine, only, if it's nothing to you, I'll remember sometimes how the moon looked that time I looked up."

She stood uncertain.

"It's kind of awkward," he said, "sometimes to make a clean break. Good luck to you. And don't feel sorry about me. And be true to yourself. And if you ever really need me for anything tell Bubbles. He knows where to find me, when anybody does."

A few minutes later Barbara was asking Bubbles if he happened to know Mr. Harry West's address.

"He won't be coming back here," she said, "and I want to send him a book."

"I'll deliver it," said Bubbles. "He don't keep no regular *ad*dress. You have to catch him on the run."

"Very well," she said, "take him this, with my very best thanks and my very best wishes."

And she gave Bubbles a charmingly bound copy of Rostand's "Far-Away Princess," and when Bubbles had trotted off, she dropped into her chair and cried because she thought she had broken poor West's heart. But there was stern stuff in his heart, and exultation, for he knew that in the supreme test of his life, he had thought only of—her.

XIX

"THERE, everything is understood," said Blizzard; "we are agreed upon the 15th of next January. And you can bring enough men on from the West to do the work?"

O'Hagan, thick-set, black, bristling, nodded across the table. "You have guaranteed the money and the hats," he said; "I will guarantee the men. What's behind that door?"

"Nothing but a junk-closet," said Blizzard. "Drink something."

O'Hagan poured three fingers of dark whiskey into a short glass and drank it at one gulp. "After that one," he said, "the wagon until the 15th."

"Yes," said Blizzard with some grimness. "There must be no frolicking. And mind this, Jimmie: the more good American citizens who don't speak English that you can corral the better. We don't want intelligence. We want blind obedience with a hope of gain. And they mustn't know what they are to do till it's time to do it. They should begin to come into the city by the middle of December, a few at a time. Let 'em come to me half a dozen at once for money, weapons, and orders."

Again O'Hagan nodded. This time he rose, and the two shook hands across the table. O'Hagan seemed to labor under a certain emotion; but Blizzard was calm.

"Keep me posted," he said, "and for God's sake, Jimmie, cut out the little things. You're in big now. Forget your troubles and your wrongs. Leave liquor alone and dynamite. Remember that on the 15th of next January you and I'll be square at last with law and order and oppression. Good luck to you!"

When O'Hagan had gone Blizzard moved his chair so that it faced the door of the junk-closet. And he smiled occasionally as if he were one of an audience at some diverting play. From time to time he took a drink of whiskey and licked his lips. An hour passed, two hours, and always the legless man kept his agate eyes upon the closet door.

When two hours and fifteen minutes had gone, he drew an automatic pistol from his pocket, and held it ready for instant use. A few minutes later, finding his original plan of humor a little tedious in the working out, he spoke in a clear, incisive voice:

"Better come out of that now or I shall begin to shoot."

The door opened, and Rose staggered into the room. After a short pause, during which she swayed and gasped for breath, an automatic pistol fell with a clatter from her nerveless fingers. She sank to the floor all in a heap and began to cry hysterically.

Blizzard slid from his chair and secured her pistol. His face wore an expression of amused tolerance. "Tell me all about it," he said. "Crying *can't* do

The door opened, and Rose staggered
into the room

any good, and talking may. You hid in the closet to listen. It's not the first time. I found one of your combs, and saw where you'd brushed away the dirt so's not to spoil your dress. Now I'd like to know how much you know, and whom you've told it to?"

"What's the use?" said Rose with sudden desperation. "You've got me—nobody'll ever know from me what I've heard to-night. You're going to kill me."

"I doubt it," said Blizzard. "Now look up and tell me all about everything."

"Well," she said, "I've been spying on you."

"I know that. I knew that the day you came. When you said you loved me I knew you were lying."

"At first," she said, "I passed over everything I could find out about you. It wasn't much."

"I took care of that."

"Then I made up things—just to keep the others from knowing I wasn't playing fair. I wanted to put that off as long as I could. Anything I really found out—like your first talk with O'Hagan—I just kept to myself. I know I lied to you the first day. But I'm not lying now."

The legless man smiled tolerantly. "Why did you keep on trying to find out things—if you didn't mean to use them?"

"Because I wanted to know all about you, what you were doing, what your interests were. I thought I could be more useful to you that way."

"It's a good thing for you, Rose," said Blizzard, "that I guessed all this. If I hadn't you wouldn't be alive now. And so, now that you've gotten to know me pretty well, there's something about me, is there, that's knocked your ambitions galley-west?"

"I had friends that trusted me," she said, "and I've played double with them. And now I've got only you."

"Tell me one thing," and Blizzard asked the question with some eagerness, "what particular quality of mine got you to feeling this way about me?"

"I guess it's every quality now," said Rose, "but it started with me the first time I heard you play, and knew that, whatever you'd been and done, and were planning to do, you had a soul above it all. And I knew that if your soul had ever had a fair chance you'd have been more like a god than a man."

"Well, well," said Blizzard after a long silence, "perhaps. Who knows! And so it was the music that changed your heart? Well, why not? Nobody makes better music—unless it's Hofman."

The idea of appealing to the heart of quite another girl through his music filled the legless man with a wild hoping. Why not? If he could play himself clean out of hell whenever he pleased, why not another? He would not tell her the possibilities of nobility that yet remained in him. He would play them to her.

"Rose," he said, "you're the best pedaller I ever had. You've got music in you. We'll practise up and give a concert. I'll ask some nobs in. We'll turn the piano so that seeing how the pedalling is done won't distract their attention from the music. But they won't hear our music, Rose. It will be better than that. They shall roll in it, bathe in it, see heaven!"

"That's what I saw."

Blizzard's agate eyes glinted with a strange light. It was as if the beast in him was fighting with the God. But gradually all mercifulness, all pity, went out, and the fires which remained were not good to see.

He kissed her and she kissed him back.

XX

FEELING that she had been working too hard, being in much distress about Harry West, and in some for herself, and learning that Wilmot Allen was to be of the party, Barbara told Blizzard, at the end of his sitting on Friday, that he need not come Saturday, as she was going to spend the week-end with the Bruces at Meadowbrook.

"I'm dog-tired," she said, "and that's the same as being discouraged. We both need a rest. Things have been at a stand-still nearly all the week."

"I think you are right about yourself," said Blizzard, "but won't your gay friends keep you up till all hours?"

"They will *not*," said Barbara, "and it won't be gay. During a falling market there are never more than two happy people at the largest Long Island house-party. The men will sit by themselves and drink very solemnly. The women will sit by themselves and yawn till ten o'clock. It will be very boring and very restful."

"Speaking of falling markets, is my friend Mr. Allen to be among those present? I understand that he has been very hard hit."

"I don't know about that," said Barbara. "He often is. Yes, he is to be among those present, and

I'm really going just to have a chance to talk to him."

"*With* him or *to* him?" asked Blizzard with one of his sudden, dazzling smiles.

"*To* him," said Barbara, also smiling. "I, too, have listened to tales out of school, and since he is my oldest friend, and probably my best, he must be straightened out."

"A little absence from New York, perhaps," suggested Blizzard, and watched her face closely.

"Do you think so? It doesn't seem to me necessary to run away in order to straighten out."

"Mr. Allen," said Blizzard, "should swear off stock-gambling, and marry a rich girl."

"He's not that kind," said Barbara simply. And this swift, loyal statement did not please the beggar, since it argued more to his mind of the faith that goes with love than of that appertaining to friendship. He felt a sharp stab of jealousy, and had some ado to keep the pain of it from showing in his face.

"Well," he said, "if anybody can help him, you can. And if you can't, send him to me. Oh, we've had dealings before now. I was even of real service to him once."

"If that is true," Barbara thought, "it's rather rotten of Wilmot to keep running this poor soul down."

Blizzard left with obvious reluctance. Two whole days without a sight of Miss Ferris seemed a very long time to him. "I shall miss these morning loafings."

"Is that what you call posing?"

"What else? You loaf now. Good luck to the tired eye and hand."

"Thank you," said Barbara. "Next week we'll see if we can't really get somewhere."

"We shall try," said Blizzard. He turned at the door. "I want to play for you some time," he said. "May I?"

"Why, yes—of course."

"At my place," he said. "I have a new piano in; it's very good. You see, I pound four or five of them to pieces in the course of a year. I thought perhaps you'd bring two or three or more of your friends who like music. I know *you* do. I'll give you supper. Your friends might think it was a good slumming spree to come to a concert at my house. And I particularly want to play for you. I go for weeks without playing, and then the wish comes."

She longed to ask him how he worked the pedals, and had to bite the question back.

He laughed, reading her mind. "If you come," he said, "I will try to make you forget what I am— even what I look like. I should like you to know what I might have been—what I still might be." He went out abruptly and closed the door after him.

Barbara mused for a minute and then rang for Bubbles. "I'm going out of town for over Sunday," she said. "What will you do?"

"Me and Harry," said he, "is going down to the sea swimming."

"Please give Harry my best wishes, Bubbles."

The great eyes held hers for a minute and were turned away. He was sharp enough to know that through one of his idols the other had been hurt. And he found the knowledge sorrowful and heavy.

"I'll do that," he said solemnly.

That afternoon Wilmot Allen drove Barbara down to Meadowbrook. He had borrowed a sixty-horse-power runabout for the occasion, but displayed no anxiety to put the machine through its higher paces. "I've had a rough week," he said, "and my nerves are shaky. Do you mind if we take our time?"

"No," said Barbara, "my nerves are shaky, too. And I want to talk to you without having the words blown out of my mouth and scattered all over Long Island."

He bowed over the steering-wheel, and said: "It's good to know that you *want* to talk to me. Is it to be about you, about me—or us?"

Barbara leaned luxuriously against the scientifically placed cushion, all her muscles relaxed. "You," she said, "are to play several parts, Wilmot."

"And always one," he answered softly.

"Not now," she said, "please. First you are to play priest, and listen to confession. Then you are to confess, or I am to do it for you, and receive penance."

"While I'm priest," he said, "do I impose any penance on you?"

"I'll listen to suggestions," said she, "that point toward absolution."

"I am now clothed in my priestly outfit," said Wilmot; "you have entered the confessional. I listen."

Very simply, without preamble, she plunged into her affair with Harry West. And Wilmot listened, his head bent forward over the steering-wheel. It was not pleasant for him to learn that she had thought herself seriously in love with another man, and was not now in the least sure of her feelings toward him.

"I cried almost all night," she said; "it didn't seem as if I could bear it."

"How about the next night, Barbs?"

"Oh, I slept," she said, "or thought about work."

"And he told you that you mustn't see each other any more?"

"Yes."

"I think he was right, Barbs. I don't believe you really love him, dear. If you did you would have cried for many nights and days—felt like it, I mean, all the time. Men attract you—they drop out for some reason or other—and so on. I know pretty well."

"That's just what he said," said Barbara, "and it's true, Wilmot. I'm almost sure now that I don't really love him. And that's ugly enough. But it's worse to think that he really loves me, and that it's my fault."

Wilmot Allen did not make the mistake of saying that it was not her fault. "It just shows, Barbs dear," he said, "that it's time to pull up. You've got more darned temperament than anybody I ever saw. It's a great weapon, but you've got to learn to control it, and not swing it wild and hurt people."

"That's what he said."

"Well, he seems to be a sensible fellow, and a fine fellow, and to have thought of you rather than himself. You told him you'd marry him if he asked you? Now, Barbs, listen to me. That was a fool thing to say."

"I know it."

"Do you realize how lucky you are to have said it to West instead of to some other fellow who happened to be on the make? You've come through your young life almost entirely by good luck, not by good management. You've run up against honorable men, instead of rotters. That's the answer."

"I should think, feeling this way, you'd hate and despise me."

His hand left the steering-wheel and gave hers a swift pat.

"Well, it's over," she said, "and I wanted you to know. I'm going to pull back in my shell and be very dignified and honorable. If anybody wants to get hurt through me, they've got to hurt themselves."

"You'll not try to see West any more?"

"No," she said rather wearily, "that's over. And it's for the best. I've had a good lesson. No man ought ever to take me seriously until I've told him every day for a year that I love him. Maybe two years."

"Just tell me *once*—" he began

"Don't," she said, "please. Now you confess."

"Well, Barbs," he said, "this week-end is a sort of good-by. I'm in very deep, and I'm going to a new place to live a new life."

"Well!" she exclaimed, "you're not running away?"

"Only from temptation," he said. "I have spoken to all my creditors but one, and they have behaved decently and kindly. Wherever I go I take my obligations with me, and, God willing, they shall all be paid."

"Oh," she said, "I think a man ought to make good in the midst of his temptations."

"Might just as well say that you ought to finish your bust of Blizzard with one hand tied behind your back, since it's a constant temptation to you to use both. You ought also to be blindfolded and to work in the dark, since you are constantly tempted to look at your model and see what you are doing."

"I shall miss you," she said simply, "like everything. Why——"

"Why what?"

"It fills the future with blanks that can't be filled in."

"That may or may not be, Barbs. If they can't be filled in, you will write to me, and I will come back."

"But I don't mean——"

"I don't believe you know what you mean. But you aren't Barbs now; you are my confessor. I confess to you, then, that I am in pretty much the same boat with Harry West. I am going away, partly, to get over you—if I can. Love is a fire. Feed it, and it grows. Let it alone, and it dies. Confessor, there is a certain girl—one Barbara Ferris. I love her with all my heart and soul and have so done for many years. Since this leads to happiness for neither of us, I am going to cut her out of my life."

"Wilmot! Are you speaking seriously? You're not going to write to me? I'll have no news of you? Not know how you are getting on? Not know if you are sick or well?"

"The first night," said Wilmot, "you cried. The second you slept and thought about work."

"But you are my oldest friend and my best. Whatever we are to each other, we are that—best friends. We have our roots so deep in the happenings of years and years that we can't be moved—and get away with it."

"We shall see," said Wilmot almost solemnly. "It isn't going to be easy for me, either. But time will soon show. If after a year we find that we cannot do without each other's friendship—why, then we must see each other again. That's all there is to it."

"At least you'll write?"

He shook his head.

"But I will."

"No, Barbs. The sight of your writing would be too much fuel for the fire."

She was silent for a quarter of a mile. She did not enjoy the idea of being deliberately cut out of Wilmot

Allen's life and heart. "Suppose," she said, "that at the end of the year the fire is still burning bright?"

He slowed the car down so that he could turn and look at her. His face looked very strong and stern. "In that case," he said, "I will come back and marry you."

"And supposing that meanwhile, in a fit of loneliness and mistaken zeal, I shall have married some one else?"

"If I feel about you as I do now," said Allen, "I will take you away from him."

Once more the car began to run swiftly, so swiftly that Wilmot could not take his eyes from the road to look at Barbara's face. If he had, he would have seen in her eyes an extraordinary look of trouble and tenderness.

XXI

Dᴜʀɪɴɢ the week-end Barbara and Allen were much together, to the amusement of the other guests, who said: "*It's* on again." But it was not really.

If Wilmot was going away, Barbara wished him to have good memories of last times together to carry with him. And Wilmot, like a foolish fellow who is going to swear off Monday, and in the meanwhile drinks to excess, saw no reason why he should dress his wounds in the present, since, in time to save his life, he was going to give them every attention possible. That he was going to "get over" Barbara in a year he did not believe. But observation and common-sense told him that life without her must become easier and saner as time passed, and that to be forever caught up or thrown down by her varying moods toward him had ceased to be a self-respecting way of life. This is what common-sense and experience told him; but his heart told him that he would love her always, and that if he could not have her he must simply die.

Sunday night, after she had gone to bed, Barbara lay in the darkness and asked herself questions. Wilmot's life had not been fine, but his love had been very fine, and for longer than she could remember. Would it not be well to trust herself to such a love as

that? Had she the right to send it away begging?
Would it not be better, since marriage is a lottery, to
grasp some things that in this case would be sure, instead of leaving everything to chance? If he kept
away from her long enough, his love would probably
die, or at least reduce itself to a state of occasional
melancholy agitation. But if she belonged to him it
would never die. Of this their whole past seemed a
sure proof. If she married him he would always love
her and be faithful to her; for her part she was wonderfully fond of him, and she believed that if she once
actually committed herself to his care, she would be
a good wife to him, and a loving. Then why not?
She tried the effect of pretending that she had promised to marry him and meant to keep her word, and
she found that the position, if only mentally, was
strategically strong and secure. She would make him
happy; she herself would cease from troubling him
and other men. For her sake he would turn over
new leaves and be everything that was fine. She
would be obedient and have no more difficult knots
to untangle for herself. Wilmot would simply cut
them for her with a sure word, one way or the other.

She had not for a long time enjoyed so peaceful a
night. Hours passed, and she found that, without
sleeping, she was becoming wonderfully rested. For
it is true that nothing so rests the thinker as unselfish
thinking.

She had breakfast in her room, but was down in
time to catch the business men's train for town, or

to be driven in Wilmot's borrowed runabout, if he should ask her. He did, and amid shouts of farewell and invitations to come again soon, they drove away together into the cool bright morning.

"Wilmot," Barbara said, when they had passed the last outpost of the Bruces' shrubbery and whirled into the turnpike, "I spent most of last night thinking."

"You look fresh as a rosebud."

She shook her head as if to shake off the dew, and said: "I feel more rested than if I had slept soundly. If you will marry me, Wilmot, I will make you a good wife."

Wilmot's heart leaped into his throat with joy, and then dropped as if into a deep abyss of doubt. For all her confessions to him, and for all her promises of amendment, here was his darling Barbs unable to resist the temptation of hurting him again. "One of her impulses," he thought, and at once he was angry with her, and his heart yearned over her.

"Are you going to be able to say that, Barbs," he said gently, "a year from now, after we've been out of sight and hearing of each other all that time?"

"Wilmot," she said, "I'm not up to my old bad tricks. I am ready to give you my word this time, and to keep faith. Only I'd like everything to be done as soon as possible. I've been a very foolish girl, and perplexed and tired, and I want to lean on you, if you'll let me. We'll have a good life together, and I will keep my eyes in the boat."

"A few days ago, Barbs," he said, "you thought that you were seriously in love with another man."

"I know," she said, "but I wasn't."

"Are you in love with me now?" he asked wistfully.

"I know that you will always be good to me, and love me. And that is what I *know* that I want."

"Poor little Barbs," he said.

"It seems to me rather," she said, "that I am now rich with chances of happiness for us both. I want to make my oldest and most deserving friend happy, and I trust him to make me happy."

"It isn't love, dear?"

"It's so much affection and friendship that perhaps it's better." She turned her face away a little. "The best that marriage can end in is affectionate companionship; why not begin with that, and so be sure of it for always?"

"If I had ever dreamed," said Wilmot unsteadily, "that you were going to say things like this to me, I'd have dreamed that I went wild with happiness, and drove you to the nearest clergyman. But now that you have actually said what you have said, in real life, I find that I love you more than ever, and that it is not compatible with so much love to take you on a basis of friendship. You feel that you have hurt me more than is possible for your conscience to bear, and you wish to make up for it. Is that right?"

"That's not all there is to it, Wilmot, by any means. But for heaven's sake believe that I'm being altogether unselfish: but you know me too well to believe anything so ridiculous."

"I know you well enough," said Wilmot, "to worship the ground you walk on. Not because my heart urges me, but my understanding. And I know you would play the game, once you had given your word, and make me a splendid wife. But what I have for you cannot be given to mere friendship and submission. I should feel that I had sinned against my love for you too greatly to be forgiven. You are closer to me than you have ever been, my dear—and yet so far away that I can only look upward as to a star, and despair of the distance. If there has been anything fine in my life, it has been my love for you. And behold, you, with every opposite intention, are tempting me to let that go rotten, too. But, O my Barbs, if you could only love me!"

Barbara drew a long breath. "I thought I was doing right."

"You *have* done right. It is for me to do right."

"Well," she said, "I'm bitterly disappointed, and that's all there is to it. Ought I to thank you for letting me off?"

"Yes, dear."

"Then I thank you."

Neither spoke for a long time. At last Barbara said: "When do you go West?"

"In a very few days."

"Then you will be able to go to Mr. Blizzard's party and hear him play."

"Are you still determined on that?"

"Why, yes. It will be fun. And besides, I haven't any husband to forbid me."

Wilmot's temper rose a little. "I'll go," he said shortly. "When will the bust be finished? And the whole Blizzard episode?"

"I'm sure I don't know," said Barbara patiently. "But I think the Blizzard episode—as you call it— is rather a permanent friendship. I find reasons to like him, and to admire him."

Wilmot made no comment. He longed to speak evil of Blizzard, but the fact of his financial obligation to the man kept him silent. He contented himself with saying: "I'm glad that I haven't your artistic judgment of character. One of these days you will learn, to your cost, that men's judgment of a man is usually correct."

"I wish he had legs," said Barbara. "I'd like to do Prometheus bound to the rock."

Wilmot's disgust was intense. "Do you mean to say—" he began, and then checked himself. "Why not have your father graft a pair on him? He's succeeded, by all accounts, in doing so for all sorts of beasts."

"Do you know," said Barbara sweetly, "that is just what my father would try to do for Mr. Blizzard if some interested person would only step forward and supply the legs."

"I dare say Blizzard would find a pair quickly enough, if he thought they could be attached."

"But how could he?"

"Oh, I'm just joking, Miss Innocence. But, seri-ously, he could buy a pair for a price. You can buy anything in this world—except love."

Blizzard, sitting in the sun on the steps of 17 Mc-Burney Place, watched the pair approaching in the runabout, noted as they drew near the affectionate seriousness of their attitude toward each other—for they had stopped talking of him and returned to themselves—and his whole being burned suddenly with a rage of jealousy. Controlling the expression of his face, he rose upon his crutches and descended the steps to greet Barbara at the curb.

"Glad to see you!" said she. "And how about Wednesday night for the party? Mr. Allen is coming, and I have asked three or four other people."

The legless man bowed and said: "Thank you. Wednesday at half-past nine."

He nodded affably to Allen, who returned the salute with all his charming ease and courtesy. You might have mistaken them for two men who really valued each other.

"Miss Ferris," said Blizzard, "I shall be ready for work as soon as you. I wish to ask Mr. Allen a question."

Wilmot winced, since he noted a tone of com-mand in Blizzard's voice, and it jarred on him, and he said good-by to Barbara and watched her disappear into the studio-building with a feel-ing of strong resentment against the man who had to all intents and purposes dismissed her from the scene.

"Well?" he said curtly.

But Blizzard, enjoying the childish satisfaction of having separated the pair, was no longer in the mood to take offence. "I wish to make a proposition to you," he said, "but at some length. Will you come to my place at three o'clock this afternoon? It is easier for you to get about than for me."

"I am very busy," said Wilmot; "I am getting ready to go West."

"So I have gathered. Have you anything definite in view?"

"Not very," said Wilmot. "Nor any money to put it through with. About the loan you were so kind as to make me, I can only say that I am going to turn over a new leaf, and to work very hard at something or other. If I have any luck you shall be paid."

The legless man dismissed the matter of the loan with a backward toss of his head. "If you've nothing definite in view," said he, "please come at three o'clock. I have interests in the West—legitimate interests, and influence. Perhaps I can put you in a way to clear up your debts."

"Well, by George," said Wilmot, his good nature returning, "if that's the idea, I'll turn up at three sharp. Sure thing."

XXII

BLIZZARD had upon his desk a specimen of the straw hats which the young ladies of his establishment were kept so busy plaiting. At exactly three o'clock he thrust it to one side, and at exactly the same moment the bell of his street door clanged, and Wilmot Allen came in out of the sunlight.

"On time," said Blizzard, "thank you. Are you a judge of hats? Try that one."

Obediently Wilmot removed his own heavy yellowish straw, and substituted the soft and pliant article indicated. It fitted him to perfection, and the legless man smiled.

"It's yours," he said; "fold it up, and put it in your pocket."

"It'll break it."

"Here. Let me show you." And Blizzard folded the hat as if it had been a linen handkerchief. "Very handy thing," he said, "and only to be obtained as a gift. Sit down." Wilmot thrust the hat into his inside pocket and sat down on the beggar's left, facing the light. The faint hum of girls talking at their work came from the back of the establishment. A whirling fan buzzed and bumped. The weather had turned very hot.

"Young man," the beggar began abruptly, "if I

had your legs I'd engage in something more active
and adventurous than the manufacture of straw hats.
Have you ever had the wish to be a soldier of fortune?
To go about the world redressing wrong, fighting upon
the side of the oppressed?"

"Of course," said Wilmot simply.

"You are heavily in debt?"

"Very."

"Whatever I may say to you will go no further?"

"No further."

The legless man stroked his chin strongly with his
thick fingers. "I am engineering a little revolution,"
he said. "My own morals are negligible. Any revolution that offered a profit would look good to me.
But in this case the revolutionary party *is* oppressed,
down-trodden, robbed, starved, and murdered by conditions created by the party in power. I am not yet
at liberty to name you the part of the world in which
this state of affairs exists, that will be for later.
Meanwhile, if my proposition interests you, will you
take my word for the place and for the abuse of
power? Indeed, the latter smells to heaven."

"South America," said Wilmot, "is full of just such
rottenness as you describe. I suppose you're speaking of some South American republic?"

"Maybe I am," said Blizzard, "and maybe I'm
not. That will be for later—for January 15th. On
that date my soldiers of fortune will be gathered in
New York and told their destiny. I am hoping that
you will be one of the leaders."

"I know nothing of soldiering."

"Your record proves that you are a great hand with a rifle. It stands to reason that you can teach the trick to others."

"Possibly," said Wilmot, "to a certain extent."

"I have," said Blizzard, "a number of scattered mining interests in Utah. I wish you to travel among them teaching the men in relays to shoot accurately and fast. This can be done without greatly interfering with the working of the mines. You would be nominally under the command of a man named O'Hagan, to whom I have written a letter introducing you, on the chance that you might care to use it."

"Where," said Wilmot smiling, "does the business end of the affair begin? I'm rotten with debts."

"For teaching my men to shoot," said Blizzard, "I will pay you the money that you owe me. That's one debt written off."

"And how shall I live in the meanwhile?"

"I have empowered O'Hagan to pay you five hundred dollars a month."

"And the rest of my debts? How about them?"

"You will fight for down-trodden people," said Blizzard gravely. "If you win, you will find them grateful—possibly beyond the dreams of avarice. In the republic of which we are speaking there is wealth enough for all. It is one of the richest little corners of God's footstool—gold, diamonds, silver. If you succeed you will be on Easy Street. If you fail, you will very likely get a bullet through your head."

Wilmot's face brightened. "If I got killed trying to pay 'em," said he, "my creditors couldn't feel very nasty toward me, could they?"

A look of strong admiration came into Blizzard's hard eyes. "I like the way your mind works," said he. "If you get killed in my service, I'll pay your debts myself."

"I owe nearly a hundred thousand," said Wilmot.

"I've been worse stung," said Blizzard.

"Where the devil do you get all your money, Blizzard?"

"I've lived for money and power. I've been lucky, clever—and unscrupulous."

"I like your frankness. But you are not letting me in for anything rotten?"

"Your Revolutionary ancestors fought against just such forces as you are to fight against—unjust taxation, abuse of power, and corruption in high places. Are you going to serve?"

"I'm going it pretty blind, but I think so. I like the idea of fighting. I like the idea of paying my debts. And at times I think a bullet in the head would be a matter for self-congratulation."

"That," said Blizzard, "is the feeling of two classes of young men—those who are tangled up with women and those who aren't."

Wilmot laughed, though the legless man's words brought the ache into his heart.

"You will return to New York," Blizzard went on, "during the first half of January."

"I had rather promised myself to keep out of New York for a year."

"It will be for only a few days. If you don't wish your presence in the city known, I'll put you up in my house. Parts of it are as secret as the grave."

"All right. But supposing the revolution falls through before it ever gets started?"

"I'll make you a bet," said Blizzard, smiling. "Please reach me that black check-book." He wrote a check, blotted it, and showed it to Wilmot. "This," he said, "against a penny! It will pay your debts. It's payable at the City Bank on January 16th. Put it in your pocket."

"When do I start for Utah?"

"Wednesday afternoon."

"I hoped to come to your concert that night."

Blizzard shook his head. "You will hear better music," he said, "in the West—rifles on the ranges. And by the way, don't lose that hat I gave you. It must be where you can get it on the 15th of January."

To Wilmot a straw hat suggested the palm-groves of a South American republic rather than the streets of New York in midwinter, and he said so; but the legless man only smiled.

XXIII

DURING those last days Barbara and Wilmot were together a great deal. Tuesday morning, by invitation, he watched her at work upon her bust of Blizzard; afterward he took her to lunch and for a long drive through Westchester County. That night they dined with Mr. Ferris, who, immediately after dinner, excused himself, and withdrew to his laboratory. Wednesday morning Barbara did no work, but drove about in a taxicab with Wilmot and helped him shop. They lunched together, and she went to the Grand Central to see him off. Where Wilmot found the time to pack the things which they had bought in the morning was always something of a mystery to them both.

As train-time approached the hearts of both these young people began to beat very fast. Each felt that the good-bys presently to be said might be forever. In his resolution not even to write to Barbara, Wilmot was weakening pitiably. He wished that he had taken her at her word and married her Monday when she was in the mood. Better Barbara unloving, he thought, than this terrible emptiness and aching. His heart was proving stronger than his mind. Short, more or less conventional phrases were torn from him. Barbara, her heart beating faster and faster, said very little.

The attention of her wonderful eyes was divided between the crowds and the station clock. She could see the minute-hand move. Once in a while she snatched, as it were, a look at Wilmot. His eyes were never lifted from her face.

The gate for Wilmot's train was suddenly slid wide open with a horrid, rasping noise, and people began to press upon the man who examined the tickets. It was then that Barbara's roving and troubled eyes came to rest, you may say, in Wilmot's, with a look so sweet, so confiding, so trusting, that it seemed to the young man that the pain of separation was going to be greater than he could bear. He lifted his hands as if to take her in his arms, and stood there like a study in arrested motion.

"Best friend in the world," she said, the great eyes still in his, "most charming companion in the world —man I've hurt so much and so often—only say the word."

"What word? That I love you—love you—love you?"

They spoke in whispers.

"Stay with me," she said, "and for me—or take me with you. I can't bear this. I can't bear it."

"You'd come—now—just as you are?"

"Yes."

"Do you love me?"

Slowly, like two things in anguish, her eyes turned

from their steady gazing into his. And, "I dare not say it," she said, "but I will go with you—and try."

They were aware of something pressing toward them, and turning with a common resentment against interruption, they found themselves looking down upon the legless man.

"Just dropped in to say good-by and wish you good luck," he said. His face wore a good-natured smile, and, quite innocent of self-consciousness, brought confusion upon their last moments together. The tentacles of unreasoning passion that each had been putting forth were beaten down by it and aside.

"Better get a move on—time's up."

"Good-by, Wilmot," said Barbara swiftly. "Everything's all right. Good luck to you and God bless you."

She turned, her lovely head drooping, and walked swiftly away.

A young man took off his hat and held it in his hands until she had passed. He had been watching her and Wilmot, and incidentally the legless man, for the last ten minutes. He hoped that she would look up and speak to him, but her mind was given singly to sorrow. And she went through the station to the street without knowing if it was crowded or deserted. Harry West's sad eyes followed her until she was out of sight. Then with a sort of wrench he turned once more to observe the actions of the legless man. This one, however, having said cheerful good-bys to the sulky and heartsick Wilmot, and having at the same time noted the obtrusive nearness of the secret-service agent, had made swift use of his crutches and stumps and was at the moment climbing into a waiting taxicab.

Whatever West's opinion may have been, Blizzard was making a sufficiently innocent disposition of time. He had prevented an elopement, perhaps. And he was on his way to a prominent florist to fill his cab with flowers for the evening's entertainment.

He was in a curiously shy and nervous state of mind. There was perhaps no man living whose hands were more nearly at home upon the key-board of a piano, or whose mind was more disdainful of other people's opinions. But of the fact that he was suffering from incipient stage fright there could be no doubt whatever. Would this inoculate his playing, keep the soul out of it? Or worse, would it cause him to strike wrong notes, and even to forget whole passages, so that his guests, and of course Barbara, would go away in the impression that they had heard a boastful person make an ass of himself? He was almost minded to begin his concert with an imitation of a virtuoso suffering from stage fright. If there was going to be laughter, let it be thought that he was not the irresponsible cause of it, but the deliberate and responsible. What should he play? Violent things to get his hands in and his courage up, and then Chopin? Let Chopin speak up on his behalf to Barbara; tell her how he had suffered; how you must not judge him until you understood the suffering;

how there was still in him a soul that looked up from the depths, and aspired to beautiful things? Yes, let Chopin speak to her, plead with her, reason with her, show her, lead her.

He descended from the cab, and entered the florist's.

XXIV

BARBARA paid Blizzard the compliment of inviting
only people who were really fond of music to hear
him play. The Bruces, Adrian Savage, Blythe the
architect, young Morton Haddon, and Barbara herself, composed the party. They dined on a roof, and
then, occupying two taxicabs, started for Marrow
Lane in the highest spirits. But the East Side had
its way with them, and they reached their destina-
tion in a serious mood, ashamed, perhaps, of being
rich and fortunate, unhappy at feeling themselves
envied and hated. Bruce, Adrian Savage, and Barbara were in the leading cab, a brand-new one smell-
ing of leather, and of the gardenia which Barbara was
wearing. The filth of the East Side came no nearer
to them than the tires of the cab. They were, you
may say, insulated, enfortressed against squalor, pov-
erty, crime, and discontent. They were almost free
to do as they pleased, as indeed their expedition
proved, and yet, such is the natural charity of the
human heart, they could not look from the windows
of the cab and remain untroubled, or fail to understand a little of those motives which turn the minds
of the unfortunate to thoughts of anarchy. There
was no whole tragedy unrolled before their eyes, not
even a completed episode in one. It so happened

that they saw no one in tears or in liquor; on the contrary, they saw many who laughed, many children playing games with and tricks upon one another. Yet in its mirth the region was mirthless; its energy was not physical, but nervous. It had an air of living intensely in the present, for fear of remembering, for fear of looking ahead. And it needed but a misunderstanding or a catchword to turn in a moment from recreation to violence. Indeed, the mere fact of their own passing in the highly polished cab with its wake of burned gas and Havana tobacco turned many a smile into a scowl or a jeer.

Often the driver throttled his car to a snail's pace or brought it to a full stop to avoid running over one of those children who, so far as self-preservation goes, appear to be deaf, dumb, blind, and without powers of locomotion; and during one of these halts a little girl, walking slowly backward, her eyes upon another little girl who for no apparent cause was making a series of malevolent faces at her, collided with one of the tires and fell on her back directly in front of the stationary car. Instantly she began to screech, and the street, hitherto but scatteringly occupied, filled with raging people.

The driver from his seat, Bruce from one window, Savage from the other, attempted to explain to deaf ears. Their voices were drowned in a torrent of abuse.

Barbara, at first only exasperated by the stupidity of the crowd, sitting very still and erect, had upon her face that expression of bored contempt with which aristocrats in the French Revolution are said to have gone to the guillotine. Then that was shouted in her ear which, though but half understood, turned her scarlet with anger. Unfortunately Savage, hitherto patiently self-controlled, had heard the compounded epithet hurled at Barbara, and in a moment his fighting blood was beyond control, and he was out of the cab raining heavy blows upon a bloated chalky-white face, and receiving worse than he gave from a dozen fists and feet. Strong as a bull, always in training, his strength was beaten and kicked from him in twenty seconds, and with Bruce and the driver—who, bravely enough, if reluctantly, had leaped to his assistance—things were no better.

A whistling, shrill and metallic, brought the fight to a sudden end. The crowd drew back sullen and reluctant, no longer shouting and cursing, but muttering, explaining, and discreet.

Barbara took from her lips the whistle which Kid Shannon had given her. She was very white, but her eyes blazed with the light of success and power. The bringing of the whistle had been an accident, the blowing it an act of desperation; but perceiving the sudden effect of that blowing she could not but feel that she had done something strategically good and in the nick of time. Savage began to straighten his collar and necktie, Bruce to nurse a sprained thumb. The second cab came up. Blythe and Morton Haddon got out and, full of perplexity but not unamused,

fell to asking questions of their dishevelled friends.
These, winded and bruised, could give but an ejacu-
latory explanation, mostly of what they would do to
such and such a one if they could isolate him from
his fellow cutthroats for five minutes; and Blythe
and Haddon, not bruised and winded, told them to
pull themselves together.   Meanwhile the crowd had
disintegrated before the possible arrival of Kid Shannon; had vanished like a lump of sugar in a cup of
tea.   Even the little child who had been the cause
of the uproar had disappeared.   So a colony of prairie-
dogs vanishes into its burrows at the shadow of a
hawk.

The short street was deserted save for the figure of
a rapidly approaching policeman.   Why this guardian
of the peace had not been upon his beat during the
fracas could have been best explained perhaps by the
proprietor of a disorderly house, from whom at the
time he had been levying a weekly stipend of lust
money and a glass of beer.   For his lapse of duty,
however, he made such amends as were possible.   In
short, he took the numbers of both taxicabs, the
names of their occupants, and told them, with stern
condescension, that they were now at liberty to pur-
sue their interrupted way.

But first Barbara received praise for having blown
the whistle, and Bruce and Savage were made to say
repeatedly that they insisted on going on with the
evening's entertainment; that they were not really
hurt, and that they wouldn't think of being driven

to a doctor. Everybody wanted to know more about Kid Shannon, and in just what consisted the terror and efficacy of his name. But Barbara could only say that he was a friend of hers, and a sort of henchman of their host for the evening. Then she said, smiling:

"I'm sorry he didn't come himself, but anyway his whistle is a perfectly good whistle, and another time I'll know enough to blow it before anybody gets hurt."

Mrs. Bruce insisted on having her husband ride with her, so Blythe took his place in Barbara's cab, and they reached Marrow Lane without further molestation. Indeed, it seemed as if rumor had gone ahead of them, saying that they were not as other swells, but East-Siders in disguise, integral parts of the master's organization, armed with the whistle of his lieutenant. They were stared at, it is true, and commented upon, but with awe now and childish admiration.

The door of Blizzard's house was opened for them by Kid Shannon.

"Why, Mr. Shannon," exclaimed Barbara, "I blew your whistle, and you never came."

"And wasn't the whistling enough?"

"Why, yes."

He smiled the smile of a general who knows that his troops are in a state of perfect discipline. "The boss is expecting you," he said. "Please step right in."

A faint odor of roses greeted them.

XXV

ONE light, not strong, illuminated the legless man's face. Barbara and her friends sat in half-darkness. Kid Shannon went out of the room on tiptoe, closing the door softly behind him. Of Rose, crouched under the key-board of the grand piano, her hands on the pedals, nothing could be seen, owing to a grouping of small palms and flowers in pots. The stump of Blizzard's right leg touched her shoulder. She was trembling. So was Blizzard. He was trembling with stage fright; she with Blizzard fright. His hands, thick with agile muscles and heavy as hams, though he had just been soaking them in hot water, seemed powerless to him, and stiff.

He struck a chord, and it sounded to him not like the voices of a musical instrument, but like a clattering together of tin dishes. This enraged him. His self-consciousness vanished. Those ivory keys and well-tempered wires had fooled him. He hated his piano. And he began to punish it. The heavy hands, rising and falling with the speed and strength of lightning strokes, produced a volume of tone which perhaps no other player in the world could have equalled.

Blythe, a great amateur of music, had come in a sceptical mood. He now sat more erect, his face, eyebrows raised, turned to Blizzard, his ears recalling to him certain moments of Rubinstein's playing.

But Blizzard no longer hated his piano. It had stood up nobly to his assault. It was a brave instrument, well-bred, a friend full of rare qualities—for a friend to show off. And, the swollen veins in his forehead flattening, he began to make his peace with his piano. It could do more than shout and rage. It could sing like an angel in all languages; it could be witty, humorous, heart-rending, heart-healing, chaste, passionate, helpful, mischievous. And it could be wise and eloquent. It could stand up for a friend, and explain his sins away, and get him forgiven in high places.

And even as Blizzard thought, so he played. He was no longer conscious of himself or his guests, not even of Barbara. As for Rose, she was merely a set of pedals in perfect mechanical adjustment. He was not even conscious of his thoughts. They came and went without deliberation, and were expressed as they came and dismissed as they went in the terms of his extraordinary improvisation.

But it came to this at last, that he thought only of beautiful things, so that even his face was stripped of wickedness, and his fingers loosed one by one the voices of angels, until it seemed as if the whole room was full of them—all singing. And the singing died away to silence.

The legless man looked straight ahead of him into the dim room. Then, smiling, his head a little on one side, he caressed his piano so that it gave out Chopin's 7th Prelude, which, as all the world knows, is a little girl who smiles because she is happy; and she is happy because so many of the flowers in the garden are blue. It is not known why this makes her happy, only that it does.

And forthwith he played Chopin and only Chopin: brooks and pools of sound to which you did not listen, but in which you bathed. And in his soul the legless man was playing only for Barbara, and only to Barbara. And so powerful was this obsession that it stole out of him like some hypnotic influence, affected the others, and gave him away. First Blythe looked toward Barbara, not realizing why, then Haddon looked, then Mrs. Bruce.

Barbara felt the warm blood in her cheeks. She was troubled, unhappy, touched. A man, his face full of unhappy yearning, his soul quick with genius, was making love to her; asking her to forget his shortcomings, to forgive his sins, to give him a hand upward out of the dark places into the light. He followed her, always pleading, by brooks, into valleys, through flowery meadows in the early morning, into solemn churches, into groves of cypress flooded with moonlight.

Blythe could have sworn that a woman sobbed, but his eyes, used by now to the obscurity, told him that it was neither Mrs. Bruce nor Barbara. The piano burst into a storm of sound, under cover of which Rose, still at her post, torn with jealousy, continued to pedal at the direction of her lord and master, and sobbed as if her heart would break. Devils filled the room, whirling in mad dances; they screamed and yelled; the souls of the damned screeched in torment; and the face of him who invoked the inferno, swollen, streaming with sweat, the eyes glazed, protruding, was the face of a madman.

Rose, for whom her master's playing had the eloquence and precision of speech, forgot her jealousy in fear of those consequences which her ill-timed sobbing must bring upon her. Her tears dried as in a desert wind; her sobs ceased, and in a moment or two the madness was going out of Blizzard's music and out of his face. He rested, preluded, and then began to play Beethoven, quietly, with a pure singing tone, music of a heavenly sanity.

The jarred feelings of his audience were soothed. Into his own face there stole a high-priest look. And when he had finished playing, this look remained for a few moments. Then he laughed quietly and, speaking for the first time, expressed the hope that he had not made them listen too long.

He reached for the wall behind him, and turned a switch so that the room became brightly lighted. Then, reluctantly, he came out from behind the piano, swinging between his crutches, and leaving Rose to escape at the first favorable opportunity. His descent from colossus to cripple had an unpleasant effect. And the question, "How the deuce do you work the pedals?" was jerked from Blythe, usually a most tactful person.

"Why," said Blizzard simply, "I have an assistant."

He caught Barbara's eye and reddened a little. "A young man who is musical and intelligent. We have a system of signals, and—but I think there is a sort of thought communication that comes of much rehearsing together. And in our best moments we do pretty well. But sometimes when our minds are not tuned together we make a dreadful hash of things."

He might have added: "At such times I drag her about by the hair and beat her." But he didn't. He looked instead the picture of a very patient man who makes the best of things.

"Whatever you do at times," said Barbara gently, "you have done wonders to-night. But you know better than we do how good your playing is. So what is the use of praising it—to you?"

She felt that he was her own private discovery—almost her property. And knowing that her friends were still profoundly affected by his playing, she was filled with honest pride. Her eyes flashed, her cheeks glowed.

"What did I tell you?" she exclaimed. "Was I right? Didn't I promise that he would make good? Did he?"

She was delighted with Blizzard, delighted with herself, delighted with the whole party. She had forgotten the madman face that he had showed. She forgot that he was a cripple, a thing soured and wicked. She thought of him only as a great genius, which she herself had discovered.

The childlike pleasure which she felt communicated

itself to the others, and Blizzard, escaping an ovation
of honest praise, led them into the next room, where,
among palms and roses, such a supper was spread as
gamblers, the big men of the profession, spread for
their victims.

The mere sight of the champagne-glasses loosened
the men's tongues. Talk flowed. Mrs. Bruce and
Barbara, seated right and left of their host, made
much of his music and his hospitality. For once in
his life he was genuinely happy. He looked very
handsome, very high-minded, very modest, a man's
man. Sitting, he was much taller than the others.
You forgot that, standing, he was but a dwarf. He
towered at the head of his table, his mind working in
swift, good-natured, hospitable flashes. It was obvious that he had been born a gentleman, and that
he had never "forgotten how." It was obvious, too,
that he was a man of power and position, who when
he wished could spend money like a great lord, and
who was accustomed to give orders.

In his manner to Barbara there was (perhaps no-
ticeable only to herself) an air of long-proved friendship and a kind of guardianly tenderness, and he
managed somehow to convey to her that she had an
immense influence over him; that he looked to her
for help—for inspiration.

The desire to make a great man of him invaded her
mind. Her heart warmed toward him.

"I wonder," said Bruce suddenly, "where our wan-
dering Wilmot is to-night?"

"I drink to him," said the beggar quickly, "wherever he is, and wish him luck."

But the poison had been spilled on Barbara's evening. For three hours she had not once thought of the man whom twelve hours ago she had really wanted to marry. And her heart meanwhile had warmed and expanded toward one who at best was a prodigiously successful crook and rascal, and she was ashamed. But for all that neither the warmth nor the triumphant sense of influence and conquest went out of her heart. And later, when Mrs. Bruce said: "I really think we ought to go," Barbara, outwardly all sweetness and agreement, was inwardly annoyed. She wanted very much to stay, for she knew that the moment she was alone her conscience would give her no peace, and that she would make resolutions which she would not, judging from past experiences, be able to keep. She would resolve to abandon her bust of Blizzard, resolve never to see the creature again, since it seemed that he had in him power upon her emotions—dangerous power.

"Do we work to-morrow, Miss Ferris?"

The words, "No, I'm afraid not to-morrow," rose to her lips. The words, "*Please*, at the usual time," came out.

And she felt as if his will, not her own, had caused her to say those words. Her heart gave a sudden leap of fear.

XXVI

BARBARA knew very well that she was doing wrong. Summer had descended, blazing, upon the city. Without exception her friends had gone to the country. Her father had gone to Colorado upon an errand of which for the present he chose to make a mystery. She made a habit of lunching at the Colony Club, and occasionally saw some friend or other who had run into town for a face massage, a hair wave, a gown, or a hat. But the afternoons and evenings hung very heavily upon her hands. So that she got to living in and for her mornings at the studio. With the appearance of Blizzard, clean, thoughtful, and forceful, her feelings of loneliness and depression vanished. If her vitality was at low ebb, his was not. The heat appeared to brace him, and he had the faculty of communicating something of his own energy, so that it was not until she had finished working and dismissed him that she was sensible of fatigue and discouragement.

The man was on his best behavior. He could not but realize that he had established an influence over her; that she was beginning to take him at his own estimate of himself, and to believe in his pretended aspirations. And while he credited her with no affection for himself, he had the presumption to imagine that his maimed condition and his low station in life no longer made the slightest difference to her, and that finally her friendliness would turn into a warmer feeling. But if not, he had but to wait until the maturity of his plans should throw the city into chaos, when she would be at his mercy.

The hand which he had dealt himself was so full of high cards that the occasional losing of a trick did not disturb him in the slightest. He had through her father's hideous mistake a hold on Barbara's conscience. As a personage whose power over certain sections of the city was stronger than the law, he had a hold upon her imagination. As the inspirer of her best work, he had a hold upon her gratitude. He had, or thought he had, a chance to win her affection in open and equal competition. And, highest card of all—ace of trumps—he had persuaded her that her influence upon him was such that with all the strength of remorse he was shaping his life toward high ideals.

In his heart she was usually, but not always, the first consideration. Sometimes the passion of ambition overlapped the passion of love. And sometimes he felt that he would forego the fruition of all his plans if only by some miracle his legs could be restored to him.

But on the whole, he had reached a high-water mark of self-satisfaction. He had found it easy to carry corruption into high places. A list of those who were in his power—willing or unwilling—would have horrified the whole nation. From O'Hagan in the West came reports that all went well with the organization, and that Wilmot Allen was displaying genius in teaching inexperienced Polacks to shoot.

On his walks through the city the legless man carried a high head, and looked about him with the eye of a landlord. His imagination was so strong that he had already the feelings of a genuine conqueror, and not of a man confronted by the awful possibilities of failure. And by some subtlety of mental communication Barbara was coming more and more into this same opinion of him. And in realizing this, and in allowing their relations to continue, she knew that she was doing wrong.

She compared her model with all the men she had known, always to conclude that there was in him a sort of greatness utterly wanting in the others. If he had revealed his plans to her, she would have believed him not only capable of carrying them out, but sure to do so—if he wished. He might be Satan fallen, but he was still a god. In the early days of their association she had felt herself the important person of the two, and her bust of him the most important thing in the world. He and she would surely die, but the bust had a chance to live. But now she had the feeling that the work was of less importance than the man; and that she herself was an insignificant spoiled person of no importance whatever. When Blizzard entered the studio she had the feeling that a great and busy man was, out of pure good nature, wasting his time upon an unknown artist.

But she knew very well that such was not the case. She knew that he came to the studio because she attracted him, and for no other reason. And at times she felt keenly curious to know just how much she attracted him, and the morbid wish, for which she hated herself, of leading him into some sort of a declaration.

XXVII

HOWEVER unnecessary the hot waves of the New York summer may appear to some people, they were never wasted on Bubbles. He had a passion for the water, and to his love of swimming was added a passion for the underworld gossip with which the piers of the East River reek in bathing weather. For just as mice are more intimate with the details of houses than landlords are, so the small boys of a city have the best opportunities for being acquainted with its workings, and with the intimate lives of its inhabitants. The street-boy's mind matures while his body is still that of a child. Births and deaths are familiar spectacles to him. He knows and holds of high import hundreds of things which men have forgotten. He can see in the dark. He can hide in a handful of shadow. And when he isn't overhearing on his own hook, he is listening to what somebody else has overheard. Second-story men fear him, lovers loathe him, and nature, who has been thwarted in her intention that he should run in sweet meadows, sleep in fresh air, and bathe in clean water, sighs over him.

It was so hot that the policeman whose duty and privilege it was to see that no small boy cooled himself from Pier 31A, disappeared tactfully into the family entrance of a water-front saloon. The city had many laws which to this particular officer appeared unreasonable and which he enforced only when he couldn't help himself. In men there is the need of gambling and some other things. As for small boys, they *must* play baseball and they *must* swim.

Bubbles went overboard at about three o'clock. There were twenty or thirty boys of all sizes already in the water, and the addition of one to the struggling group of wet heads was not to be noticed. Nor was the disappearance of that head noticed, nor the fact that it appeared to remain under water for nearly three-quarters of an hour, nor that when it finally did emerge it looked on the whole as if it had seen a ghost.

Bubbles, it seems, was less interested in the waters around Pier 31A than in the waters underneath. And for this reason: on the previous night, while stripping for a swim, he had heard a muffled sound of voices coming from directly under the pier, followed by a long subdued roaring as of a load of earth being emptied into the water. Now, under Harry West's tuition Bubbles had formed the habit of investigating whatever he did not understand. And he wished very much to find out why people should talk under piers at night, how they could get under Pier 31A except by swimming, and *if* they were throwing earth overboard *why* they were doing so, and where they got the earth.

His head filled with vague and highly colored no-
tions of a smugglers' cave, his narrow lungs filled
with air, Bubbles dove, swam between two slimy bar-
nacled piles, and came up presently in a dark, dank,
stale, gurgling region, wonderfully cool after the blazing sunlight which he had just left.

Toward the shore the light that filtered between
the supporting piles of Pier 31A became less and less,
until completely shut off by walls of solid masonry.
Into this darkness Bubbles swam with great caution,
accustoming his eyes to the obscurity and holding
himself ready to dive in retreat at the first alarm.

The shore end of Pier 31A had originally been a
clean wall of solid masonry. The removal of half a
dozen great blocks of stone had made a jagged opening in the midst of this, and into this opening, pulling
himself a little out of the water, Bubbles strained and
strained his eyes and saw nothing but the beginning
of a passageway and then pitch darkness.

His heart beat very hard and fast like the heart of
a caught bird. Here, leading into the city from the
shore of the East River, was a mysterious passageway. Who had made it and why? There were two
ways of finding out. One was to wait patiently until
some one entered the passage or emerged from it.
The other way, and the better, was to forget how
very much the idea of so doing frightened you, climb
into the opening, and follow the passage to its other
end. Bubbles compromised. He waited patiently for
half an hour. Nothing happened. Then he pulled

himself into the opening and crawled through the darkness for perhaps the length of a city block.

"What," he then said to himself, "is the use of me going any further? I can't see in the dark. I've got no matches, and if anything happens to me, there'll be nobody to tell Harry about this place. Better make a get-away now, find Harry, and bring him here to-night. Then if we find anybody there'll be something doing."

He had turned and was crawling rather rapidly toward the entrance of the passage.

XXVIII

BUBBLES'S problem was to locate Harry West. And
he wrestled with it, if trying to cover the whole of a
scorching hot city on a pair of insufficient legs and a
very limited amount of carfare may be called wres-
tling. His search took him into many odd places
where you could not have expected to cross the trail
of an honest man. He even made inquiries of a
master-plumber, of a Fourth Avenue vender of an-
tiques, of a hairy woman with one eye who ran a
news-stand, of a bar-tender, of saloon-keepers and
bootblacks. He drifted through a department store,
and whispered to a pretty girl who sold "art pictures."
She shook her head. He spoke a word to the negro
sentinel of a house in the West Forties, and was admitted to quiet, padded rooms, containing everything
which is necessary to separate hopeful persons from
their money. In one room a number of book-makers
were whiling away the hot afternoon with poker for
small stakes. In another room, played upon by an
electric fan, sat Mr. Lichtenstein, the proprietor. He
was bent over a table on which he had assembled
fifteen or twenty of the component parts of a very
large picture-puzzle. He was small, plump and earnest. He may have been a Jew, but he had bright
red hair and a pug nose. His eyes, bright, quick,

small, brown, and kind, were very busy hunting among
the brightly colored pieces of the puzzle.

"'Dafternoon, Mr. Lichtenstein," said Bubbles.

"'Dafternoon, Bubbles," said Mr. Lichtenstein,
without looking up.

"How d'je know it was me?"

"I saw you in the looking-glass. What's the
news?"

"It's for Harry."

"And Harry is—where?"

"Don't you know where Harry is?"

"I do. But you can't get to him." Mr. Lichtenstein lowered his voice. "He's gone West, Bub, on
the trail of O'Hagan. The plant the old one is growing hasn't put its head above ground yet, and the
roots are in the West. Out in Utah they're teaching
all kinds of Polacks to shoot rifles. Why? O'Hagan
is travelling from one mine to another as a common
laborer. Why? While here in little New York, the
old one is sitting for his portrait and getting a perfectly innocent young girl talked about. No use to
watch the old one till later."

"But," said Bubbles, "suppose some one was to
find a secret passage leading from the East River
to—to——"

"To where?"

"He doesn't know where. He wanted to get
Harry to go with him to find out."

"Where does the passage begin, Bubbles?"

"Under Pier 31A."

"'D afternoon, Mr. Lichtenstein." said
  Bubbles

"Come over here, Bub," said Mr. Lichtenstein and led the way to a mahogany table covered with green baize. Upon this he spread a folding-map of New York City that he took from his inside pocket. With the rapidity of thought his stubby forefinger found Pier 31A and passed from it to the crook in Marrow Lane. And he said:

"Hum! The bee-line of it leads straight to Blizzard's place. There are two things to find out, Bub. Is the passage straight? And how long is it? A light in the entrance to sight by will answer question No. 1, and a ball of twine to be unwound at leisure will answer No. 2."

"You'd ought to have a compass," Bubbles suggested, "to know just how she runs."

"True," said Mr. Lichtenstein. "Happy thought. And you could borrow one mounted in tiger's eye from a friend."

He laughed, took the little compass in question from its watch chain, and gave it to Bubbles. Then, his voice losing its bantering tone and taking on a kind of faltering sincerity, he asked:

"Do you want to play this hand, Bubbles, or do you want me to delegate some one else?"

"It's my graft," said Bubbles, "I'd like to see it through."

Mr. Lichtenstein looked upon the boy with a certain pride and tenderness. "I'd like to go with you," he said, "but I can't run *any* risks. There's the strings of too many things in my head. In every battle there has to be a general who sits on a hill out of danger and orders other people to do brave things. Remember that you've worked for us ever since Harry came in and said, laughing, 'Governor, I've made friends with a bright baby that knows how to keep his mouth shut.' You've only to step up to Blizzard and say, 'Abe Lichtenstein is the head,' to bring the gun-men down on me. But you'd die first."

The boy's breast swelled with pride and martial ardor. "Betcher life," he said, and then: "If I get the news will I bring it here?"

Mr. Lichtenstein considered for a minute. Then shook his head. "I'll be in Blicker's drug-store between 'leven and midnight," he said.

"If I don't show up it'll be because I can't."

Mr. Lichtenstein smiled encouragingly. "Don't look on the dark side of the future," he said, "but don't take any chances, and don't show a light till you have to."

XXIX

THE night was hot, but the rising tide had brought in cold water from the ocean, and what with his excitement and trepidation it was a very shivery small boy that began to investigate the passage under Pier 31A. Mindful of Mr. Lichtenstein's advice not tó show a light till he had to, Bubbles felt his way forward very slowly in the inky darkness, unrolling, as he went, a huge ball of twine. It would be time to take the bearings of the place by compass when he had ascertained its general extent and whether it was free from human occupants. On this score he felt comparatively safe, since it seemed likely that the passage had been constructed with a view to emergency rather than daily use.

Having advanced a distance of about three short city blocks, it seemed to Bubbles as if the passage had opened suddenly into a room. If so, he had to thank instinct for the knowledge, since he could see but an inch in the blackness. He had the feeling that walls were no longer passing near him, and, groping cautiously this way and that, he found it to be fact and not fancy. During these gropings he lost his sense of direction, and, after considering the matter at some length, he concluded that the time had come to flash his torch. But first he listened for a long

time. At last, satisfied that he was alone, his thumb
began to press against the switch of his torch. A
shaft of light bored into the darkness, and he saw two
wildly bearded men, who sat with their backs against
a wall of living rock and looked straight at him.

It was as if he had been suddenly frozen solid, so
dreadful was his surprise and horror, but the men
with the wild heads showed no emotion. They had
a pale, tired, hopeless look; and though one was dark
and one blond, this expression, common to both, gave
them an appearance of being twin brothers. They
had gentle soft eyes in which was no sign of surprise
or agitation. It seemed as if they were perfectly
accustomed to having light suddenly flashed into
them. One of the men leaned forward and began to
run his hand this way and that over the hard dirt
floor.

"Lost something?" said the other suddenly.

"Dropped my plug," said the first in a dull weary
voice, and he continued to feel for and repeatedly
just miss a half-cake of chewing-tobacco. Bubbles
could see it distinctly, and another thing was clear
to him: the men were both blind.

With this knowledge certain frayed and tattered
fragments of courage returned to him, and, what was
of much greater importance, his presence of mind.

The excavation in which he stood was nearly forty
feet square. His torch showed him the passage by
which he had entered, and opposite this a flight of
steps leading sharply upward. Here and there, lean-

ing against the walls, were picks and shovels and other tools used in excavating. Near the centre of the passage was a tall pile of dirt and loose stones, together with two small wheelbarrows of sheet-iron.

Just as Bubbles had ascertained these facts and got himself into a much calmer state of mind, he had a fresh thrill of horror. The two blind men sighed, and as if moved by a common impulse got up, and the little boy saw that, like Blizzard, the beggar, they had no legs. With perfect accuracy of direction they turned to the great pile of dirt, and taking up two shovels which leaned against it began to fill the two little wheelbarrows.

They labored slowly as if time was of no moment, as if the work in hand was a form of punishment instead of something that it was intended to complete.

Bubbles had begun to wonder what they were going to do with the dirt, when one of them, having filled his barrow, trundled off with it into the passageway leading to the river. And to Bubbles, feverishly listening, there came after what seemed a very long interval a sound as of earth being dumped into water.

The second excavator, having filled his barrow, waited the return of his companion, since the passage was too narrow to admit of the two barrows meeting and passing each other.

And that simple fact was very alarming to Bubbles, since virtually it made a prisoner of him. One man with his barrow full or empty was always in the passage.

Nor was there any possibility of escape by the flight
of stairs which he had noticed, for a hurried examination revealed a door of sheet-iron which did not give
to his most determined efforts. There was nothing
for it but to wait until the blind men should rest from
their labors.

He got used to them gradually; lost his fear of
them. Once in a while they spoke to each other,
always with a kind of lugubrious gentleness in their
voices. He began to feel sorry for them. He wished
to be of service to them in some way or other. Their
wild beards and shaggy, matted hair no longer ter-
rified him. They were two lambs made up to represent wolves, but the merest child must have seen
through the disguisement.

Upon the ball of twine which Bubbles still held in
his hand there was a sudden tug. It fell to the ground
with a thump and rolled toward the blind laborer
who had just filled his barrow. He was much startled
and turned his blind eyes this way and that; then
called to his mate, at that moment coming from the
passageway.

"I heard something drop," he said; "somebody
dropped something. I thought I heard steps on the
stairs, and now I know I did."

But the other had found the twine lying the length
of the passage. "Some one's come in from the river,"
he said, "and dropped all this string."

He began to gather it in, hand over hand, paused
suddenly, and then, with a kind of bravado of terri-

fied politeness, and with a bob of his wild, dark head, exclaimed:

"Good evening, Mr. Blizzard!"

Then the pair cowered as if they expected to be struck, and after a long while the blond one said:

"It ain't him."

Then the dark one:

"Don't be scared of us. We couldn't hurt a fly if we wanted to. Who is it?"

Now it seemed to Bubbles all of a sudden (though the mention of Blizzard's name had once more given him the horrors) that any risk run in revealing his presence to the blind men was more than compensated by the consequent possibility of "finding out things" from them. So he said:

"It's only me—just a boy. I found this hole swimmin' and come in to see what it was for."

"It's only a boy," said the blond man.

"He wouldn't hurt us," said the dark one.

"Maybe you'll tell me what all this cellar work is for," said Bubbles.

The dark man scratched his matted head. "We don't know," he said; "we was just put in here to dig. At first there was ten of us; but we was kep' on to give the finishin' touches."

"What became of the others?"

"Oh, Mr. Blizzard, he's got other work for them."

"Is this place under his house?"

"No, sir, it ain't. But the cellar at the head of them steps is."

"Maybe he's hollered this out to hide things in?"

The blind men turned toward each other and nodded their heads.

"That's just presactly what we think," said the blond one.

"What do you do when you aren't working?"

"Oh, we sleeps and eats in Blizzard's cellar."

"How long you been on the job?"

"We don't know. We lost track."

"See much of Blizzard?"

"Oh, he's in and out, just to keep things going."

"Is the passage to the river just to get rid of the dirt?"

The dark man laughed sheepishly. "We don't think so," he said—"we gets lots of time to think. And it ain't always dirt that goes into the river. Twicet it's been men, and once it were a woman. There was lead pipe wrapped round the bodies to make 'em sink. And oncet Blizzard he tumbled a girl down the stairs to us. But she weren't dead, and me and Bill took the lead off her before we throwed her in."

His comrade interrupted. "She said she could swim. She said if we'd take the lead off and untie her and give her a chanst, we could have a kiss apiece. But we let her go fer nothin'."

"Did she get away?" Bubbles was tremendously interested.

"No, sir. It was dark night, and she couldn't find a way out from under the wharf. She just swam round and round, slower and slower, like a mouse in a wash-tub. Then she calls out she'll come back and we can hide her till daylight. But she don't make it. We has to stand there and listen to her drown."

"When she's dead she gets out into the open river, and when Blizzard hears she's been found without any lead on her he raises hell."

"When he gets through with us we was most skinned alive."

"He wouldn't dig that hole to the river," said Bubbles, "just to get rid of people. What do you think it's for?"

"You ain't goin' to tell Blizzard you been here, nor get us in trouble?"

"I'll get you out of this some day, but you can't get in no trouble through me."

"Then," said the blond man, "this is what we thinks out and concludes: Blizzard he's calculatin' to receive stolen goods wholesale. First he stores 'em in here until this cellar is full, and then he takes 'em down to the river and puts 'em aboard a ship bound fur furrin' ports, and we thinks and concludes that he'll make his get-away about the same time."

"Well," said Bubbles, "I'm obliged. I won't forget your kindness. But it's time I was off."

"Come close first," said the blond man.

Bubbles was instantly alarmed. "Why?"

"Only so's we can feel your face, so's to know what you look like."

He stood impatient and embarrassed while they pawed his face with hard, grimy hands.

At last they let him go, he whose barrow was full accompanying him to the end of the passageway, and speeding him on his way with this comfortable remark:

"If you was to dive deep and feel around, you might find those as is leaded to the bottom."

It took every ounce of nerve that Bubbles had at command to let his legs and body slip down into the cold and tragic current. It seemed certain that dead hands were reaching for him. But he screwed his courage up to the sticking point, and called to his acquaintance in the passage-mouth a whispered but nonchalant, "S'long!"

XXX

WHEN Bubbles entered Blicker's drug-store, the city clocks were striking a quarter to twelve, but the place was still brightly lighted, and at the soda-counter a young man was treating his flame to a glass of chocolate vanilla ice-cream.

Bubbles marched to the prescription counter, and began to unwrap a bloody handkerchief from his left hand. Then he began to clear his throat. This brought Mr. Blicker from a region of mortar pestles, empty pill-boxes, and glass retorts.

"What you want?" he asked aggressively.

"I want me thumb bandaged."

"You cut him—eh?"

Bubbles lowered his voice. "On a barnacle."

"Come in back here," said Mr. Blicker roughly. "I fix him." But once out of sight in the depths of the store, his manner changed, and he patted Bubbles enthusiastically on the back. "You have found out some things?"

"Sure—lots."

The chemist, without commenting, began to treat the cut thumb, washing, disinfecting, and bandaging. Then, very loud, for the benefit perhaps of the lovers

235

at the soda-counter, "So," he said, "I let you out the back door."

And he actually opened a door, slammed it shut, and turned a key in the lock. But it was a closet door. Then with a finger on his lips he pointed to a narrow staircase and, his own feet making a great tramping, led the way up it. Upon the top steps they found Mr. Lichtenstein, nervously puffing clouds of tobacco smoke.

"'Bout given you up," he said. "Good boy!"

"Better talk by the parlor," said Blicker; "here is too exposed."

When the door of the stuffy little parlor had closed behind them, the proprietor began to smile and beam. But Mr. Lichtenstein looked grave and troubled. It was not for pleasure that he sometimes found occasion to put dangerous work in the hands of children.

"Hurt your thumb bad?" he asked.

Bubbles shook his head and plunged into his story. Now and then the German laughed, but the red-haired, pug-nosed Jew appeared to sink deeper and deeper into his own thoughts, only showing by an occasional question that he was following the boy's narrative. Bubbles wished to dwell at length and with comment upon the use of the passage for disposing of dead bodies, but to Mr. Lichtenstein this appeared to be merely a natural by-product of its construction.

"It wasn't dug for that," he said. "How big is the main excavation?"

"''Bout as big as a small East Side dance-hall."

Mr. Lichtenstein turned to the German. "Hold a lot of loot—what?"

"I bet me," said the German, and washed his hands with air.

"Lot o' what?" asked Bubbles.

"Loot—gold, silver, jewels, bullion."

"Your ideas," said the German, "is all idiot. No mans is such a darn fool as to think he can get away by such a business—no mans, that is, but is crazy."

"Blizzard is crazy," said Mr. Lichtenstein simply. "It wasn't until we hit on that hypothesis that we made any progress. Bubbles, did you ever hear of the Massacre of Saint Bartholomew?"

"Sure," said Bubbles, "they shot him full of ar- rows."

"That was Saint Sebastian," corrected the Jew. "Now listen, this is history. On the night of August 24, 1572, two thousand men, distinguished from other men by white cockades in their hats, on the order of a crazy man, at the tolling of a bell, drew their swords, murdered everybody in a great city who opposed their leaders, and made themselves absolute masters of the place. What two thousand men did in Paris during the Middle Ages, ten thousand men acting in concert could do in New York to-day. If a man rose up with the power to command such a following, with the ability to keep his plans absolutely secret, with the genius to make plans in which there were no flaws, he could loot Maiden Lane, the Sub-Treasury,

Tiffany's, the Metropolitan Museum—*and get away with it.*"

Mr. Lichtenstein's small eyes glittered. He was visibly excited. And so was Mr. Blicker.

"He will loot the Metropolitan Museum," said this one, "but what will he do with the metropolitan police?"

"Well," said Mr. Lichtenstein, "I am only supposing. But suppose some fine night a building somewhere central was blown up with dynamite. Suppose the sound was so big that it could be heard in every part of greater New York. Suppose at the sound every policeman in greater New York was shot dead in his tracks——"

Bubbles's hair began to bristle. "Say," he cried in his excitement, "the straw hats—the soft straw hats that Blizzard makes and don't sell—they're the white cockades!"

Mr. Blicker guffawed. Mr. Lichtenstein rose and paced the room.

"And that proves," he exclaimed, "that nothing is to happen when you and I are wearing straw hats—but in winter. Bubbles, you're a bright boy!"

"You are both so bright," said Mr. Blicker, "you keep me all the time laughing."

"Well," said Mr. Lichtenstein, "that may be, but suppose you tell me why Blizzard makes straw hats and don't sell 'em. Tell me why he's dug such a great hole under his house with a passage leading to the river, and ships. Tell me why O'Hagan is drilling men in the West. Tell me why Blizzard has gone out of the white-slave business. It fetched him in a pretty penny."

"I think I can answer the last question," said Bubbles.

"Do then."

"I think," said the small boy, "that he's got some good in him somewhere, and I know he's dead gone on my Miss Ferris. I think he's ashamed o' some o' the things he's done."

Mr. Lichtenstein considered this at some length. Then he said: "Well, that's possible. But it's an absolutely new idea to me. Blizzard *ashamed?* Hum!"

XXXI

"TRUE that policemen take money in exchange for protection? True that they practise blackmail and extortion? Of course it's true. Whenever a big temptation appears loose in a city half the people who get a look at it trip and fall. Oh, I'd like to reform this city, Miss Barbara—and this country. I'd like to be dictator for six months."

"Who wouldn't?" said Barbara. "But what would you do? Where would you begin?"

"I should be drastic at first," said the legless man, "and kind later. I'd begin," he went on, his eyes smiling, "with a general massacre of incompetents—old men with too little money, young men with too much—old maids, aliens, incurables, the races that are too clever to work, the races that are too stupid, habitual drunkards, spreaders of disease, the women who abolished the canteen, the women who wear aigrettes. After that I should destroy all possibilities of graft."

"How?" asked Barbara.

"Why," said he, "the simplest way in the world—legalize the business that now pays for protection. There would be no more of them than there are now, and they could be regulated and kept to confined limits of cities. Don't blame the police for graft:

blame all who believe that human nature can be abolished by law. But," and this time his whole face smiled, "I shall never be dictator. The thing to do is to start a new country, and make no mistakes."

And he proceeded, sometimes seriously but for the most part whimsically, to outline his model republic, while Barbara worked and listened, sometimes with amusement, sometimes with a sense of being uplifted and thrilled by the man's plausible originality. Since she had but the vaguest recollection of history, and none whatever of economics, it was easy for the man to play the constructive statesman. Nor were his schemes always foolish and illogical, since the book of human nature had been always in his library, and of all its volumes had been most often read.

"Ah!" said the legless man at last, "if I were younger, and whole!"

Whenever he referred to his maimed condition Barbara, to whom it was no longer physically shocking, was uncomfortable and distressed, changing the subject as swiftly as might be. But now, stopping her work short off, her hands hanging at her sides, she began to speak of the matter.

"I suppose," she said, "it's almost life and death to you—sometimes, that you'd give almost anything, take any chance to be—the way you were meant to be. My father believes that some day people can have anything that they've lost restored—a hand or an arm. He's made experiments along those lines ever since he made his mistake with you, and it all works out beautifully with monkeys and dogs and guinea-pigs and rabbits. Just now he is in Colorado to try it on a man. There's a man out there in jail for life, who has a brother that lost his right hand in some machinery. The well brother has offered to let father cut off his hand, and graft it on the maimed brother's wrist. I've just had a letter—it's been done. He thinks it's all right, but he can't be sure yet. Please don't say anything about it because—well, because people are still queer about these things. In the old days people burned the best doctors, and now they want to lynch vivisectors and almost anybody who's really trying to make health more or less contagious."

"Do you believe I could be made whole?" exclaimed Blizzard, his eyes glittering as with a sudden hope. "My God! Even if they weren't much use to me, I'd give my soul to look like a real man—my soul! Do you know what I'd rather do than anything in this whole world—just once? I'd rather draw myself to my full height—just once—than be Napoleon Bonaparte. If all the treasure in this city were mine to give, I'd give it to walk the length of a city block on my own feet, looking down at the people instead of always up—always up—until the leverage of your eyes twists the back of your brain in everlasting torment."

"When my father comes back," said Barbara quietly, "talk to him. And if only it can be done—why, you'll forgive us, won't you, for all the suffering you've had and everything?"

She said in a small, surprised voice,
  "Why, it's finished"

"Yes, yes," he said quickly. "But it isn't true—it isn't possible. It won't work. It's against experience."

"It is *possible*," said Barbara gently. "That's all I know. And even if—even if it can't be done yet awhile, I thought it would comfort you to think that some day—almost surely——"

"You are always thinking of my comfort," he cried. "In this pit that we call life, you are an angel serene, blessed and blessing. Oh," he cried, "what would you say if I stood before you on my own feet, and told you—told you—" He broke off short and hung his head.

Barbara bit her lips and lifted her hands with a weary gesture to resume work. But the bust of Blizzard was a live thing, and seeing anew the strength and hellish beauty of it, suddenly and as if with the eyes of a stranger, her heart seemed to leap into her throat, her whole body relaxed once more, and she said in a small, surprised voice:

"Why, it's finished!"

XXXII

Upon Blizzard, who had been looking forward to many mornings during which he should unobtrusively advance his cause, this quiet statement fell with disturbing force. It meant that his opportunities for intimate talks had come to a sudden and most unprepared-for end. He knew that Barbara was tired out with the steady grind of creation, and that she had been going through an equally steady grind of discouragement and uncertainty. He believed that she would make no delay in carrying her triumph and her trouble out of the heat-ridden city, to cool places, to her own people. He believed, not that she would forget him, but that, free from his influence, she would see with equal vision how wide the gulf between them really was.

He had made a slip in his calculation. He had been spreading his arts thinly, you may say, to cover what he supposed was to have been a much longer period of time. And he should have come sooner and with all his strength to the point. There had been moments of supreme discouragement, when, if there was to be a miracle in his life, he should have spoken. There were to be no more of those golden moments. She would close the studio, go away, and return by way of exercise and fresh air to a sane and

244

normal state of mind—a state of mind in which such a physical and moral cripple as himself could have no place except among the curiosities.

She stood looking steadily at the head which had come to life under her hands. Her eyelids drooped heavily. She looked almost as if she was falling asleep.

Blizzard watched her as a cat watches a mouse, not knowing what was best for him to dare. Now he was for pleading his cause with all the passion that inspired it; now for boldly claiming her as the expiation for her father's fault; and now he was for passing over all preliminaries and felling her with a blow of his fist.

And then she suddenly turned to him, and smiled like a very happy and very tired child. "You've been very good to me," she said, "and so patient! I don't know quite how to thank you. I owe you such a lot."

"Do you?" he said, his hard eyes softening and seeking hers.

She nodded slowly. "Such a lot. And there's no way of paying, or making things up to you, is there?"

"Only one," he said.

There was quite a long silence; his eyes, flames in them, held hers, which were troubled and childlike, and imbued the two words that he had spoken with an unmistakable intelligence.

"Don't let me go utterly," he said, "and slip back into the pit. You have finished the bust. If you wished you could finish the man: put him back among the good angels. . . . If your father died owing money, you couldn't rest until you had paid his debts. . . . I could be anything you wished. And I could give you anything that you wanted in this world. There is nothing I couldn't put over—with you at my side, wishing the good deed done, the great deed—or——"

He began to tremble with the passion that was in his voice, slipped from his chair, and began to move slowly toward her with outstretched arms, upon his stumps of legs.

It was no mirth or any sense of the ridiculous that moved Barbara, but fear, disgust, and horror. She backed away from him, laughing hysterically. But he, whose self-consciousness in her sight bordered upon mania, mistook the cause of her laughter, so that a kind of hell-born fury shook him, and he rushed at her, his mouth giving out horrible and inarticulate sounds. And in those lightning moments she could move neither hand nor foot; nor could she cry for help. And yet she realized, as in some nightmare, that if once those horrible hairy hands closed upon her she was lost utterly. And in that same clear flash of reason she realized that for whatever might befall she had herself alone to blame. She had touched pitch, and played with fire—and all that men might some day call her great.

The speed for which the fury of the legless man called was more than the stumps of his legs could furnish. He was like a man, thigh-deep in water, who attempts to run at top speed. Yet his hands were within inches of her dress, when daring and nerve at last thrilled through Barbara, and returned her muscles into the keeping of her mind. She darted backward and to one side. In that instant the legless man overreached himself and fell heavily. Here seemed an inestimable advantage for Barbara, and yet the great body, shaken with curses and already rising to its stumps, was between her and the door.

XXXIII

For once the legless man had been deserted by the power of cool reasoning. And his fury was of a kind that could not wait for satisfaction. He was more like a mad dog than a man. And this, although it added to the horror of Barbara's situation, proved her salvation.

Occupying a point from which he could head off her escape by either of the studio doors, he abandoned this, and attempted to match the stumps of his legs against her swift young feet. And must have overcome the disparity, but that in the lightning instinct of self-preservation she overturned a table between them, and during the moments thus gained dashed into her dressing-room and locked the door behind her.

Blizzard vented his rage upon the locked door, splintering its panels with bleeding fists; but in the meanwhile his quarry had escaped him, and was already in the street walking swiftly toward Washington Square. He leaned at last from a window, and saw her going. And in his heart shame gradually took the place of fury. Why, when she laughed at him, had he not been able to dissemble his emotions for a few seconds? to mask his dreadfulness? For then, surely, he must have got her in his power. He should have hung his head when she laughed, begged her to forgive him for daring to lift his thoughts to her; and begged her as a token of forgiveness to shake hands with him. Her hand once clasped in his——

Well, he had made a fool of himself. Perhaps he had frightened her utterly beyond the reach even of his long arm. Fear would carry her out of the city, out of the State, out of the country, perhaps. To prevent the least of these contingencies he must act swiftly and with daring wisdom.

He passed into the studio, glanced upward at the bust of himself, stopped, and looked about for something heavy with which to destroy it. Later he would tell her that he had done so, and let that knowledge be the beginning of her torment.

But the thing that he planned to destroy looked him in the eye, smiling. The thing smiled in the full knowledge of good and evil, the fact that it had chosen evil, the fact that it was lost forever. It was no contagious smile, but a smile aloof and dreadful. So a man, impaled, may smile, when agony has passed beyond the usual human passions—and even so the legless man smiled upward at the smiling bust of himself. And he found that he could not destroy the bust: for the act would have about it too ominous a flavor of self-destruction.

He caught up his crutches, his little hand-organ, and hurried from the studio. By now Barbara must be well on her way up-town. He entered a public telephone station and gave the number of her house.

He asked to speak with Miss Marion O'Brien, and
when after an interval he heard the voice of Barbara's
maid in his ear, he said: "She's been frightened. Let
me know what she's going to do as soon as you know.
Don't use the house 'phone. Slip out to a pay station.
I must know when she's going and where, and if she
says for how long." He hung up the receiver, and
hurried off.

An hour later Barbara's maid telephoned him the
required news, but all of it that mattered was that
Barbara was not going out of town until the next day.
There was a whole afternoon and night in which to
act.

The legless man sank at once into deep and swift
thought. And ten minutes later he had abandoned
all idea of kidnapping Barbara for the present. Certain dangers of so doing seemed insurmountable. He
must possess his soul in patience, and in the meanwhile discount, if possible, the fright that he had
given her. To this end he wrote the following letter:

"It wasn't your fault that I lifted my eyes to you,
and hoped that you would lower yours to me. But
now I know what a fool I have been. I forgive you
for laughing at me, though at the time it made me
mad like a dog, and I only wanted to hurt the woman
I love. I won't trouble you any more, ever. Indeed
I am too ashamed and humbled ever to wish to see
you again. Only please don't hate me. If I had
any good sides, please remember them. Some time
you will hear of me again; but never again from me.

I have work to do, but I have given my time to
dreaming.

"When your father comes back will you ask him
to let me know if he will see me? You thought he
could do something for me—or hold out some hope.
I would risk my life itself to be whole, even if I could
never be very active. And science is so wonderful;
and I know your father would like to help me if he
could.

"If you don't think I am being punished for threatening you, and going crazy, you don't know anything
about the unhappiest beast in this world. But it is
terrible for a cripple when the one person he looks up
to laughs at him. I have a thick skin; but that
burnt through it like acid."

The messenger who carried the letter to Barbara
brought him her answer:

"I will give your message to my father. You are
quite wrong about the laughing. I didn't laugh at
you or anything about you. I laughed because I
was nervous and frightened. But it can't matter
much one way or the other. I am sorry that you have
been hurt twice by my family. But the second hurt
is not our fault. And I do not see that there is anything to be done about it. As for the first, my father
would end his days in peace if he could make you
whole. I shall hope to hear nothing but good of
you in the future."

The shame and remorse to which Blizzard pretended, Barbara actually felt. All her friendships

with men had been pursued by disasters of some sort or other. But her most disastrous experiment in friendship had been with Blizzard. She had been bluntly told by truth-speaking persons that he was not a fit acquaintance for her. His own face had warned her. But she had persisted in meeting him without precautions, in treating him like an equal, in overcoming her natural and just repugnance to him, and in calling him her friend. It was humiliating for her to realize and acknowledge that she had made a fool of herself. It was worse to remember the look in his face, during those last awful moments in the studio. Even if the bust she had made of him was a great work of art, she had paid too high for the privilege of making it.

XXXIV

Dr. Ferris was delighted to learn that Barbara had left town. Her meetings with Blizzard had been horribly on his mind and conscience. He had dreaded some vague calamity—some intangible darkening of his darling's soul.

A few days in the country had worked wonders for her. Her skin had browned a little, and her cheeks were crimson. But dearer to the paternal heart than these evidences of good health was the fact that she seemed unusually glad to see him. She seemed to him to have lost a world of independence and self-reliance, to be inclined to accept his judgments without dispute. She seemed more womanly and more daughterly, more normal and more beautiful.

For a man with a heavy weight always upon his conscience, the excellent surgeon found himself wonderfully at peace with the world and its institutions. There was no doubt that the hand which he had come from grafting was going to live and be of some use to its new owner. His mail was heavy with approbation. And it seemed to him that the path which he had discovered had no ending.

"In a hundred years, Barbara," he said, "it will be possible to replace anything that the body has lost, or that has become diseased and useless or a menace—not the heart, perhaps, nor the brain—but anything else. What I have done clumsily others will do to perfection."

"What are the chances for Blizzard?"

"Even," said the surgeon. "They would be more favorable if he had not lost his legs so long ago. At the worst the experiment wouldn't kill him. He would merely have undergone a useless operation. At the best he would be able to walk, run perhaps, and look like a whole man. If anything is to be done for him, the time has come. He has only to tell me to go ahead."

"I think he'll do that," said Barbara. "But there's one thing I don't understand," and she smiled; "who is to supply the spare legs?"

"That's the least of all the difficulties," said her father, "now that ways of keeping tissues alive have been discovered and proved. In time there will be storages from which any part of the human body may be obtained on short notice and in perfect condition for grafting. Just now the idea is horrible to ignorant people, but the faith will spread. Only wait till we have made a few old people young—for that will come, too, with the new surgery."

"You will be glad," said Barbara, "to hear that I have severed friendly relations with Mr. Blizzard. He behaved in the end pretty much as you all feared he would."

And she told her father, briefly, and somewhat shamefacedly, all that had happened in the studio.

"He thought I was laughing at him," she said. "Of course I wasn't. And he came at me. Do you remember when poor old Rose went mad, and tried to get at us through the bars of the kennel? Blizzard looked like that—like a mad dog." She shuddered.

The surgeon's high spirits were dashed as with cold water.

"He ought not to be helped," said Barbara; "he ought to be shot, as Rose was."

But Dr. Ferris shook his head gravely. "If he is that sort of a man," he said, "who made him so? Who took the joy of life from him? Barbara, my dear, there is nothing that man could do that I couldn't forgive."

"And I think that your conscience is sick," said Barbara. "I used to think as you think. But if you had seen his face that day! . . . The one great mistake you have made has ruined not his life, but yours. If he had had the right stuff in him, calamity would not have broken him! It would have *made* him. Give him a new pair of legs, if you can; and forget about him, as I shall. When you first told me about him, I thought we owed him anything he chose to ask. At one time I thought that if he wished it, it would be right for me to marry him."

"Barbara!"

"Yes, I did—I thought it strongly. Shows what a fool a girl who's naturally foolish can make of herself! Why, father, what if he has suffered through

your mistake? That mistake turned your thoughts
to the new surgery—and for the one miserable man
that you have hurt you will have given the wonder of
hope to the whole of mankind."

She slid her hand under her father's arm.

"Let's potter 'round the gardens," she said, "and
forget our troubles. It's bully to have you back.
There's not much doing in the floral line. The
summer sun in Westchester doesn't vary from year
to year. But there are lots of green things that smell
good, and the asters and dahlias are making the most
extraordinary promises of what they are going to do
by and by."

They passed out of the house and by marble steps
into the first and most formal of their many gardens,
and so down through the other gardens, terrace below
terrace, to the lake.

The water was so still as to suggest a solid rather
than a liquid; to the west shadowy mountains of
cloud charged with thunder swelled toward the zenith.
The long midsummer drought was coming to an end,
and all birds and insects were silent, as if tired of
complaining. Across the lake one maple, turned pre-
maturely scarlet, brought out the soft greens of the
woods with an astounding accent. Directly in front
of this flaming tree, a snow-white heron stood motionless upon a gray rock.

To Barbara it seemed on that day that "Clovelly"
was the loveliest place in all the world, and her father,
who had fashioned it out of rough farm lands, one of

They passed out of the house and by
marble steps into the first and most
formal of their many gardens

the world's most charming artists. "Why paint with oils, when you can draw with trees and flowers and grass and water?" she asked herself.

"In the time it took me to do Blizzard's bust," she said, "I could have planted millions of flowers and seen them bloom."

"At least," said her father, "you can finish a bust, but a garden that is finished isn't a garden. What are you going to do with it?"

"The bust? Why, sometimes I think I'll just leave it in the studio, and let it survive or perish. Sometimes I want to take a hammer and smash it to pieces."

"It didn't come out as well as you hoped?"

"Of course not. Does anything ever? But it's the best that I can do. And I shall never do anything better."

"Nonsense."

"I shall never even try. I want to recover all the things I've thrown away, and put them back in my head and heart where they belong, and just live."

"Well," said her father, smiling, "if you feel that way, why that's a good way to feel. But I'm afraid art is stronger in you than you think. Just now you're tired and disillusionized. In a month you'll be making sketches for some monumental opus."

"If I do," said Barbara, "it will be executed here at Clovelly. I never want to leave Clovelly. I feel safe here, safe from myself and other people. I think," and she smiled whimsically, "that I should almost like to settle down and make you a good daughter."

"A good daughter," said the surgeon, "marries; and her father builds a beautiful house for her, just over the hill from his own—remember the little valley where we found all the fringed gentian one year?— and the shortest cut between the two houses is worn bare and packed hard by the feet of grandchildren. Good Lord, my dear, what's the good of art, what's the good of science? I would rather have watched you grow up than have made the Winged Victory, or discovered the circulation of the blood. Come now, Barbs, tell me, who's the young man?"

For the first time in her life she told him of the wild impulsiveness and the shocking brevity of her affections for various members of his sex; naming no names she explained to him with much self-abasement (and a little amusement) that she was no good. "A nice wife I'd make!" she concluded.

But her father only laughed. "The only abnormal thing about you," he said, "is that you tell the truth. The average girl shows men more attentions than men show her. I don't mean that she demonstrates her attentions; but that she feels them in her heart. To be absolutely the first in a woman's heart a man must catch her when she's about three months old."

"But a girl," said Barbara, "who thinks she's sure and then finds she isn't, hurts the people she's fondest of. In extreme cases she breaks hearts and spoils lives."

"Hearts," said her father, "that can be broken are very weak. Lives that can be spoiled by disappointment and injured pride aren't worth preserving. If you have nothing more serious on your conscience than having, in all good faith, encouraged a few young men, found that you were wrong, and sent them away with bees in their bonnets, I'm sure I envy you."

Barbara simply shook her head.

"When you do find the right man, Barbara, you'll make up to him with showers of blessings for whatever cold rains you've shed on others. . . . What is Wilmot doing with himself these days?"

"He went away," said Barbara, and she sat looking steadily across the lake, her chin on her hand, her eyes troubled.

XXXV

IN many ways the life which Barbara led at Clovelly was calculated to rest her mind. She developed a passion for exercise, and when night came was too full of tired good health to read or talk. Since the estate was to be hers one day, she found the wish to know her way intimately about it, and since there were three thousand acres, for the most part thick forests spread over rocky hills, she could contemplate weeks of delightful explorations. To discover ponds, brooks, and caves that belong to other people has its delights, but to go daily up and down a lovely country discovering lovely things that belong to yourself is perhaps the most delightful way of passing time that has been vouchsafed to any one.

On these explorations Barbara's chosen companion was Bubbles. He was no longer a mere Buttons: her interest and belief in the child had passed beyond the wish to see him develop into a good servant. She wished to make something better of him—or if there is nothing better than a good servant, something more showy and ornamental.

He was sharp as a needle; and he was honest. He was not too old to be moulded by good influences, schools, and associations into a man with proper manners, and an upper-class command of the English language. He should go to one of the New England church schools, later to college, then he should choose a career for himself and be helped into harness. So she planned his future. In the meanwhile she wished to see the thin, spindly body catch up with the big, intelligent head. Although his muscles were tough and wiry he had a delicate look which troubled her, and a cough which to her inexperienced and anxious ears suggested a consumptive tendency.

Dr. Ferris laughed at this, but to satisfy her he gave the boy a thorough questioning and a thorough looking over. "Any of your family consumptives, Bubbles?"

"Don't think so, sir."

"Well, you're not. Heart and lungs are sound."

"Miss Barbara says she doesn't like my cough."

"Yes," said the surgeon, "it worries her quite a good deal. And I advise you to stop it."

"But my throat gets tickling, and——"

"Your throat gets tickling because you are an inveterate cigarette smoker. And that's the reason why you are undersized and under-nourished. How long have you smoked?"

"I don't remember when I didn't."

"Can't you stop?"

"I stopped once for two days, and then I took a pack of smokers that wasn't mine. That was about the only thing I ever stole."

"But if you gave me your word not to smoke any more till you're twenty-one, couldn't you keep that promise?"

"I could try," said Bubbles, evincing very little confidence.

"Will you try?" said the surgeon. "Hello, what's this?"

The boy in lifting his left arm had disclosed a dark-brown birthmark shaped like the new moon. All amusement had gone out of Dr. Ferris's eyes; and he had that look of tragic memories that so often put an end to his smiling and optimistic moods.

"Do you remember your father?"

"No, sir."

"Mother living?"

Bubbles hesitated. "She's in an asylum. She's crazy."

"What was your father's name?"

Bubbles shook his head.

The surgeon considered for a moment. "Well," he said, at length, and once more smiling, "put your clothes on, and then go to Miss Ferris and promise her that you won't smoke any more. What asylum did you say your mother was in?"

"Ottawan."

"Do you ever see her?"

"No, sir. She don't like to see me."

"What is her name, Bubbles?"

"Jenny Ward."

Dr. Ferris ordered a car, and in less than two hours

he was talking with the superintendent of Ottawan about the patient, Jenny Ward.

"The boy," he was saying, "is a protégé of my daughter's. She means to educate him, and we are naturally interested in his antecedents. I wonder if she has any lucid recollection of the father?"

"When she first came she seemed to have lucid moments. Even now she never makes trouble for any one, except that sometimes she wakes in the night screaming. She has been very pretty."

"H'm!" said Dr. Ferris. "You think she couldn't tell me anything about the boy's father?"

"I know she couldn't. When she was examined after being committed, it was found that her tongue had been cut out."

The woman, upon being visited, proved a meek, gentle, pathetic creature, eager to please. As the superintendent reported, she had been very pretty. She would have been pretty still, but for her utterly vacant look.

The doctor questioned her, but she made no effort, it seemed, even to understand the questions. Given a pencil and paper she seemed to take pleasure in making dots, dashes, and scrawls; but she made no mark that in any way represented a letter of the alphabet. Confronted with a printed page, she thrust it aside.

"Very likely she never could read or write," said the superintendent; "usually when you give 'em a pencil they make letters by an act of muscular memory."

In the corridor outside the woman's room, they encountered one of those nurses who are used in man-
aging the violent insane. He was a huge fellow, with
a dark, strong, and somewhat forbidding face. He
nodded to the superintendent and passed. Dr. Ferris looked after him down the corridor, had a sudden
thought, and communicated it to his host in a quick
undertone.

"I say, Gyles! Look here a moment."

The huge nurse turned on his heel, and came tower-
ing back to them.

"Have you ever assisted in looking after the
woman Jenny Ward?" and he pointed toward the
door of her room.

"No, sir."

"Dr. Ferris wishes to try an experiment."

"Yes, sir."

"He wishes you to throw open the door of her
room, and to enter quickly—upon your knees."

"On my knees?"

"Yes."

"All right, sir." The man shrugged his big shoulders, and, his face sullen and annoyed, knelt at the
door of Jenny Ward's room, unlocked it, flung it
open, and entered quickly.

Over his head the doctors saw an expression of fear,
almost unearthly, come over the woman's face. And
she filled her room and the corridor without with a
hoarse and horrible screaming.

Instantly the big nurse rose to his feet, and came

out of the room. His face was passionately angry.
And he said:

"It's a shame to frighten her like that."

The superintendent's eyes fell before the glare in
those of the employee, and he murmured something
about "necessary experiment—had to be done."

XXXVI

"THERE's no room for doubt in my mind," said Dr. Ferris. "The coincidence of the birthmarks, most unusual in shape and texture, the poor woman's behavior at sight of a man who at first glance appeared to be without legs——"

"Yes," said Barbara, "but I go more on a certain expression that Bubbles sometimes has and that makes him look like his father. You see, I've done both their heads, and studied them closer than anybody else."

"Do you suppose the boy knows?"

She shook her head. "I think not. He's too— too decent. If he thought that Blizzard was his father, he wouldn't say the things that I have heard him say about him. He's the most loyal child."

"Do you suppose Blizzard knows?"

"Why, of course. A man could hardly have a son without knowing him—especially a man who lives with his ears to the ground and his mind in touch with everything in the city."

Dr. Ferris smiled a little. "Well," he said, "shall we tell Bubbles?"

"Why should we? I shouldn't like to be told out of a clear sky that I had such and such a father. It doesn't seem in the least necessary."

But before the day was out Barbara thought best to tell Bubbles. He came to her, with a slightly important air, which he did his best to conceal, and said that he wished to go to the city for a few days, on business.

"Sure the business isn't free untrammelled smoking?"

Bubbles was offended. "If I hadn't given you my word," he said, "you might think that. I told you when we came that I might have to go back any time on business. I got to go. Honest, Miss Barbara."

"Well, that settles it, Bubbles. But don't you think as long as I'm trying to give you some of the things you've missed, that you might take me a little more into your confidence?"

She maintained a discreet and serious countenance, although she wished very much to laugh.

The boy studied her face gravely with grave eyes. "The ABC of my business," he said presently, "is knowing who to trust. I know you won't blab, Miss Barbara, 'r else I wouldn't tell you. There's a society in New York City for putting down grafts and crimes. There's a rich man back of it. And there's more kinds o' people working for it than you'd guess in a year. There's even policemen workin' for it——"

"But it's their business to put down crime."

Bubbles shook his head sadly. "The chief business of the society is to put down police graft in crime," he said. "But there's heaps o' side businesses. Harry West, he's one of us. He's way high up. I'm way low down. But when I'm called to do what I can, I got to do it. There's one member younger'n me. And there's Fifth Avenue swells belongs, and waiters, and druggists, and bootblacks, and men in hardware stores, and barkeepers——"

"What sort of work do you have to do?"

"To go places and find out things."

"Why, then you're a detective, Bubbles."

A look of contempt swept into the child's face. "Detectives is in business," he said, "for what they can get out of it. We're in it because the house we live in is dirty and full of rats, and we want to make it clean."

The boy had raised his voice a little, and Barbara found herself thrilling to it.

"But, Bubbles," she objected, "you can't go to school and college and keep up this work at the same time."

"If I get education," said Bubbles, "it's so's to be fitter for the work when I come out. But I can't give the work up till the job I'm on is finished. It wouldn't be square."

"Can you tell me the job?"

"I'm one o' them that's helpin' to get the old un where he's wanted."

"What old one?"

"Blizzard."

Barbara was very much taken aback. "The man I made the bust of?"

"We can send him to the chair any time. But

what's the use? He knows things that we got to know before we pass him up."

"But, Bubbles, how can you help?"

"Oh, I'm little. I can get into little places. They wouldn't want me if I weren't of use."

"But I don't like the idea of your running down Blizzard, Bubbles."

"Why not, Miss Barbara? There's no one in the city that's *needed* as much as him."

"Aside from that, Bubbles—I'm willing to grant that—there's a reason why I think you should have nothing to do with running him down."

"It's got to be an awful good one, Miss Barbara—not just good to you, and maybe to me, but to men higher up."

"I think it would be good enough for the very highest up, Bubbles. Will you take my word for it?"

"Yes, Miss Barbara. But *they* won't take my word for your word."

"No," she said, "of course not."

She considered for a few moments. Then she said: "Bubbles, I'm going to tell you my reason. I hope I'm not doing wrong. It's a serious thing for me to tell you and for you to know. There is very little doubt but that Blizzard is your father."

"Say that again, please," said Bubbles.

"Blizzard is probably your father."

Bubbles took the news very coolly. His eyes sparkled; but he made no exclamations of surprise or chagrin. Instead he said: "*That* accounts for it."

"Accounts for what?"

"Oncet he caught me in his house. He said the
next time he'd skin me alive. If I hadn't been his
son he'd a skun me that time. Do you get me, Miss
Barbara? He's my father, sure. But—" Now chagrin, wonder, and perplexity were written in Bubbles's
face. "Why," he said, "it makes everything different. He never done anything for me; but if he's
my father——"

"You can't very well spy on him, can you, Bubbles? You've got to stand aside and leave all that
to others."

"I got to see the Head, Miss Barbara. I got to
ask him."

"Who is the head, Bubbles?"

"I'd tell you in a minute, Miss Barbara, only we're
all swore to tell no one. But what he says goes with
me. It's got to be that way, else we'd never get
nowhere."

XXXVII

Mr. Abe Lichtenstein looked up from a mass of writing. "So," he smiled, "you got your few days off?"

"Mr. Lichtenstein," said Bubbles, his eyes big, his voice trembling, "an awful thing has happened."

"You can tell me nothing bad but I can tell you something worse. What has happened?"

"The old un is my father!"

"Yes," said Lichtenstein, "I have thought of that. You are sure?"

"I'm sure enough not to want to have anything more to do with huntin' him. But that's for you to say. I do what you say."

"I won't ask you to go on," said Lichtenstein; "but you're still with us, Bubbles? You're still for cleaning up the dirty house and making it fit for human beings to live in?"

"Yes, sir."

"As far as your father's concerned you'll be neutral."

"Meaning I won't do nothing against him, nor for him?"

The red-headed Jew nodded. "You won't do like Rose?"

"Rose?"

Lichtenstein's face became very cold and grim. "She's gone over to him body and soul, Bubbles, and heart and mind. For weeks she's fooled us with non-sense—stuff they've made up together. Worse, she's broken every oath she ever swore. Our strength was secrecy. Well, your father knows the name of every agent in our society. Oh, he's got it all out of her! Everything!"

"Does he know that you are——"

"Yes, confound him, he does. And my life is about as safe in this city as that of the average cat in the Italian quarter. My life isn't the important thing. It's what I've got in my head—cold facts. See all this stuff? That's what's in my head going down on paper for the first time. It's to guide the man that takes my place—to help him over some of the hard places—three hundred sheets of it already, and only a week since I began."

"Rose!" exclaimed Bubbles.

"There was none better—none smarter—till she fell in love—*fell* in love!"

"Does he know I'm one of us, Mr. Lichtenstein?"

"Why, yes. I suppose she'll have given even the children away." Mr. Lichtenstein's eye roamed over the suite of rich rooms with their elaborate gambling-paraphernalia. "Not much doing," he smiled, "since Rose went over. The tip's out that I'm wanted. Nobody drops in for a quiet game. Bubbles, you tell people when you're a man and I'm gone, that I wasn't only a gambler. Tell 'em I took money from people who had plenty but wouldn't take the trouble to do right with it, and tell 'em I used that money to do right—to help make dirty things clean."

He turned and regarded the face of the black marble clock on the mantel-piece. As he looked the face of the clock was violently shattered, and so, but on a lower level, was a pane of glass in the window immediately opposite.

Abe Lichtenstein fell face down upon his unfinished manuscript.

· XXXVIII

THEN he began to speak in a quiet voice. "Never touched me, Bubbles. Pull that cord at the right of the window. That will close the curtains. Careful not to show yourself. The man that fired that shot thinks he got me. I fell over to make him think so and to keep him from shooting again. Now then"— the curtain had been drawn over the window with the broken pane—"let's see what sort of a gun our friend uses, and then perhaps we can spot our friend. Did you hear the shot?"

"No, sir. There was a noise just when the clock broke like when a steel girder falls on the sidewalk."

"That noise was just *before* the clock broke, Bubbles. And it was loud enough to drown the noise of our friend's gun. Clever work, though, to *have* to pull the trigger at a given moment, and to make such a close shot. Probably had his gun screwed in a vise."

Meanwhile Lichtenstein had extracted from the ruined clock a .45-calibre bullet of nickel steel. A glance at the grooves made by the rifling of the barrel from which it had been expelled caused him to raise his colorless eyebrows and smile cynically.

"New government automatic, Bubbles," he said, "and the funny part of it is they've only been issued to officers so far, and the factory hasn't put 'em on sale yet."

"Must have been stole from an officer, then," said Bubbles.

"You steal her jewels from an actress," said Lichtenstein, "her mite from the widow, its romances from the people, but you don't steal his side arms from an American army officer. No. Somebody in the factory has let the weapon that fired this slip out. It doesn't matter—it's just a little link in the long chain."

He seated himself calmly at the table and set down in black and white the fact that he had been very nearly murdered by a bullet fired from the new army pistol. Then he began to gather up the sheets of his manuscript.

"Now I wonder," he said, "where I can go to finish this document? I don't want them to 'get' me until I've paved the way for the man that comes after me. Now then—the secret passage isn't only for the wicked."

Kneeling on the clean hearth, Mr. Lichtenstein caused the ornamental cast-iron back of the fireplace to swing outward upon a hinge. Reaching a long arm into the disclosed opening, he unfastened and pushed ajar the iron back of a fireplace in the next house.

Bubbles, crawling through first, found himself in a somewhat overdressed pink and blue bedroom. The lace curtains were too elaborate. The room was luxurious and vulgar. Among the photographs on the centre-table reposed a champagne-bottle, three parts empty, and two glasses, in which a number of flies were heavily crawling.

Lichtenstein, having carefully replaced the fire-backs, rose smiling, and clapped a hand upon Bubbles's shoulder.

"Now then, Bubbles," he said, "push that bell-button by the door four times, and we'll see what Mrs. Popple can do to get us out of this. Never met Mrs. Popple? She's one of us, and at heart a good one."

The lady in question came swiftly in answer to the four rings. At first sight she passed for a woman of hard and forbidding aspect; filmy laces and a cling-ing kimona of rose-pink silk neither softened nor made feminine the alabaster-colored face with its thin, straight mouth, heavy hairy eyebrows, and clean-cut Greek nose. Only her costume and her hair, inde-scribably fine, and indescribably yellow, betrayed that there were follies in her nature. But the moment she spoke you liked her. She had a slow, deep, beautiful voice, and the slowness of her speech was offset by the fewness of her words.

"What's wrong, Abe?"

Lichtenstein explained briefly, and added: "Now how are we to get out of this without being spotted and followed?"

"Easy," said Mrs. Popple. She went to a vast wardrobe painted white, and pulled the creaking doors wide open. "Wedge the man into one dress," she said, "pad the boy into another. Send 'em off in a taxi. Now, boy. Is this Bubbles? Pleased to meet you. I'm old enough to be your grandmother."

The words were a command, and the boy, much embarrassed, began to take off his coat.

"Get busy, Abe. Can take your own things along in a suit-case. I don't look, see? I'm looking out duds for you. What's that? Razor? Find everything in medicine-closet over wash-basin in bathroom."

Lichtenstein disappeared, and gave forth presently the rasping sounds of a man shaving in a hurry. And in the meanwhile, always swift and sure, Mrs. Popple initiated Bubbles into the ABC's of female attire.

"No trouble about a straight front for you," she chuckled, and gave a sudden strong tug at the laces of Bubbles's corsets. He gasped, and the tears came to his eyes.

"Mind to take little steps," she said, "and don't swing your arms." She clasped a blond wig upon his head, and drew back to see the effect.

"Abe," she called, "she's a pippin!"

A moment later she frowned, almost savagely, laid her finger on her lips, knelt at the fireplace, thrust her head far in and listened intently.

Lichtenstein, one side of his face in lather, appeared at the bath-room door. His eyes on the crouching figure of Mrs. Popple, he continued calmly and methodically to shave himself.

After an interval the woman rose, and shook her head.

"Can't make out who's in there," she whispered. "Have Lizzie watch front window see who goes out."

Lichtenstein nodded, washed the tag ends of lather from his face, and proceeded in dead silence to dress himself as a lady of somewhat doubtful age, looks, and position. But Bubbles would have made a very pretty girl, if Mrs. Popple had not insisted on powdering his face till it was as white as that of a clown.

"Won't do to be conspicuous," she explained.

Lichtenstein packed the things which he and Bubbles had taken off into a suit-case marked "A. P." (Amelia Popple), and led the way downstairs. A little later a taxicab drew up at the curb, and the two disguised secret-service agents sauntered down the high steps of Mrs. Popple's brownstone house, looking neither to the right nor to the left, and got in.

"Where to?" said the driver, with rather a bold leer. The average lady who descended or ascended Mrs. Popple's steps, was not considered respectable even by taxi-drivers.

It had been agreed that Bubbles, having of the two the more feminine adaptabilities of voice, should do the talking.

"Grand Central," he said.

XXXIX

BARBARA was reading "Smoke" and did not wish to be interrupted by a "young person" (in the footman's words) who refused to give her name. Nevertheless she was weakly good-natured in such matters, and closing her book said: "Very well—in here, John."

A moment later the young person was shown into the living-room. Barbara was still more annoyed, for young faces covered with powder were odious to her. But suddenly the young person's mouth curled into a captivating grin, and the young person trotted forward in a very un-young-personish way, and cried triumphantly:

"It's me—Bubbles."

And Bubbles followed Barbara's gratifying exclamations of surprise and inquiry with a syncopated outburst of explanation, finishing with: "And Mr. Lichtenstein said I was to throw us on your mercy, and ask if he could stay to finish his writing, and he's stepped into some bushes off the driveway to put on his own clothes. And please, Miss Barbara, he's just the finest and bravest ever, and don't care what happens to him, only he says they're bound to get him now everything's found out, and he's just got to finish writing down what he carries in his head."

"Of course," said Barbara, "we'll have to tell my father; but all will be well. Mr. Lichtenstein shall stay. Bring him to me when he's finished changing, and then you'd best change, and if you don't want to have a sore face wash all that nasty stuff off it."

Lichtenstein had already changed, and was coming up the driveway carrying a suit-case. Bubbles brought him at once, and with great pride, to Barbara. Mr. Lichtenstein had never seen her before. In his bow there was a trace of Oriental elaboration. And his curiously meagreish, pug-nosed sandy face beamed with pleasure and admiration.

"I thought I knew my New York, Miss Ferris," he said, "but it seems I was mistaken."

Since the compliment was obviously sincere, Barbara took pleasure in it, and the pleasure showed in her charming face. "And Bubbles says," said she, "that you are the 'finest ever.' I'm glad if staying here is going to help the cause. You can be as private as you like—" But a sudden change had come over Lichtenstein's face, the smile had vanished, the eyes grown sharp, even stern. "What is your maid's name?" he asked abruptly.

"My maid? Why, what about her?"

"She passed just now—by that door. I saw her in the mirror at the end of the room. What's her name?"

"Marion—" Barbara hesitated.

"O'Brien?"

"Yes, O'Brien."

"I thought so. She's in Blizzard's pay. If she has recognized me— Shut the door into the hall, Bubbles."

The door being shut, Lichtenstein crossed the room and stood near it, his hand on the knob. For nearly a minute he neither moved nor changed expression. Then a smile flickered about his mouth, and, sure of his effect, with a sharp gesture he flung the door wide open, and discovered Miss Marion O'Brien kneeling in the opening. He caught her by the wrist, drew her to her feet, and into the room.

"Marion!" exclaimed Miss Ferris.

XL

THERE was a long silence during which Miss O'Brien tried to look defiant, and succeeded only in shedding a few tears. Barbara had always liked the girl, and now felt profoundly sorry for her. Lichtenstein, too, seemed sorry and at a loss for words. The position was difficult. The O'Brien's eavesdropping warranted her discharge, and nothing more. She would go straight to Blizzard and disclose Lichtenstein's whereabouts. But this in itself was merely an annoyance, as in the meanwhile the secret service head could go elsewhere. There was nothing for it but to discharge her and let her go. So Lichtenstein said presently, and then wrote with a pencil on a card. This card he handed to the maid.

"Give that to your employer," he said. On the card was written: "If anything happens to me you will be indicted for the Kaparoff business, and there is enough evidence in a safe place to make you pay the penalty. Lichtenstein."

"And now, Miss Ferris," he said, "it will be as well to let this girl first telephone to her master to say that I am here, and second to pack her trunks and go."

Barbara smiled, but not unkindly, at Marion, and

nodded her brightly colored head. "I think that will be best, Marion."

The maid turned without a word and started for the hall-door, but was brought to a trembling stop by sudden words from Bubbles.

"Miss Barbara," said he, "ask her where your diamond bow-knot went!"

"Oh," exclaimed Lichtenstein, "an excuse for keeping an eye on her, perhaps. That was what we needed. How about this bow-knot, Marion?"

The guilt in the girl's face must have been obvious to the dullest eye.

"Oh," said Barbara, "is it good enough? She'd communicate with him somehow. This isn't the Middle Ages. Marion, if by any chance any of my things have gotten mixed with yours, please leave them on my dressing-table."

Marion, very red in the face, lurched out of the room.

"I can't very well give her a character," said Barbara.

Lichtenstein laughed. "Plenty of worse girls," he said, "receive excellent characters daily. And now I suppose I ought to put distance between this house and myself."

Barbara lifted her eyebrows. "Why?"

"Why? She's probably working the telephone now."

"I know," said Barbara, "but if you pretend to go, and then come back, this would be the last home in the world that Blizzard would suspect you of hiding in. Marion will tell him her story. And he certainly won't look for you here."

Lichtenstein's face was wreathed in smiles. "So be it," he said, "and I shall sit at your feet to learn."

"Can you drive a car?" asked Barbara.

"What kind of a car?"

"A Stoughton? But if you can drive any kind you can drive a Stoughton. We'll lend you a car and you shall take a long run and come back when it's dark. If you start at once, Marion will know of it. Meanwhile I'll tell my father all about everything. But first of all I'm dying with curiosity to know what you wrote on that card. That's all I can say. Of course if I'm not to be told——"

Had she asked for his dearest secret Lichtenstein could not have refused it, and he told her what he had written on the card.

"But why," said Barbara, "if you have a criminal, so to speak, where you want him—why let him be free to make more mischief? I ask merely for information."

"If he were punished for an ordinary crime," said Lichtenstein, "justice would be cheated. But if we can really get him where we want him, why, not only crime will be tried and found guilty, but the whole fabric of the police—yes, and the administration of the law. Therefore," and his voice was cold as marble, "it would be inadvisable to run him in for such picayune crimes as twisting lead pipe round young women and throwing them overboard, or otherwise delicately quieting tongues that might be made to wag against him. And now if you are going to lend me a car——"

XLI

WILMOT ALLEN was surprised and annoyed at being called back to New York by his employer. He had not "gotten over" Barbara in the least, but the great West had entered his blood. Thanks to financial arrangements with Blizzard he had lived a life free from care, and indeed had grown and developed in many ways, just as a forest tree will, to which air and sunlight has been admitted by removing its nearest neighbors, together with all their claims upon the rain-fall and the tree-food locked up in the forest soil.

He had grown in body and mind. Wall Street, that had seemed so broad and important to him, now seemed narrow and insignificant. It was better for a man, a good horse between his knees, to find out what lay beyond the Ridges than whether steel was going up or down. He looked back upon his past life, not, it is true, with contempt and loathing, but with amused tolerance, as a man wise and reliable looks back upon the pranks of his boyhood.

He loved Barbara with all his heart, but no longer with the feeling that the loss of her would put an end to all the possibilities of life. Indeed he was coolly resolved in the event of her marrying somebody else to marry somebody else himself. The thought of children and a home had grown very dear to him.

In short, he had assimilated a characteristic of the great unsettled West, where the ratio of the male of the species to the female is often as great as ten to one.

But if the year did not cure him of Barbara he would get her if he could.

To the main line was a day's journey over a single-track road abounding in undeveloped way stations, at which an insatiable locomotive was forever stopping to drink. At one of these stations a young man taller and broader even than Wilmot himself, and like him bearded and brown as autumn leaves, boarded the train laboriously and came down the aisle occasionally catching at the backs of seats for support.

A second look assured Wilmot that the stranger was not drunk, but sick or hurt, and he was wondering whether or not to offer him assistance, when the stranger suddenly stopped and smiled, steadied himself with one hand, and held out the other.

"I heard that you would be on this train," he said simply, "so I managed to catch it, too. May I sit with you?"

Wondering, Wilmot made room for the stranger and waited developments. But as these were not at once forthcoming he felt that he must break a silence which seemed awkward to him. And he turned his head and saw that the man had fainted.

A request for whiskey addressed to a car containing a dozen men accustomed to wrest metals from the earth was not in vain. Wilmot chose the nearest of twelve outstretched flasks, and was obliged to refuse a thirteenth in the kindly hand of the conductor.

"Feel better?"

"Thanks, I'm all right."

The twelve miners withdrew tactfully to their seats.

"Sure?"

"Sure. Just let me sample that brand again. Good. Now if you don't mind I'll say what I came to say."

"But aren't you hurt—isn't there something to do?"

"I've *been* hurt. I'm just weak. Don't think about it. But you're Mr. Wilmot Allen all right, aren't you?"

"Yes."

"It's hard to be sure of a man you never knew and who's grown a beard since you saw him last."

"I assure you," Wilmot smiled, "that I'm only waiting to reach a first-class barber-shop."

"Perhaps you will change your mind."

"Why should I?"

"You know a man named O'Hagan?"

Wilmot nodded.

"I had a talk with him up in the mountains— yesterday. He spoke truth for once. You know a man in New York—Blizzard?"

"He's been a good friend to me."

"Why?" asked the stranger.

"I don't know. I've asked myself that question a thousand times."

"He's helped you with your debts in return for your services in teaching a lot of foreigners to shoot straight?"

Wilmot frowned.

"Did it ever occur to you that he could have obtained half a dozen teachers for a tenth of the money?"

"That *has* occurred to me," said Wilmot stiffly.

"Obviously then he has some ulterior use for you."

"Very possibly."

"Please don't take offence. There are reasons why you shouldn't. I am coming to them. Remember, O'Hagan talked to me, and talked truth. Blizzard is planning a revolution. You are to be one of the leaders. You imagine that one of the hell-governed Latin republics is to be the seat of operations, or you wouldn't have gone into the thing. But Blizzard is after bigger game than undeveloped wildernesses. Mr. Allen, you are part of a conspiracy to overthrow the government of New York City."

"Say that again."

The stranger smiled. "O'Hagan at the last made a clean breast of everything. He had to. I came West to make him."

"At the *last*? What does that mean?"

"When a man won't talk you have to make him— even if you fix him so that he can never talk again."

"Is O'Hagan *dead*?"

"He had his choice. But he *had* to talk. If I had let him off afterward—I couldn't have gotten away

with the information. One of us had to go out, and
I had the power to decide which. I chose that
O'Hagan should be the one. He was a man steeped
in crime. I am not."

"You killed him?"

"I am a very poor talker if I have conveyed another
meaning. I tracked him into the mountains. He
shot me twice before I could get my hands on him. I
twisted the truth out of him, and then as I was about
to faint like a school-girl, and as my information was
precious, I flung him over a cliff. If I hadn't, you
see, he could have fixed me while I was unconscious."

The man's voice was very quiet, very matter-of-fact.
Wilmot stared at him with a sort of wondering horror,
for he knew that the man was telling the truth.

"He shot you twice. That was some time yesterday. You've seen a doctor?"

"There was none, and I had to ride all night to get
here."

"Are you badly hit?"

The stranger drew back his coat and disclosed a
shirt twice perforated over the abdomen and dark
with dried and thickening blood. "Please don't try
to do anything. There's no help. The damage is
where it doesn't show. Only listen, please, and believe, and be frank with me."

Wilmot nodded gravely. "I don't know who you
are," he said, "but you are hurt, and if you'd rather
talk than try to do something about it, of course
I'll listen."

"I twisted the truth out of him, and
  then flung him over a cliff"

"You are in wrong on the revolution," said the stranger. "It is not to come off in South America, but in the city of New York. If Blizzard's plans carry, this will happen. On the 15th of January there will be an explosion of dynamite loud enough to be heard from the Battery to the Bronx. At that signal two-thirds of the police force, at the moment on active duty, will be shot dead in their tracks. The assassins, distinguished from law-abiding citizens by straw hats of a peculiar weave——"

"I have such a hat in my trunk."

"Are to assemble together with that third of the police force whom it was not necessary to annihilate, at the Sub-Treasury in Wall Street. Here they will receive further orders—some to loot the Sub-Treasury, some to loot banks, some Tiffany's, some the great wholesale jewellers of Maiden Lane. You, perhaps, as a man of superior talk and breeding, would be sent with a picked crew of Polacks, dagoes, and other high-minded patriots to rifle the Metropolitan Museum of Art——"

"Look here, did O'Hagan——"

"He did. Meanwhile all communication by telephone, by telegraph, by cable between New York and the outer world will be cut off. For at least twenty-four hours the city will be in Blizzard's power, at his disposition."

"How about communication by train?"

"Trains will come into the Grand Central and the Pennsylvania, but they will not go out."

"A man could jump into an automobile and carry the news."

"Ferries will stop running. Bridges will be closed."

The idea of looting New York had fired Wilmot's imagination. It was a possibility to which he had never before given any thought.

"But," he objected, "there must be a flaw somewhere."

"Probably," admitted the stranger. "For there is a flaw in Blizzard's mind. It is the only way to account for him. He stands on the verge of insanity."

"Suppose the plan carries. The city has been looted. What next?"

"The stuff is hidden under Blizzard's house in Marrow Lane in cellars that he has been preparing for years. A passage leads from these cellars to a pier on the East River. Either he gets away with his loot in a stolen liner, or he finds that he may live on in New York, or perhaps in Washington."

"I don't see that."

"What effect would a successful revolution in New York have upon the discontented and the murderous of other cities? Are the criminals of San Francisco, Denver, Chicago to be outdone by the criminals of the effete East? I tell you, Mr. Allen, that sometimes in mad visions the legless beggar sees upon his brows a kingly crown."

"But the rest of the police—the garrison at Governor's Island?"

"O'Hagan was Blizzard's right-hand man, his gen-

eral in the West. For the honor of being his left-
hand man there are two aspirants—the mayor of New
York City and the police commissioner—nor will the
lieutenant-governor of our great State hold his hands
behind his back and shake his head when the loot is
being distributed."

"Are you *joking?*"

"No, Mr. Allen. I am dying. Now listen. I assume that you are no longer with Blizzard."

"What an ass I've been!"

"You are to find Abe Lichtenstein and tell him
what I have told you. The boy Bubbles will put you
on his track. As for money which Blizzard has advanced to you—" The stranger fumbled in his breast
pocket and brought forth a much-soiled sheet of paper.
"This locates outlying mining claims in Utah. They
will make you rich. One-third to you—one-third to
Miss Barbara Ferris—one-third to the boy Bubbles.
You will tell him that I was his brother—different
mothers, but the same father."

"*You* are Harry West," and Wilmot looked with
compassionate interest upon the man who, if only for
a brief period of time, had once stood first in Barbara's
affections.

Under the strain of talking West's voice had grown
weaker. "Miss Barbara," he said quietly, "is in
great danger from my father——"

"*Your* father?"

"Didn't I tell you? Oh, yes. He is my father—
Blizzard. That is why I don't mind dying. When

the city is in confusion, and without any laws save
of his own dictation, Miss Barbara will be in terrible
danger. Many years from now, when it can do no
harm with you, tell her, please, that in my life I had
the incomparable privilege——"

Wilmot leaped to his feet. "Is there a doctor
here? This man is dying."

But the Spartan, the wolf Death gnawing at his
vitals, had said all that it was necessary for him to
say. Wilmot Allen's strong arm about him, his mouth
vaguely smiling, he fell heavily forward as if under
the weight of a new and overpowering wonder and
knowledge.

XLII

NOTHING so makes for insomnia as a man's knowledge that he has made a fool of himself. Between Chicago and New York Wilmot Allen did not even have his berth made up. He visited the dining-car at the proper intervals, hardly conscious of what he ordered or ate. He bought newspapers, books, magazines, and opened none of them. For the most part he looked out the window of his compartment into rushing daylight or darkness. His mind kept travelling the round of a great circle that began and ended in humiliation. He had been as confiding in Blizzard's hands as an undeveloped child of seven. He had been teaching men whose creed was murder and anarchy how to handle weapons. He had taken at their face value words uttered by an emperor among scoundrels; had asked no material or leading questions, and was in his conscience paying the penalty for having snatched at tainted money with which to relieve himself of obligations that pressed till they hurt.

Beginning in humiliation, the circle of his thoughts ascended time after time to Barbara, only to fall from the high and tender lights which memories and anticipations of her brought into them, back to that darkness in which he struggled to give himself "a little the best of things" and could not.

On arriving in New York a man of more complex
mental processes would have tried first of all to get
the precious information which he carried into the
possession of Lichtenstein, but Wilmot felt that he
could have no peace until he had seen Blizzard,
spoken his mind, and washed his hands of him. That
he would then put his own life in danger did not occur
to him, and would not have altered his determination
if it had.

The lure of Barbara, however, drew him aside from
the direct path to Marrow Lane. He had resolved
not to see her for a year, but thought it right to break
through that resolution in order to tell her at first
hand of Harry West's death. But the janitor told
him that Miss Ferris had not been coming to the
studio for a long time. She had had no word from
her. She had left one day by the back stair without
her hat; a little later the legless beggar had left by
the front door. His expression had been enough to
frighten a body to death. Yes, the boy had come
one day in a taxicab and gone away with her things.
He had refused to answer any questions. She had
never thought very highly of him as a boy. No, the
bust upon which Miss Ferris had been at work had
not been removed. No, the gentleman could not
see it. Orders were orders. . . . Yes, the gentleman
could see it. After all there had been no orders recently.

She led the way upstairs, her hand tightly closed
upon a greenback. She unlocked and flung open the

door of Barbara's studio, remarking that nothing in it had been touched since that lady's departure.

Wilmot noticed much dust, an overturned chair, and then his eyes rose to the bust of Blizzard as to a living presence. The expression of that bestial fallen face made his spine feel as if ants were crawling on it. And he turned away with disgust and hatred. "Oh, Barbs, Barbs, what a wrong-headed little darling you are!" But he added: "And Lord, what a talent she's got!"

Blizzard was not in his office. But he was upstairs and expected Mr. Allen.

A girl who had been wonderfully pretty told Wilmot these things. She would have been wonderfully pretty still, for she was very young, if she had not looked so tired, so unhappy, so broken-spirited. Did Rose still love the man for whom she had betrayed her friends and her own better nature? Yes. But she had learned that she was no more to him than a plaything—to caress or to break as seemed most amusing to him. At first until the novelty of her had worn off he had shown her a sufficiency of brusque tenderness. Latterly as his great plans matured he had been all brute. Sometimes he made her feel that he was so surfeited with her love that he considered killing her.

Sideways, with eyes haunted by shame and tragedy, she gave the handsome bearded youth a look of compassion. "In here, please," she said.

The door closed behind Wilmot with an ominous

click, and he found himself face to face with the legless beggar. In this one's eyes, seen above a table littered with pamphlets and writings, was none of that mock affability to which he had formerly treated Wilmot Allen. He looked angry, dangerous, poisonous. And he broke into a harsh, ugly laugh.

"It takes you," he said, "to rush in where angels fear to tread. Welcome to my parlor! What a fool! My God! You heard what Harry West had to say before he died, and you came straight here."

"I don't know how you know it. But I did talk to your son. I did hear what he said. And I came here to tell you. And to tell you that there will be no more dealings between us. I am going straight from here to tell the proper authorities what I know."

"Aren't you going to punch my face first? That's what you'd like to do. It's in your eyes. But you're afraid."

"I am not afraid," said Wilmot, "and you know it."

For answer the legless man picked up a silver dollar from among the papers in front of him, and broke it savagely into four pieces. "Afraid!" he said. "Afraid! Afraid!"

Wilmot took a step forward. "It would give me the greatest pleasure," he said quietly, "to knock your head off. Unfortunately you are a cripple."

Blizzard said nothing, and presently, white with anger and contempt, Wilmot turned and tried the handle of the door by which he had entered. Blizzard laughed.

"This door is locked," said Wilmot.

"You are a prisoner in this house."

"I am, am I?"

Quick as lightning he had drawn and levelled at the legless man an automatic pistol of the largest calibre. The legless man did not move an inch, change expression, or take his eyes from Wilmot's.

Wilmot advanced till only the table separated them. "You will," he said, "climb out of that chair, and let me out of this house, walking in front of me."

The legless beggar appeared to consider the matter. There was silence. Wilmot shifted the position of his feet, and the floor boards under them creaked.

Blizzard appeared to have made up his mind. He spread his hands on the table as if to help himself out of his chair. The palm of his right hand, unknown to Wilmot, covered an electric push-button.

"Perhaps," said Blizzard, "you won't be in such a hurry to go after you hear that Miss Barbara Ferris is also a prisoner in this house——"

In horror and bewilderment Wilmot allowed the muzzle of his automatic to swerve. In that moment the palm of the legless man's right hand pressed upon the button, and the square of the floor upon which Wilmot stood dropped like the trap of a gallows, and he fell through the opening into darkness.

He was neither stunned nor bruised, and he began to grope about for the pistol which in the sudden descent had been knocked from his hand. The only light came from the open trap in the floor above.

Something fell softly at his feet; he picked it up. It was a cloth, saturated with chloroform. He flung it from him, and began with a new haste to grope and fumble for his pistol.

Another cloth fell, and another. Distant and ugly laughter fell with them. More cloths, and already the air in the place reeked with chloroform.

He no longer knew what he was looking for, and when at last his hand closed upon the stock of the automatic, he did not know what it was that he had found.

Another cloth fell.

XLIII

HE came to in a narrow iron bed, weak, nauseated, and handcuffed. He could rub his feet together, but he could not separate them. He had been dreaming about Barbara—horrible dreams. His first conscious thought was that she, too, was a prisoner in the house of Blizzard, and that somehow or other he must save her. Having tried in vain to break the bright, delicate-looking handcuffs, he tried in vain to think calmly. Hours passed. Nobody came. He worked himself gradually into a fever of impotent rage. Civilization slipped away from him. He was ready, if necessary, to fight with his teeth, to gouge eyes, to inflict any barbarous atrocity upon his enemy.

Gradually, for the air in the room was fresh, the feeling of sickness passed away, and was succeeded by weakness and lassitude. As a matter of fact, being a strong man, in splendid health, he was faint from hunger. But he did not know this.

An elderly woman came softly into the room. She wore a blue dress, a white apron, a white kerchief, white cuffs, a white cap. Her face was disfigured by a great brown protruding mole from which a tuft of hair sprouted; she had an expression of methodical kindness, but small shifting eyes in which was no honesty.

She carried a cup that smoked. She put the cup on a table, lifted Wilmot to a sitting position, as if he had been a child, and asked him if he was hungry.

For a moment he did not answer; he was getting used to the discovery that he had been undressed and was wearing a linen night-gown. Then he nodded toward the smoking cup.

"How do I know it isn't poisoned?"

"Come—come," said the woman, "you'd have gone out under the chloroform if that had been the intention. Better keep your strength up."

After a few spoonfuls of the soup, Wilmot suggested that he should prefer something solid.

The woman shook her head.

"If I'm to be kept alive," he said petulantly, "why not comfortably ?"

"Nothing solid. That's the doctor's orders."

"Blizzard's?"

"No. The doctor."

"What doctor?"

"Why, Dr. Ferris."

"Where is he? I want to speak to him."

"He isn't here. He's coming when everything's ready."

"Everything ready?" A nameless fear began to gnaw at Wilmot's vitals. And at that moment the door swung open, and he saw, beyond the bulking head and shoulders of the legless man, a narrow iron table, white and shining, in a room all glass and white paint.

On the entrance of Blizzard, the woman took up the remains of the soup, and passed noiselessly out of the room.

Blizzard climbed to the foot of Wilmot's bed, and sat looking at him. In his eyes there was a glitter of suppressed excitement. "When our last talk was interrupted," he said, "I had just told you that Miss Ferris is a prisoner in this house. You don't like the idea?"

Wilmot shuddered and made a convulsive effort to break the handcuffs. He struggled with them in desperate silence for nearly a minute.

."I might break them," said Blizzard, "but you can't. Try to be as reasonable as you can. Miss Ferris is in no immediate danger. I am going to let her go, if you and I can agree."

"What do you want *me* to agree to?"

"I've had it in mind for a long time. It was why I relieved you of money cares, and sent you West. I wished to put you in a state of perfect health before trying an experiment of the utmost interest and value to science. Only your consent is now wanting. Upon that consent depends Miss Ferris's fate. Refuse and I leave your lover heart to imagine what that fate may be. She is absolutely in my power—absolutely. Do you know her writing?"

He smiled a little and held before Wilmot's eyes a sheet of note-paper.

"She has just written it," he said, "of her own free will."

Wilmot read: "I will marry you, as soon as I know that Wilmot Allen is out of your power and safe in life and limb."

A sort of ecstasy, half anguish and half delight, thrilled through Wilmot. The writing was unmistakably Barbara's—and she was ready to make that sacrifice for him!

"She sha'n't do that," he said, "so help me God. What must I do—to save her?"

"Young man," said the legless man, "you must give me your legs."

Wilmot was at first bewildered.

"My legs?"

"They are to be grafted on my poor old stumps," said Blizzard. "You won't die. You'll just be as I am now. And I—I," his eyes shone with an unholy light, "shall be as you are now—a biped—a real man —a giant of a man. You are going to consent?"

"How do I know that you will let Miss Ferris go?"

"You shall have news of her freedom and safety in her own writing."

"When I have that assurance," said Wilmot, "I will consent to anything. Any decent man would give his life for a woman—why not his legs? Is Dr. Ferris to operate?"

"He will be the chief of three surgeons."

"But he won't cut off my legs. We're old friends. He——"

"Won't know you in that beard. I have told him that you are a murderer whom I have saved from the

chair. That in gratitude for this and for the further
services of smuggling you out of the country and
giving you a large sum of money—not forgetting the
crying interests of science—you have consented to
give me your legs. He will ask you if you consent
to have your legs cut off, and you will nod your
head without speaking—then when my old stumps
have been prepared—you will be put under an anæsthetic——"

"First I must know that Miss Ferris is safe."

"Give me your word of honor that when you *know*
that she is—you will consent."

"I don't know what you have to do with honor,"
said Wilmot, "but I give my word."

"Then," said Blizzard, sliding to the floor, "I go
to set Miss Ferris free."

XLIV

At first Barbara could not bear to tell her father, but at last her excitement and distress became so great that she had to tell him. In a few hours she had changed from a radiant person to one white, sick, and shadowed.

"I've seen that man," she said. "I was writing notes in the summer-house. He——"

"What man—Blizzard? Well?"

"I've promised to marry him. He has Wilmot Allen in his house—in his power. He told me that if I would marry him, he would let Wilmot go. If I wouldn't, he would kill him with indescribable tortures. I told him that I would marry him when I learned that Wilmot was safe. And so I will, and then I will kill myself. You've got to do something. I never knew till he was in this awful danger that in all the world there was never anybody for me but Wilmot—fool not to know it in time."

Dr. Ferris made her drink something that he mixed in a glass. In a few minutes her jumping nerves began to come into control.

"Wilmot," said he, "will never consent to save himself at your expense. And I think I can promise you that Blizzard will do nothing in this matter for some time. He is to undergo a very serious operation to-night. It has all been arranged. A man under obligation to Blizzard has consented to give his legs —I am to operate. Don't look at me like that, daughter. I have given my word that if I thought the thing could be done, I would do it. The man consents. There is no reason why I shouldn't. I would do more to undo what I have done, and in the interests of science."

"You don't understand. The man who *consents* is Wilmot."

"Did Blizzard tell you so?"

"Nobody has told me. I know it. He consents so that I may go free."

"Of course if Wilmot is the man——"

"You couldn't—you wouldn't do it to *him*, father."

"And you so in love with him, my dear! We must go to the police."

"No, we mustn't. He said that if we tried to play any tricks, we might get him, but never Wilmot, alive. Don't you see? Father, the man isn't fit to live. He's insane."

"Answer wanted, Miss Barbara." Bubbles entered hesitatingly, a note in his hand.

One glance at the superscription, and Barbara ripped open the envelope. She read the note and her brows contracted with pain. "Read that, father."

Dr. Ferris read:

DEAREST BARBS:

I can't help breaking my silence to say I love you with my whole heart and soul. Only tell me that you are safe

and sound in your father's house. I want much to know
that, for I am on the brink of a great, a dangerous, and I
think a noble venture.   WILMOT.

"What did I tell you!" she exclaimed. "Who
brought this, Bubbles?"

"Nobody—a messenger-boy."

"Barbara," said her father, "write that you are
safe at home. I'll tell Lichtenstein what has happened. He's our best advice. Where is Mr. Lichtenstein, Bubbles?"

"In his room, sir, writing."

Dr. Ferris left hurriedly, and Bubbles, gnawed by
unsatisfied curiosity, stood first on one foot and then
on the other while Barbara wrote to Wilmot. Somehow it was a very difficult note to write, for she felt
sure that it would not be read by Wilmot's eyes alone,
and she didn't wish by a syllable further to incite the
legless man against his prisoner. So at last she merely
wrote that she was with her father at Clovelly.
What she wanted to write was that her love for him
had grown and grown until she was sure of it.

After Bubbles had gone with the note she sat for a
long time without moving, silent and white.

When her father returned, bringing Lichtenstein,
he, too, was white. "I am going to town at once,"
he said. "God willing, I shall have only good news
for you."

Barbara turned to Lichtenstein. "You've thought
out something?"

He nodded gravely.

XLV

"My treasure! My ownest own!"

Rose cowered from the cold malice in the legless man's voice, and from the unearthly subdued excitement in his eyes.

"Sit there opposite me. Don't be afraid. Things are coming my way. To-morrow I shall have a pair of legs. Think of that! Are you thinking of it?"

She nodded.

The legless man wiped his mouth with the palm of his hand. "I told him," he said, "that she was a prisoner in this house. He said he would give me his legs if I would let her go free. He wrote a note asking if she was safe and sound. I sent it out to her place where she was all the time, and of course she answered that she was safe and sound."

He chuckled, and his agate eyes appeared to give off sparks.

"But she," he went on, "has promised to marry me, if I will let *him* go free. They love each other, Rose. They love each other! But I'm not jealous. It won't come to anything. First I will get his legs. Then, if he lives, I will make him write to her that he *is* sound and free. I will tell her that he refused to sacrifice himself. That will make her hate him, and then we'll be married and live happily ever after.

309

But if she breaks her word, why on the 15th of January she will be taken, wherever she is, and brought here, and we—we *won't* be married!" He laughed a long, ugly laugh.

"What are you going to do with me?"

The legless man considered. "I'm afraid you'll be too jealous to have about, my pretty Rose. I'm afraid your love for me will turn into a different feeling—in spite of the beautiful new legs that I shall have. In short, my dear, knowing women as I do, you are one of my greatest problems. If I could be sure that you wouldn't give anything away before the 15th—after that it wouldn't matter."

"Are you leading up to the announcement that you are going to kill me?" She looked him straight in the eyes, and began to shiver as if she was very cold.

"Wouldn't that be best," he asked, "for everybody concerned?"

"I swear to God I won't give anything away," she said.

He continued to smile in her face. "I could do it for you," he said, "so delicately—so painlessly—with my hands—and your troubles would be all over."

He took her slender white neck between the palms of his great hairy hands and caressed it. She did not shrink from his touch.

"Rose," he said presently and with the brutal and tigerish quality gone from his voice, "you're brave. But I know women too well. I don't trust you. If you'd screamed then or shown fear in any way, you'd be dead now. After the 15th you shall do what you please with your life. Meanwhile, my dear, lock and key for yours."

"You'll come to see me sometimes?"

"After to-night, I shall be laid up for a while, growing a pair of legs. Later I'll look in, now and then. How about a little music, before you retire to your room for the next few months? I'll tell you a secret. I'm nervous about to-night, and frightened. A little Beethoven? to soothe our nerves? the Adagio from the Pathétique?"

He stumped beside her, holding her hand as a child holds that of its nurse; but for a different reason.

That night, securely locked in her own room next to his, she slept at last from sheer weariness. And she dreamed that he was playing to her, for her—the Adagio, and then the "Funeral March of a Hero."

XLVI

OCCASIONALLY now, for a long time, there had been coming from the next room the clink of steel against steel, a murmur of hushed voices, and a sound of several pairs of feet moving softly. With the exception of two cups of soup, Wilmot, in preparation for what he was to undergo, had had nothing to eat. What with this and the natural commotion of revolt in his whole nervous system, he was weak and faint.

The door opened, and Dr. Ferris came quietly into the room and bent over him. He was in white linen from head to foot, and wore upon his hands a pair of thin rubber gloves, glistening with the water in which they had been boiling.

Prepared to find Wilmot, he naturally recognized him, in spite of the beard which so changed the young man's face for the worse; but of this recognition he gave no sign. The legless man, alert for any possibility of self-betrayal on Wilmot's part, had followed him into the room. Dr. Ferris spoke very quickly:

"My man," he said, "is it true that of your own free will, in exchange for immunity and other benefits received, you consent to the amputation of both your legs, as near the hip-joint as may be found necessary?"

Wilmot drew a long breath, focussed his mind upon bright memories of Barbara, and slowly nodded.

"You are quite sure? You are holding back nothing? There has been no coercion?"

"It's all right," chirped in Blizzard. "Glad of the
chance to pay me back, aren't you, my boy?"

For a moment Wilmot's eyes rested with a cold
contempt on the beggar's. And he thought, "to save
her from that!" and once more nodded.

"Shall I tell them to bring the ether, doctor?"

Dr. Ferris turned his head slowly.

"What are *you* doing here?" he said, in his smiling
professional voice. "You ought to be undressed,
scrubbed, and ready for the anæsthetic yourself."

"But I thought—I thought you'd make sure of the
legs first, before you did anything to me."

"The success of graftage," said the doctor, "lies in
the speed with which the parts to be grafted can be
transferred from one patient to the other. In this
case, the two operations will proceed at the same
time—side by side. There are four of us, and two
nurses to do what is necessary—now if you will go
and get ready."

"Frankly, doctor, do you think the chances of
success are good?"

Dr. Ferris's voice rang out heartily. "Splendid!"
he said, "splendid!" He turned once more to Wilmot. "I am sorry for you," he said kindly, "but
you are willing that we should go ahead, aren't you?"

Blizzard stood, hesitating.

"Not losing your nerve?" asked the surgeon, and
there was the least hint of mockery in his voice.

"Hope this is the last time I have to walk on stumps," Blizzard answered, and he began to move toward the door.

"I hope so, too, Blizzard," said Dr. Ferris, "with all my heart." And with an encouraging nod to Wilmot he followed the beggar out of the room, and closed the door behind him.

In the operating quarter were two nurses on whom Dr. Ferris had been able to rely for many years, and three clean-cut young surgeons, in whom he had detected more than ordinary talents.

"He said he'd send word when he was ready," said one of the nurses.

"Good," said Dr. Ferris, "for I have a few words to say to you all, knowing that, because of the etiquette of our profession, these words will not go any further."

For five minutes he spoke quietly and gravely. He told them his relations with Blizzard since the beginning. And something of Blizzard's relations, subsequent to the loss of his legs, with the rest of the world. Then he explained the operation which he was expected to perform, enlarging upon both its chances for success and for failure. And then, much to the astonishment of his audience, he brought his talk to an end with these words:

"But in this instance the operation has no chance whatever of success. The stump of a limb amputated in childhood does not keep pace with the rest of the body-growth. And we should be trying to graft the legs of a grown man upon the hips of a child. It seems, therefore, that I have brought you here under false pretenses. Technically I am going to commit a crime—I am going to perform an operation not thought of or sanctioned by the patient. But my conscience is clear. When I examined the child Blizzard after he had been run over, I did not give the attention which would be given nowadays to minor injuries, bruises, and contusions which he had sustained. From all accounts the boy was a good boy up to the time of his accident. In taking off his legs I have blamed myself for the whole of his subsequent downfall. I think I have been wrong. The man was once arrested for a crime, and freed on police perjury. During his incarceration, however, accurate measurements and a description of him were made. Only to-day a copy of this document has been shown to me, by a gentleman high in the secret service. And it seems that Blizzard is differentiated from other legless men, by a mole under one arm, and by a curious protuberance on the back of his head—and I believe that his moral delinquency is not owing to the despair and humiliation of being a cripple, but to skull-pressure upon the brain."

The three young surgeons looked at each other. One of them started to voice a protest.

"But, doctor—it's—you're asking a good deal of us. I don't know that I personally——"

Three knocks sounded quietly on a door of the room. Dr. Ferris, breaking into a smile of relief, sprang to open it.

In the rectangle appeared Lichtenstein; he was dripping wet from head to foot and carried in one hand a heavy blue automatic.

"'Fraid you couldn't make it," exclaimed the surgeon.

"Had to dynamite a safe down in the cellar—hear anything?"

Dr. Ferris shook his head, and turned to the others.

"Mr. Lichtenstein," he said, "of the secret service. . . . Lichtenstein, some of these youngsters don't want to mix up in this. Tell them things."

Lichtenstein smiled broadly. "Then I'll have to operate," he said. And he lifted his pistol ostentatiously. "Young men," he went on, "if you aren't willing to make a decent citizen of Blizzard, why I must arrest him, and send him to the chair, or if he resists arrest, I must make a decent dead man of him——"

In the distance there rose suddenly the powerful cries of the legless man. "All ready," he cried, "bring on your ether."

"Who's going to help me?" asked Dr. Ferris.

The three young surgeons stepped quickly forward.

"Good," said Dr. Ferris. "He's strong as a bull. You come with me, Jordyce, and you two wait within hearing just outside the door."

"One moment," said Lichtenstein, "where's young Allen?"

"In there," said Dr. Ferris.

"I'll just introduce myself," said the Jew, "and

tell him what's up. He must be in a most unpleasant state of mind."

To Wilmot there appeared the figure of a little stout man with red hair and a pug nose, who was dripping wet, and who smiled in an engaging fashion.

"You're safe as you'd be in your own house," said the kindly Jew; "no ether—no amputation—no nothing. And here's a note from Miss Barbara. I'm dripping wet, but I guess the ink hasn't run so's you can't read it."

Wilmot read his note, and a great light of happiness came into his eyes.

"After a while," said Lichtenstein, "I'll hunt up more clothes for you, and you can jump into a car and run out to Clovelly. Don't let Miss Barbara see you in that beard, though."

"I won't," said Wilmot. "Tell me what's happened. Has Blizzard been arrested? You're——"

"I'm Abe Lichtenstein——"

"Good Lord!" exclaimed Wilmot, "if I'd only gone straight to you——"

"If you had you might never have known that Beauty would have married the Beast—just to save young Mr. Allen pain. But why come to me?"

"With information from Harry West. He had run the whole conspiracy down. It seems——"

"Names—did he give names?"

"Yes—unbelievable names."

Lichtenstein's eyes narrowed with excitement.

In the next room there arose suddenly the sound

of many feet shuffling, as if men were carrying a heavy weight, and presently the smell of ether began to come to them through the key-hole. And they heard groans, and a dull, passionless voice that spoke words of blasphemy and obscenity.

XLVII

It was rare in Dr. Ferris's experience to see a man, after an operation, come so quickly to his senses. It was to be accounted for by perfect health and a powerful mind. The patient lay on his side, because of the wound on the back of his head, and into his eyes, glazed and ether-blind, there came suddenly light and understanding, and memory. Memory brought the sweat to his forehead in great beads.

"Is it over?" he asked quickly. "Have you done the trick?"

"It couldn't be done."

"When did you find that out?"

"I knew it before you went under ether."

"Then you haven't mutilated young Allen?"

"No."

The legless man's eyes closed, and he smiled, and for perhaps a minute dozed. He awoke saying: "Thank God for that." A moment later: "I'm all knocked out of time—what have you done to me?"

"I took the liberty of freeing your brain from pressure—result of an old accident. It can only do you good. It was hurting your mind more and more."

"I'd like to sleep, but I have the horrors."

"What sort of horrors?"

"Remorse—remorse," said the legless man in a strong voice.

Dr. Ferris was trembling with excitement.

"But thank God my deal against Allen didn't go through. That's something saved out of the burning. Where is Rose? I want Rose."

"Rose?"

"I remember. I locked her up—in that room. The key's in the bureau top drawer, left. I'd like her to sit by me. I want to go to sleep. I want to forget. Time enough to remember when I'm not sick. . . . That you, Rose? Sit by me and hold my hand, there's a dear. If I need anything she'll call you, doctor. Just leave us alone, will you?"

He clung to the hand, as a child clings to its mother's hand; and there was a tenderness and trust in the clasp that thrilled the girl to her heart.

"Say *you* forgive me, Rose." His voice was wheedling.

She leaned forward and kissed him.

"We got a lot to live down, Rose. Don't say we can't do it. Wait till I'm up and around, and strong."

He fell asleep, breathing quietly. Two hours later he woke. Rose had not moved.

"We'll begin," he said, "at once by getting married. I've dreamed it all out. And we'll set up home in a far place. That is, if *they'll* give me a chance. But I've never asked you—Rose, will you marry me?"

"Do you want me?" She leaned forward and rested her cheek against his.

"Do you understand?" he said. "We're beginning all over. You can't undo things that you've done; but you can start out and do the other kind of things and strike some sort of a balance—not before man maybe—but in your own conscience. That's something. I want to talk to Ferris. Call him, will you, and leave us."

"Doctor, was everything I *was* bone pressure? Ever get drunk?"

Dr. Ferris nodded gravely. "In extreme youth," he said.

"Well, you know how the next day you remember some of the things you did, and half remember others, and have the shakes and horrors all around, and make up your mind you'll never do so and so again? That's me—at this moment. But the past I'm facing is a million times harder to face than the average spree. It covers years and years. It's black as pitch. I don't recall any white places. Everything that the law of man forbids I've done, and everything that the law of God forbids. I won't detail. It's enough that I know. Some wrongs I can put finger to and right; others have gone their way out of reach, out of recovery. Maybe I don't sound sorry enough? I tell you it takes every ounce of courage I've got to remember my past, and face it. Was it all bone pressure? Am I really changed? Am I accountable for what I did? Was it I that did wicked things right and left, or was it somebody else that did 'em? Another thing, is the change permanent? Am I a good man now, or am I having some sort of a fit? Fetch me a hand-glass off the bureau, will you?"

Blizzard looked at himself in the mirror.

"'Seems to me," he said, "I've changed. Seems to me I don't look so much—like hell, as I did. What do you think?"

"I think, Blizzard," said Dr. Ferris, "that when you were run over as a child you hurt your head. I think that even if I hadn't cut off your legs you would have grown up an enemy of society. I think that up to the time of your accident, and since you have come out of ether just now, are the only two periods in your life when you have been sane, and accountable for your actions. Between these two periods, as I see it, you were insane—clever, shrewd—all that— but insane nevertheless. I think this—I *know* it. Even the expression of your face has changed. You look like an honest man, a man to be trusted, an able man, a kind man, the kind of man you were meant to be—a good man."

"You really think that?"

"It isn't what I think, after all; it's what *you* feel. Do you wish to be kind to people—friends with them? To do good?"

"That is the way I feel *now*. But, doctor—will it last?"

"It's got to last, Blizzard. And you've got to stop talking."

"But will they give me a chance? Lichtenstein could send me to the chair if he wanted to."

"He won't do that. He will *understand*."

"I should like Miss Barbara to feel kindly toward me."

"She will. I hope that your mind has changed about her, too?"

"That," said Blizzard, "is between me and my conscience. Whatever I feel toward her will never trouble her again."

XLVIII

WITH O'Hagan dead and Blizzard turned penitent, the bottom of course fell clean out of the scheme to loot Maiden Lane and the Sub-Treasury. But the work of Lichtenstein and his agents had not been in vain. Like the man in the opera Lichtenstein had a little "list." The lieutenant-governor soon retired into private life. He gave out that he wished to devote the remainder of his life to philanthropic enterprises. The police commissioner resigned, owing to ill health. Others who had counted too many unhatched chicks went into bankruptcy. Some thousands of discontents in the West who had been promised lucrative work in New York, about January 15th, were advised to stick to their jobs, and to keep their mouths shut. The two blind cripples who had delved for so many years in Blizzard's cellars were brought up into the light and cared for. Miss Marion O'Brien went home to England with an unusually large pot of savings, and married a man who spent these and beat her until she had thoroughly paid the penalty for all her little dishonesties and treacheries. It was curious that all the little people in the plot received tangible punishments, while the big people seemed to go scot-free. Blizzard, for instance.

No sooner recovered from the operation on the back of his head than the creature was up and doing. In straightening out his life and affairs he displayed the energy of a steam-boiler under high pressure and a colossal cheerfulness.

His first act was to marry Rose; his second to let it be known throughout the East Side that he was no longer marching in the forefront of crime. This ultimatum started a procession of wrongdoers to Marrow Lane. They came singly, in threes and fours, humble and afraid; men of substance, gunmen, the athletic, the diseased, fat crooks, thin crooks, saloon-keepers and policemen, Italians and Slavs, short noses and long (many—many of them), two clergy-men, two bankers, sharp-eyed children, married women who were childless, unmarried women who weren't—and all these came trembling and with but the one thought: "Is he going to tell what he knows about us?"

He was not. Some he bullied a little, for habit is strong; some he treated with laughter and irony, some with wit, and some with kindness and deep understanding. He might have been an able shep-herd going to work on a hopelessly numerous black and ramshackle flock of sheep. He couldn't expect to make model citizens out of all his old heelers; he couldn't expect to turn more than fifty per cent of his two clergymen into the paths of righteousness. But with the young criminals he took much pains, giving money where it would do good, and advice whether it would do good or not. Among the first to come to him was Kid Shannon.

"Now look a-here," said the Kid, "I bin good and bad by turns till I don't know which side is top side. But this minute I'm good—d'you get me? If you want to jail me you kin do it, nobody easier; but don't do it! You was always a bigger man than me, and when you led I followed—for a real man had rather follow a strong bad man than a good slob any day. You out of the lead, I got nothing to follow but me own wishes, and they're all to the good these days."

"A woman?" said Blizzard sternly.

"She ain't a woman yet," said the Kid, "and she ain't a kid—she's about half-past girl o'clock, and she thinks there's no better man in the United States than always truly yours, Kid Shannon. I got a good saloon business, and nothing crooked on hand but what's 'past and done with, and I looks to you to give a fellow a chance. Do I get it? Jail ain't goin' to help me, and it would break her. Look here, sport: I *want* to be good."

"Kid," said Blizzard, "no man that *wants* to be good need be afraid of me. You'd have been a good boy always—if it hadn't been for me. *I* know that as well as you. I've got the past all written down in my head. I can't rub it out. But any man that's got the nerve can put new writing across and across the old, until the old can't be read, or if it could would read like a joke. You can tell whomsoever it con-

cerns to do well and fear nothing. At first I thought
to tell Lichtenstein every first and last thing that I
knew about this city, and he tried to make me tell.
We had a meeting, Old Abe and I did. I was always
afraid of the little Jew, Kid. Well, face to face, I
wasn't. He talked, and I talked. And I was the
stronger. He lets me go scot-free, and I don't tell
anything. If others get you for what you've done, it
can't be helped. But none of you'll be got through
me. The past is buried; but if in the future any of
you fellows start anything, and I hear of it—look
out."

Kid Shannon wriggled uncomfortably. "Say," he
said, "what changed you?"

"I'm not changed," said Blizzard; "according to
Dr. Ferris I'm just acting natural. I was a good boy.
I had a fracture of the skull. The bone pressed on
my gray matter and made me a bad man. I'll tell
you a funny thing: *I can't beat the box any more!* I
had a go at it the other day, the missus all ready to
work the pedals, and Lord help me there was no more
music in my head or my fingers than there is in the
liver of a frog. It was the same when I was a two-
legged little kid—no music."

"Are you going to close the old diggings?"

Blizzard shook his head. "Yes and no. I'm going to pull down the old rookery; and I'm going to
put up in its place a model factory."

"Hats?"

"Hats and maybe other things. I'm going to show

New York how to run a sweatshop—you wait and
see—the most wages and the least sweat—and the
girls happier and safer than in their own homes. The
missus and I were planning to bolt to a new place
and begin life all over. That was foolish. I'd always
feel like a coward. Don't forget that old friends
meditating new crimes will be welcome at the office
—advice always given away, money sometimes and
sometimes help. Pass the word around—and when
you and Miss Half-past Girl send out your cards
don't forget me and Mrs. Blizzard in Marrow
Lane."

He leaned forward, his eyes very bright and mischievous.

"Kid," he said, "artistically and dramatically, it's
a pity."

"What's a pity?"

"That we didn't loot Maiden Lane before we got
religion. If there was any hitch in the plan, I don't
know what it was. And, Lord, I *was* so set on the
whole thing—not because I wanted the loot, but to
see if it could be done. Some of you always said it
couldn't—said there was a joker in the pack. Well,
we'll never know now. And here's Mrs. O'Farrall
come to pass the time of day—Good-by, Kid, so-
long, pass the word around. Good luck—love and
best wishes to Half-past! Mrs. O'Farrall, your
kitchen extends under the sidewalk; the more negotiable of your delicatessen are cooked on city property."

"And 'twill be me ruin to have it found out. What I came for——"

"Was to find out what I'm going to do about it. Well, the law that you're breaking isn't hurting the city a bit, Mrs. O'Farrall—I wish I could say the same for your biscuits. If you're reported, come to me and I'll see you through. How's Morgan the day?"

"The same as to-morrow, thank ye kindly—dhrunk and philanderin'."

"I'll send him a pledge to sign with my compliments, Mrs. O'Farrall, and a good job at the same time."

"He'll never sign the pledge."

"Not if I ask him to, Mrs. O'Farrall, ask him on bended knee?"

Mrs. O'Farrall looked frightened, apoplectic, and confused. Blizzard lifted his heavy eyebrows, then a smile began to brighten his face.

"Mrs. O'Farrall," said he, "blessings on your old red face! For just this minute for the first time since I lost them, the fact that I have no knees to bend escaped me. Your religion teaches you that the Lord is good to the repentant sinner. Madam, he is!" And then he began to call in a loud voice:

"Rose—Rose, run down a minute. I clean forgot that I hadn't any legs."

She came, fresh, young, and lovely. What if she had played the traitor—thrown her cap over the wind-mills? These things are not serious matters to

her sex—when the men they love are kind. And
then Lichtenstein had forgiven her, and pretended to
box her ears—and then she had had enough tragedy
and jealousy crowded into a few months to atone for
greater crimes and lapses than hers.

XLIX

"I UNDERSTAND," said Blizzard sternly, "that when you learned I was your father, you refused to proceed further against me."

"Yes, sir," said Bubbles.

"You did wrong! Always do your duty. It was your duty to send me to the chair, if you could. A fine father I'd been to you—and to Harry—and a good honest man I was to your mother! My boy, I'm face to face with the penalty that I have to pay —you. I know all about you, Bubbles, from Lichtenstein, from Dr. Ferris, from Wilmot Allen and— and others. And you're a good boy. I drove your mother crazy, I let you drift into the streets—to sink, I thought, and perish; but you're a good boy. I gave you no education, but you have picked up reading and writing and God knows what else. Once I was going to wring your neck. I didn't. That's the only favor you ever had at my hands. You'll grow up to be a good man—a fine, clever, understanding man. And it won't be because of me, it will be in spite of me. This is the hardest thing I have to face. You've come now to pay a duty call. Well, my boy, I'm obliged. But I wish to Heaven I had some hold on your affection, some way of getting a hold. Bubbles, what can I do to make you like me?"

Bubbles wriggled with awful discomfort, but said nothing.

"Is it because of your mother that you can't ever like me?"

Bubbles drew a long breath as if for a deep dive. His voice shook. "She lives in a bug-house," he said; "you drove her into it. Dr. Ferris says you were crazy yourself and nothing you ever done ought to be held against you. He says, and Miss Barbara, she says, that I ought to try to like you and feel kind to you. And—and I thought it was my duty to come and tell you that I just can't."

He was only a little boy, and the delivery of these plain truths to a man he had always held in deadly dread unmanned him. He gave one short, wailing, whimpering sob, and then bit his lips until he had himself in a sort of control.

"That's all right, Bubbles," said the legless man after a pause. "It hits hard, but it's all right. And whether you said it or not, it was coming to me, and I knew it. Do you mind if I send you books and things now and then? There was a book I had when I was a boy. I'd like you to have it. Don't know what reminds me of it—unless it's you. It's the story of a Frenchman, Bayard—they called him the chevalier *sans peur et sans reproche*. That's French. The book tells what it means. You better go now. I'm talking against time. I haven't got the same control of my nerves I used to have. I'm all broken up, my boy. But you're dead right—dead right. I say

so, and I think so. You're to go to boarding-school.
That's good. They won't teach *you* any evil."

. He did not offer his hand, and the boy was glad.

"Well, good-by," he said uneasily, reached the door,
turned, and came back a little way. "Wish you good
luck," he said.

Blizzard lowered his formidable head almost rever-
ently. "Thank you," he said.

Poor Bubbles, he began to whistle before he was
out of the building; it wasn't from heartlessness, it
was from pure discomfort and remorse. Anyway,
his father heard the shrill piping—and he sat and
looked straight ahead of him, and his face was as that
of Satan fallen—fallen, and hell fires licked into the
marrow of his bones.

So Rose found him, and flung herself upon his
breast with a cry of yearning, and his heavy sorrowed
head nestled closer and closer to hers, and he burst
suddenly into a great storm of weeping.

L

But the legless man was not one who easily or often gave way to grief. He retained all of that will-power which had made him so potent for evil, and he used it now to force cheerfulness out of discouragement and sorrow. Just what he proposed to do with his life is difficult to expose, for his plans kept changing, as almost all plans do, in the working out.

His remodelled factory will serve for an example. It began as a place in which the East Side maiden could earn enough money to keep body and soul together without scotching either. Still keeping to this idea, Blizzard kept brightening conditions, and letting in light—figuratively and actually. And he proved that short hours, high pay, and worth-while profits may be made to keep company. It all depends on how much willingness and efficiency are crowded into the short hours. Employment in Blizzard's factory became a distinction, like membership in an exclusive club, and carried with it so many privileges of comfort and self-respect that the employees couldn't very well help being efficient.

Blizzard's office, where he held the threads of many enterprises, became a sort of clearing-house for East Side troubles. He kept free certain hours during which, sitting for all the world like a judge, he listened

to private affairs, and sympathizing, scolding, wheedling, and even bullying, he gave advice, gave money,
found work, brought about reconciliations, and turned
hundreds of erring feet into the straight and narrow
path. He preached, and very eloquently, the gospel
of common-sense. For every crisis in people's lives,
he seemed to remember a parallel. And his knowledge, especially of criminalities and the workings of
crooked minds, seemed very marvellous to those who
sought him out. And he was an easy man to speak
truth to, for there were very few wicked things that
he had not done himself. It is easier to confess theft
to a thief than to a man of virtue, and the resulting
advice may very well be just the same.

His energy and activity were endless. "It's just
as hard work," he told Rose, "to do good in the world
as to do evil. I haven't changed my methods, only
my conditions and ideals. You've got to get the confidence of the people you're working for, and to get
that you've got to know more about them than they
know about themselves. To know that a man has
murdered, gives you power over that man; to know
that another man has done something fine and manly,
gives you a hold on that man. Real men are ashamed
of having two things found out about them—their
secret bad actions, and their secret good actions.
Men who do good for the sake of notoriety aren't real
men."

"I know who's a real man," said Rose.

He regarded her with much tenderness and amusement. "Rose," he said, "there's one thing I'm keen to know."

"What?"

"Will you give an honest answer?"

She nodded.

"Well then, do you like me as much as you did when I used to maltreat you and bully you and threaten you? Or do you like me more, or do you like me less?"

"It's just the same," she said, "only that then I was unhappy all the time, and now all the time I'm happy."

"Were you unhappy because I wasn't kind?"

She laughed that idea to scorn. "I was unhappy because you liked somebody else more than me."

The amusement went out of Blizzard's face; the tenderness remained. There was one thing that he was determined to do with his life, and that was to make Rose a good husband. And he was very fond of her, and she could make him laugh, but it wasn't going to be very easy, as long as the image of another girl persisted in haunting him.

LI

WHEN Wilmot Allen left Blizzard's house, he went direct to a barber-shop, where he remained for three hundred years. During this period, he lost his beard and thereby regained his self-respect. It took him a hundred years to reach the Grand Central, and a thousand more to get from there to Clovelly.

"I got your telegram," said Barbara.

"When?" he asked anxiously.

She broke into a sudden smile. "Oh," she said, "about fourteen hundred years ago."

"Barbara," he said, "that's a miracle! If you'd said thirteen hundred or fifteen hundred it would have been guessing, but fourteen hundred is the exact time that has passed since I telegraphed."

"Have you had breakfast?"

"No," he said, "I didn't have time."

They strolled through the familiar house, talking nonsense. They were almost too glad to see each other, for there was now no longer any question of Barbara making up her mind. It had been made up for her, and Wilmot knew this somehow without being told. But when had the definite change come?—that change which made her caring for Wilmot different from all her other carings? She could not say.

He had dreaded telling her about Harry West's

337

death. And when he had done so he watched her grave face with appealing eyes. Presently she smiled a little.

"I'm *not* heartless," she said, "but I'm going to keep on forgetting all the times when there was anybody but you. I expect most girls do a lot of shilly-shallying before they are sure of themselves."

"And you are really sure of yourself?"

"Yes, Wilmot, if I'm sure of you."

"The first thing," he said, "is to look into these mining properties we've fallen heir to. West wasn't the kind of man to be easily fooled; at the same time I myself have learned something about mines."

"For instance?" Her face was very mischievous.

"Well," he said, "for instance, I have learned that there are mines *and* mines. And you know, Barbs dear, I'm not eligible yet. I owe money, I haven't made good at anything, and I've got to—first of all. Haven't I?"

"Are you going to sit right there and tell me that we're not to be married until you've paid your debts and made a fortune? Where do I come in? What life have I to lead except yours? If you are in debt, so am I. If you've got to dig holes in the ground, so have I. Whatever has got to be done, we've got to do it together. So much is clear. Of course it would be *easier* for you!"

"*Barbs!*"

A little later he asked her what she was going to do with her head of Blizzard.

"Nothing," she said. "If it is good enough, it will survive these troubled times. If it isn't, somebody will break it up."

"Are you through with art?"

"What have I to do with art?" she said. "I'm in love. I used to think that women ought to have professions and all. But there's only one thing that a woman can do supremely well—and that's to make a home for a man. That will take all that she has in her of art and heart and ambition and delicacy. Of course if a girl is denied the opportunity of making a home, she can paint and sculp and thump the piano and get her name in the papers. What I want to know is—when do *we* start West?"

"You've offered to take me just as I am, with all my encumbrances, and to help me fight things through to a good finish. And I think that is pure folly on your part. But there's going to be no more folly on mine. I'm going to be a fool. Barbs—come here!"

He held out his arms, and she threw herself into them.

"Is to-morrow too soon, Barbs?"

"We could hardly arrange things sooner, but to my mind to-morrow is not nearly soon enough."

"What will your father say?"

"Why, if he's the father I think he is he'll bless us and wish us good luck. There'll be an awful lot to do. Hadn't we better jump into a car, run over to Greenwich, and get married? That will be just so much off our minds."

LII

THE young Allens began their new life by plunging themselves still deeper in debt. Their honeymoon was very short. They spent it on Long Island Sound in a yacht which Wilmot borrowed over the telephone, just before they left Clovelly to be married. On the sixth day they went West. In Salt Lake City they foregathered with a mining engineer to whom Wilmot had secured letters. This one fell in love with Barbara, closed his office and went with them into the hills for ten days. They came out of the hills with brown faces and sparkling eyes. The engineer opened his office and dictated his report of their mines to his stenographer. During this work of enthusiasm he occasionally sighed, and the stenographer knit her brows.

"Now then," said the engineer to Wilmot and Barbara, "if my name is any good in New York, you can raise all the money you need on that document. If you can't, telegraph, and I can raise it here."

"But," said Barbara, growing very practical, "if the money can be raised here, why blow in two carfares *and* a drawing-room from here to New York and back?"

"Why," the engineer stammered a little, "I thought you'd have lots and lots of friends that you'd want to let in on the ground floor. But if you haven't,

340

and if my money is as good as another's—you see, it's a grand property—I'm not above longing for an interest in it myself."

"I can't deny," said Wilmot, who had been worrying himself dreadfully about finding the means, "that this looks like easy money to me."

The engineer made generous terms across the dinner-table, and the young Allens borrowed his money from him.

"I suppose," said the engineer hopefully, "that you'll run out from time to time to see how things are getting on?"

"Run out?" exclaimed Barbara; "we are going to live with the proposition until it goes through or under. Aren't we, Wilmot?"

"I hoped you'd feel that way about it, Barbs."

"You *knew* I would."

At first they lived in a tent, and then in a series of large wooden boxes that they called first "The House" and then "Home." Machinery began to come into the camp in the wake of long strings of mules walking two and two. Upon the report of their special consulting engineer the nearest transcontinental railroad began to lay metals across the desert, to the mines. One day came strangers with picks and shovels, and the next day came more. And these began to scratch among the sage-brush and to explode sticks of dynamite against the faces of hills. Claims were staked; shanties built; a hotel with saloon attached, all of shining tin and tar paper, arose in the night. The

first thing Barbara knew Wilmot began to talk of a
stretch of sage-brush as Main Street. And the same
day she heard a man with red beard speak of the
little town as "Allen."

One night a man was shot dead among the sage-
bushes of Main Street. Six hours later Wilmot came
in on a horse covered with lather. There was a stern,
but not unhappy, look in his eyes.

"Well?" she asked.

"He showed fight," said Wilmot; "and we had to
pot him."

"Did you——"

"Would you care? We shook hands on keeping
all details secret. I think the town of Allen will be
run orderly in the future. And by the way, have I
such a thing as a clean shirt?"

"You will have," said Barbara, "when the things
dry."

"Barbara!"

"Yes, it had to come to it. There are only two
women in town, and the other isn't fit to wash your
shirts, dear."

"Let me see your hands."

He examined them critically, then kissed them un-
critically.

"They don't look like a washer-woman's hands
yet," he said.

"No," she said, "not yet. But please say they
look less and less like a sculptor's."

"Barbara," he said, "they look more and more

like a dear's. But tell me, aren't you getting bored with it—missing New York things and all and all?"

"No," she said stoutly, "I'm not. I'm useful here in some ways. And I was about as useful there as —as all the other people. I'm not even worried about the mines."

"Neither am I. But development's a great deal slower than I thought. We've still plenty of money. And the moment we begin to ship ore, we'll have plenty of credit which is just as useful. No! I'm not worried. We're going to be rich, and we're going to live in a palace."

"And then what?"

"That *is* worrying me. What do people do when the striving's over, and the sixteen hours a day hard work? What *do* they do? Oh, Barbs, we know lots of such people, and we must find out exactly what they do, and—do something else. Living as we are living has its drawbacks; but it's not a place to hurry over."

"It's a good way to live," said Barbara. "If you've got sense enough to know that it's good while it's going on. People who speak of the good old days, or who are always looking forward to better days, are usually unhappy. All the time I've been washing your clothes and mine this morning I kept saying, 'Now this is really *good*—this is really worth while,' and once when I got the better of an ink-spot, my heart began to beat as if I'd just finished some immortal work."

They were much amused with Bubbles, who came out to them for the Christmas vacation. The short fall term had already stamped him with the better ear-marks of the great New England boarding-schools. He was quite a superior person, rather prone to quote, just as if they had been facts out of the gospel, the sayings of Mr. This and Mr. That. And he used superior words, and spoke of various Kings of England as if he had *always* known that such persons existed. He had in addition a smattering of Latin, his pride in which he strove in vain to conceal. And most of all he considered the school-boy captain of the foot-ball team a creature, on the whole, wiser and more knowing even than Abe Lichtenstein.

But by the time he had been a week in camp he was himself again. And by the time he returned to school he had forgotten the ablative singular of Rosa.

They thought best to tell him that he would have plenty of money some day. In view of this would he persist in being a secret service agent? He thought so. He wasn't sure. The service needed money often and always service. Had he seen his father? Yes, and he told them about the interview.

"And," said Bubbles, "he sent me a box Thanksgiving. There was a cold turkey and caramels and guava jelly and ginger-snaps, and walnut meats and seedless raisins, and, and as Mr. Tompkins says, it doesn't do to be *too* hard on a man."

LIII

Spring came. Their mine made its first shipments of ore and was no longer a paper success. The balance-sheet for the first month after shipments had begun made Wilmot whistle. He couldn't believe the figures, and worked till late into the night, trying to find some dreadful error. Finding none, finding that with the help of others he had really made good at last, the rough life began to lose its savor. If he still owed money it could be but for a short time. He was free as air—free to do what he pleased—almost to spend what he pleased.

"Barbs," he said, the next morning, "the mine's no good; we've got to tackle something else."

"What do you mean, no good? Why, you said——"

"I know what I said. The mine is a success. Aside from what your father has, you're a rich woman. And I'm a rich man. And that's the difficulty. There's no use working our hearts out over a thing that's a definite success—is there? No fun in it. We've got to look round for something else. Now we are always going to have money—that's certain. What are we going to do with it? Think of something hard—something worth while."

"Oh," she said, "I can't—can you?"

"No," he said almost angrily, "I can't. And that's

345

the rotten side of money. That's the stumbling-block for everybody who succeeds in collecting a lot of it. The distribution is infinitely harder than the collecting. I think we'd better pull up stakes, go back to New York, and think hard."

"Yes. Let's."

"I'd like to have a talk with Blizzard."

Barbara's eyebrows went high with surprise.

"Why not? Your father writes that the man is doing more good right in New York City where it's most needed than any six philanthropists the place ever owned. Maybe he's got something really big in view, and maybe he'll let us in on the ground floor."

"Well," said Barbara, "considering everything, I shouldn't care to have much to do with him."

Wilmot put back his head and laughed aloud. "That," said he, "is precisely the sort of advice that I used to give you."

Barbara blushed. "I'd like to forget that such a man ever came into my life in any way."

"You can't forget it, dear. You asked him in. You *would* do it. And now you can never forget. And that's one of the penalties you have to pay for going against the people who love you most."

"Well," said she, "I'm willing to keep on paying —if the right people will keep on loving. Anyway, philanthropy—good works—are none of my business. My business, sir, is to make you a home. And with the exception of one person that I know about posi-tively, the rest of the world can go hang."

"And when you think," said she, "that
some women spend the best years
of their lives making *statues!*"

"That statement," said Wilmot, "sounds very pagan and profane to me and also very, very beautiful. But, who, may I ask, is this *other* person?" His brows gathered a little jealously.

"This other person," said Barbara quietly, "is at the present moment a total stranger to us."

Then she leaned forward until her head was on his breast. And she gave a little sigh which was fifty per cent comfort, and fifty per cent courage. She could hear his heart beating like a trip-hammer. Had he burst into immortal eloquence, his words would have been of less consequence in her ear.

"And when you think," said she, "that some women spend the best years of their lives making *statues!*"

THE END